"All night I've wanted this. Just this."

Conor nibbled her lips. The words were spoken against Emma's mouth, then inside her mouth as he changed the angle and kissed her again, long, slow and deep. "I wanted to be the one holding you.... Watching your eyes as they looked into mine."

He stared down and saw the smoldering look. A look that told him she was feeling the same things he was feeling.

"I was jealous." He nibbled his way from the corner of her mouth to her ear. "Jealous." He spoke the word harshly, with a trace of wonder. "A new emotion for me. I've never known it before. Nor would I have believed myself capable of such a thing."

"Conor. Conor." Emma was so confused. It was one thing to flirt. To lead him on, in order to gain information. But now she was feeling things that had her trembling with new awareness.

She wanted him. Wanted him so much, it frightened her.

Dear Reader,

This month we're giving you plenty of excuses to put your feet up and "get away from it all" with these four, fantasy-filled historical romances.

First, *USA Today* bestselling author Ruth Langan returns with *Conor*, the second book in her sensational miniseries, THE O'NEIL SAGA—although you needn't have read *Rory* to enjoy this one. It's the thrilling tale of an Irish noblewoman sent by her evil stepmother to seduce the roguish rebel Conor, who has great influence over Queen Elizabeth. Their instant attraction is only the beginning of a successful partnership in which the two unravel a plot to murder the queen....

If you enjoy half-Apache heroes, you *must* meet Rio Santee, a world-weary single father who falls in love with the independent female who reluctantly takes him and his children into her home in *The Merry Widows—Sarah*. It's fabulous! *The Rancher's Wife* by Lynda Trent is about a "pretend marriage" that turns real when an abandoned wife moves in with her widower neighbor to care for his baby girl.

Last but not least, we have *Bride Of Trouville*, a spine-tingling, forbidden love story by rising talent Lyn Stone. Forced to wed, Lady Anne MacBain struggles to hide her son's deafness from her husband—whom she has, ironically, grown to love.

Whatever your tastes in reading, you'll be sure to find a romantic journey back to the past between the covers of a Harlequin Historical®.

Sincerely,

Tracy Farrell
Senior Editor

Please address questions and book requests to:
Harlequin Reader Service
U.S.: 3010 Walden Ave., P.O. Box 1325, Buffalo, NY 14269
Canadian: P.O. Box 609, Fort Erie, Ont. L2A 5X3

RUTH LANGAN

CONOR

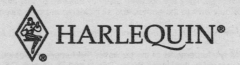

HARLEQUIN®

TORONTO • NEW YORK • LONDON
AMSTERDAM • PARIS • SYDNEY • HAMBURG
STOCKHOLM • ATHENS • TOKYO • MILAN • MADRID
PRAGUE • WARSAW • BUDAPEST • AUCKLAND

ISBN 0-373-29068-3

CONOR

Copyright © 1999 by Ruth Ryan Langan

Visit us at www.romance.net

Printed in U.S.A.

RUTH LANGAN

traces her ancestry to Scotland and Ireland. It is no surprise, then, that she feels a kinship with the characters in her historical novels.

Married to her childhood sweetheart, she has raised five children and lives in Michigan, the state where she was born and raised.

For John Ryan Langan,
the newest link in our chain of love
And his brother and sister, Tommy and Annie
And his proud parents, Tom and Maureen

And of course, to Tom, the love of my life

Prologue

Ireland, 1546

"Good morrow, young Conor." The old peasant woman beamed at the son of Gavin O'Neil, the lord of Ballinarin. "Ye've come with your family to market, have ye?"

"Aye, Mistress Garrity." Nine-year-old Conor O'Neil paused at the table laden with rich, delicate pastries.

This was his favorite stop on market day. At a nearby stall his father was sharing a bit of ale with Friar Malone and some of the men from the village. Just across the green his mother and little sister, Briana, were admiring bits of ribbon and lace that a young woman was holding aloft. In the lane his older brother, Rory, was surrounded by a cluster of lads who were pretending to ignore the pretty lasses who were giggling and blushing as they passed by.

All around were vendors hawking their wares. There were stalls filled with pens of squawking chickens, buckets of wriggling fish, wheelbarrows of mussels and other shellfish. Farmers displayed their fruits and vegetables, or bartered lambs for seafood.

"I've raised six sons of my own," Mistress Garrity was

saying in that lovely musical voice that Conor loved. "And
I know what most appeals to the heart of a wee lad."

With a wink she handed him one of the pastries. As
always he reached into his pocket for the coin. And as
always, she added a second pastry with the whispered ad-
monition, "This one's free. Just to hold ye until ye get
home, lad."

They shared a secret smile. He bit into the pastry and
gave a little sigh of pleasure. But before he could take a
second bite he felt a hand against his shoulder as he was
roughly shoved aside. As he fell to the ground, he looked
up to see more than a dozen English soldiers elbowing their
way through the crowd.

The happy voices suddenly faded into silence. Even little
children, who had been chasing each other around the stalls
laughing and shouting, went still as death.

"What do you want here?" one of the farmers demanded.

"We've come for food, old man. We're hungry." The
leader of the band of soldiers kicked over a stall and
reached for a pen of squawking, flapping chickens. While
the vendor watched helplessly, the soldier tossed it to one
of his men and said with a laugh, "While we're at it, we'll
have your gold as well."

The soldiers began snatching up buckets of fish, baskets
of bread, all the while filling their pockets with coin from
the tables.

One of the soldiers spied the pastries and began scooping
them up.

"Where's your coin, old woman?"

Mistress Garrity emptied her pocket, placing three gold
coins in his hand.

He caught her by the front of her gown, dragging her
close. Through his teeth he hissed, "I want all of them, old
woman."

She hung her head in shame. "That's all I have."

"Liar." He slapped her hard, snapping her head to one side, then gave her a shove backward.

At that a tearful little girl came forward, clutching at the old woman's skirt as though to comfort her. She was a wee bit of a lass who often played a game of tag with Conor while her family tended their stall at market.

"Hush, now, Glenna." Mistress Garrity was more concerned with soothing the child than with her own pain. "Yer old grandmother's fine."

Seeing this, the soldier snatched up the girl and pressed a knife to her throat. "You'll give me the rest of your coins, old woman, or you'll watch your brat's blood spill right here at your feet. And just to make certain that you never forget, I'll have my sport with her before I kill her."

At the soldier's words Conor, still lying in the dirt, reached for the small, sharp dirk he always wore beneath his tunic. From his youngest days he'd been taught to think like a warrior. It was in his blood, as it was in the blood of all the O'Neils. The soldier's threat had his blood running hot through his veins. Despite his tender age, he knew what would happen to his young friend, Glenna. The need to stop these monsters by any means nearly clouded his vision. But before he could attack, he looked up to see his father's hand go to the sword at his waist. Across the lane he saw Rory unsheath his knife.

Conor knew that the sword of one man and the knives of two lads would never be enough against more than a dozen armed English soldiers. It might satisfy the warrior's blood in them, but in the end it would only incite the soldiers to more brutality.

His own life mattered not to him. But he had the feeling, in that instant, that the fate of his mother and sister, and the entire village, rested in what he chose to do here. He knew, with perfect clarity, that he could save them all with the only weapon he had. And this time, it was not his knife.

Without thinking of the consequences he leapt to his feet and, in a surprisingly strong voice, asked, "Is it true that you swear allegiance to Henry of England?"

The soldier was so startled by the bold question he turned to face the lad, completely forgetting the threat to the weeping lass in his arms. "Aye. And what's it to you?"

Conor shrugged. Out of the corner of his eye he saw several of the soldiers begin to circle around him and prayed his father would hold his temper for a minute more. Though he knew he was babbling, he couldn't bear the thought of losing his brave father and brother to these foreigners' swords. Not when there might be another way, a better way, to win. "Then it can't be true what I've heard about your king."

"And what might that be?"

"That he's an honorable man."

The soldier's eyes narrowed with fury. "Are you saying he isn't honorable? Do you dare to slander the King of England?"

"If Henry of England is an honorable king, and if you swear allegiance to him, then how can you justify taking the life of an innocent lass? According to the laws of your own land, stealing food is a crime, punishable by confinement in prison. But the taking of an innocent life is a crime punishable by death."

At the look of amazement on the soldier's face, his comrades began to taunt and jeer.

"This bright Irish lad's trapped you, Ian."

"Aye, what have you to say for yourself now, man?"

"Better release the girl before good King Henry himself comes seeking vengeance."

"I've heard these Irish are gifted with words," another soldier jeered. "This lad's proved it. He's bested you, Ian."

The leader of the band hurried forward and, hearing the taunts, said angrily, "I want no trouble here. We came for food and gold, nothing more. When we leave this place, we leave with no blood on our hands. Is that clear, Ian?"

The two faced each other for long silent moments. Then the soldier dropped the girl and she scrambled to her feet and raced, weeping and wailing, into the trembling embrace of her grandmother.

In the silence that followed the soldier turned and caught Conor roughly by the arms, yanking the lad up until they were eye to eye.

"You've a glib tongue, Irish."

Conor's heart was thundering inside his chest. If the soldier felt the knife beneath his tunic, it would be turned on him. But he swallowed back his fear and met the soldier's stare in silence.

"That's better. You'd best see that your mouth stays closed if you want to keep that clever golden tongue. Else you may find it cut out by my blade." With a vicious oath he tossed the lad down in a heap, then whirled away.

Minutes later the English soldiers disappeared into the forest as quickly as they had arrived.

At once the villagers pounced on Conor, hugging him, squeezing his arm, shaking his hand and exclaiming while Mistress Garrity thanked him over and over again through a mist of tears.

"Ye saved my little Glenna, Conor O'Neil. Had it not been for yer courage, and yer fine words, he'd have brutalized her and slit her throat. I know he would. And all the swords in the land wouldn't have been quick enough to stop him."

When Conor's family gathered around, the villagers stepped aside out of respect.

His mother and sister hugged him, while his brother

slapped his shoulder in approval. And all the while his father studied him in silence.

After several minutes, Gavin O'Neil finally managed to swallow back the knot of fear that had been threatening to choke him. "How did you come by the things you said to the soldier, Conor?"

Conor shrugged, prepared for his father's famous temper to explode. "I know not. The words just seemed to come into my mind. I knew that if I didn't stop the soldiers with words, you would be forced to stop them with your sword. And Rory with his knife."

"It is our duty to defend those we love. You know that I'm a skilled swordsman, as you and Rory are skilled with a knife."

"Aye, Father. But sometimes words are better than swords. Especially if they can prevent bloodshed."

Gavin glanced over the lad's head to where his wife, Moira, was standing. A look passed between them. And in that instant they both knew. Though Gavin believed in the power of the sword, he had just witnessed an even greater power. An unbelievable power.

There were places of learning in Spain, in France, in Italy, where a lad with a fine mind could be given every advantage. Fed by the writings of the world's scholars, a fine mind could be honed until it might equal or even surpass an army of swordsmen.

Could it be that this, their middle child, might prove to be the answer to a nation's prayer? A prayer for freedom from their hated oppressors?

There was no doubt Conor would be as skilled a warrior as his father and brother, for he had the fearlessness, the steady hand, the vision. But if he could become equally skilled as an orator, he would be a formidable foe indeed.

They owed it to him, to their family, to their country, to do everything in their power to make it so.

* * *

In the years that followed, there was much to discuss around Ballinarin. There was the power of Conor O'Neil's words, for he had become a famed orator. But as skilled as he was, another was even more acclaimed. A mysterious, hooded warrior had begun waging a solitary war of vengeance against the cruel bands of English soldiers that roamed the countryside. A warrior who spoke not a word as he slit the throats of soldiers caught in the act of brutalizing helpless women and children. Because he always dressed in the garb of a monk, with the hood pulled down to his eyes, and the cowl pulled up to hide the lower half of his face, he'd become known as Heaven's Avenger.

Emma Vaughn was small and slight for her age of ten and two. Dusk had already settled over the land when she began making her way home from the village apothecary. Her beautiful mother had never regained her strength after a difficult childbirth. But Emma was determined to see her mother fully recovered. This day she carried a pouch of special herbs and potions said to have healing properties. They had taken longer to prepare than she'd anticipated, and she was anxious about the lateness of the hour. But her mother's health was worth any amount of time.

The sound of horses coming up behind her had her turning in alarm. When she caught sight of the band of English soldiers, her heart leapt to her throat, and she cursed herself for her carelessness. She knew, as did every woman and child in Ireland, what these hardened soldiers considered sport.

Hiking her skirts above her knees, she veered off the path and raced across the meadow, hoping the tall grass would slow down those in pursuit. She heard a roar of laughter as the horsemen caught sight of her and began to give chase.

Her chest heaved, the breath burning her lungs as she

pushed herself to the limit. But as she headed toward a line of trees, hoping to hide herself, she saw a second group of soldiers emerge from the cover of the forest and advance toward her. She paused. Turned. Then realized, with growing panic, that she was surrounded. The circle of soldiers narrowed as they moved in on their target, who darted from one side of the meadow to the other, like a creature of the wild bent on escape.

"I've got her." One of the soldiers reached down and scooped her up like a rag doll, holding her imprisoned in his arms as he nudged his horse toward the cover of the woods.

The others were laughing and cursing as they made their way to their encampment.

The one holding Emma slid from the saddle. "Since I caught her, I claim the right to be first. The rest of you can have what's left." He gave a mocking laugh. "From the looks of this scrawny wench, I doubt she can pleasure me much. But I'll have to make do."

The others joined in the laughter as a cask was opened and ale was passed among them.

"She's no more than a child," one of the men complained.

"All the better. We'll teach her the ways of a woman. Maybe, if she pleases us, we can keep her around." The soldier kept a firm grasp on Emma as he dragged her across the camp toward his blankets. Along the way he snagged a tankard of ale, tipping it up and draining it as he walked.

When he reached his bedroll, secured beside a fallen log, he tossed her down, then fell on top of her. Her screams died in her throat. She nearly gagged on the stench of ale and sour breath as her mouth was covered by his.

It was impossible to move. She was pinned beneath him. Still, panic gave her strength she'd never known she possessed. Her hand reached out blindly and encountered a rock. Her fingers curled around it, and she struck the back of his head with all the strength she could manage.

He gave a grunt of pain. "Little witch. I'll teach you." He grabbed both her hands, holding them above her head in one of his. Then he slapped her so hard stars danced behind her eyes. "Now you'll pay."

Emma braced herself for what was to come. But as he fumbled beneath her skirts, he suddenly went rigid with shock. She caught sight of a flash of silver as the soldier's eyes went wide, then seemed to glaze over. Blood streamed from a gaping slash across his throat in the moment before he slumped forward, pinning her beneath his dead weight.

With a sense of panic she pushed and struggled to free herself. Her hands, her gown, even her hair were smeared with his blood.

Suddenly his body was yanked roughly away. Standing over her was a figure clad in the garb of a friar, with the cowl pulled up over his mouth, and the hood pulled down to his eyes. And the bluest eyes Emma had ever seen. They glowed in the moonlight like sapphires.

"Who...? What...?"

He shook his head and touched a finger to her lips. Then, without a word, he turned away and began to crawl toward the encampment, where the voices of the drunken soldiers could be heard.

Kneeling up, Emma watched in amazement as the hooded figure moved among them, silently slitting each throat. He moved so quickly, none of his victims had time to notice his approach, or to offer any resistance.

When he returned, she was weeping in relief. Big wet tears that spilled down her cheeks. He lifted her face and wiped the tears with his thumbs. In his eyes she could read both simmering anger and heartfelt compassion for what she was suffering. Without a word he picked her up and carried her to his waiting horse. She could feel the ripple of muscle as he climbed easily into the saddle, all the while holding her against his chest.

"Thank you," she murmured when she could find her voice. "I know...I know what would have happened if you hadn't come to my rescue."

Again he touched a finger to her lips to silence her words. Then he gathered her close, allowing her head to rest on his shoulder. They rode across the meadow in silence. In fact, it seemed to Emma, the whole world had gone suddenly silent. No breeze stirred the leaves of the trees. No night birds sang. Even the frogs in the pond made no sound as the horse splashed through the water, then climbed the embankment and headed toward her village in the distance.

In the circle of this stranger's arms she felt warm and safe. No harm would come to her, she knew, as long as he held her like this.

When they reached the village he slid from the saddle and set her on her feet.

"I need to know your name, sir, so that my father can properly thank you."

He shook his head.

"Are you mute? Is that why you don't speak?"

He merely remained silent.

She offered her hand. "Then I thank you, sir. I will never, ever forget you, or what you did this night."

Though the lower half of his face was covered by the cowl, she could see the smile in his eyes. He pressed her hand between both of his, then turned and pulled himself into the saddle.

He waited until she ran up the lane and let herself into her house. Then, as she stood in the doorway and waved, he saluted smartly and wheeled his mount. Minutes later he blended into the darkness.

From that day on, Emma Vaughn told all who would

listen about the mysterious warrior who had saved her honor and her life. When asked to identify her champion, she could describe only his eyes. Deep blue eyes, filled with ageless wisdom and courage and compassion. Though she was little more than a child, she had already lost her heart to this stranger. To emulate him, she put aside her fears and mastered the art of defense with a knife, vowing that no man would ever again find her helpless.

Throughout all of Ireland the legend grew. And all spoke in awe of the courage of Heaven's Avenger.

Chapter One

Ireland, 1563

"I wish you weren't going to England, Conor." Moira O'Neil struggled to keep the emotion from her voice as she hugged her son. But the pain and fear were there, just beneath the surface. She knew that her middle child was widely regarded as Ireland's most persuasive orator. Knew, also, that he was a warrior second only to his older brother, Rory. A man adept with both word and sword could surely take care of himself in any situation. Still, the worry persisted. He was going to the land of their enemy. Into the very den of the lion.

It had been his father's plan since Conor was a lad. And gradually, Conor had accepted the plan as his own. His gift was this wonderful ability to persuade people, through logic and pretty words, to use common sense over emotion. To negotiate rather than fight. To make peace rather than war.

He had another gift, as well. Moira had seen the looks of approval in the eyes of the young women when he passed, and knew that he was a dashing ladies' man who had caught the eye of the queen. But Elizabeth of England was no innocent. She was a worldly monarch, famous for

keeping charming young men around her only so long as
they amused her. Once she lost interest they could find
themselves in grave peril.

Moira sighed. In her eyes Conor would always be that
blue-eyed laughing charmer who had captured her heart
when he was born, and owned it still.

"It seems like only yesterday since you and Rory returned from that hellish place. And now you're going back,
to the very palace where your brother nearly lost his life."

"I'll be fine, Mother. I'm going at the invitation of the
queen. What harm could possibly come to me?"

What harm indeed? She had heard of the villainies and
betrayals among those who surrounded Elizabeth at court.
But she kept such things to herself as she hugged her son.

"I'm proud of you, Conor." Gavin O'Neil clapped a
hand on his son's shoulder and dragged him close. "You'll
do us all proud. Your family. Your countrymen. And all
those who will come after us will bless your name because
of this sacrifice you make for Ireland. If you can't persuade
the English queen to leave us in peace, at least you'll have
your ear to the throne, so that we'll be prepared for what
is to come."

"I'll do my best, Father." Conor turned to his older
brother, Rory, and the two men clasped hands. "You'll see
to everything on this side of the sea?"

"Aye." Rory grinned. "And gladly leave the other side
to you." He gave Conor a cool, measured look. "There
was another attack last night upon a group of English soldiers. Heaven's Avenger found them abusing a wench, and
without a word, slit all their throats with a very small, very
deadly knife."

Conor took a step back. "Is that so?"

Rory nodded. "Like all the others, this wench insists her
avenger had superhuman strength, subduing all seven soldiers before even one could lift a hand in defense. She is

telling all who will listen that he was as tall as a giant, and as handsome as a young god, even though she couldn't see his face.''

"Thus are legends born," Conor scoffed. "If she couldn't see his face, he could be either fair of face, as the wench insists, or perhaps scarred so badly he hides his disfigurement beneath a mask." Conor's tone was dry as he turned to kiss his sister-in-law's cheek. "Continue taking care of my brother, AnnaClaire, for he is surely losing his senses.''

She laughed. "I'll see to Rory. You'll give my father my love?''

"Aye. If I should see him before he sets sail." James Lord Thompson, AnnaClaire's father, was Conor's only friend among the queen's counselors. But he had just sent word that he was being sent by the queen to Spain. Some suggested he was being banished because he had dared to cross words with the queen's favorite, Lynley Lord Dunstan.

Conor turned to the lad who stood between Rory and AnnaClaire. The orphan, Innis Maguire, had become a son to them, living in their household, blossoming under their loving care. In the past months he had grown more than an inch in height. The beginnings of muscles could be seen beneath the sleeves of his tunic.

Conor tousled the blonde hair and dragged the lad close. "Next time I leave, maybe you can go with me."

"You mean it?"

"Aye, lad. Though I think, when I return from England, I'll be home to stay.''

Conor turned to his little sister, Briana, who was openly weeping. "No tears now, lass. I'll be home before you have time to miss me.''

"I miss you already." She threw her arms around his neck and hugged him fiercely. "I don't want you to leave."

"I know." He pressed a kiss to her temple. "But when the Queen of England issues an invitation, it's really a royal command. I must go."

"She isn't my queen." Briana pushed from his arms and stomped her foot. She'd inherited her temper, as fiery as her hair, from her father. "Nor is she your queen, Conor."

"True enough. But I've learned that 'tis ofttimes more prudent to lull an enemy with sweet songs than to approach with sword raised. So I'll go to England, lass, and watch and listen." He shot her that charming smile that had broken the heart of many a colleen. "And even croon a minstrel's song of love to the lady on the throne, if that's what it takes to keep my people safe from English swords."

He pulled himself into the saddle and saluted his family smartly. Then, with a last wave at the servants who had assembled to wish him godspeed, he turned his mount toward Dublin.

Before he reached the village he turned for a lingering look at Ballinarin. The sun had burned away the last of the morning raindrops. The sky was awash with feathery clouds that seemed to brush the highest peaks of Croagh Patrick. A waterfall cascaded down the side of the mountain, sending up a misty spray. A flock of sheep undulated across a hillside. This land was so green, so beautiful, it seemed like an artist's rendering.

He thought of his little sister Briana's words to him and felt a sigh well up from deep inside. He wasn't yet gone, and already he missed the land of his birth. At times he felt like a nomad. Since boyhood he'd spent as much time away as he had at his beloved home. He'd lived with a tutor in a villa in Rome, where he'd mastered the classics. Learned to speak fluent Spanish in a monastery. Could converse in French after two years in Paris. What he longed for, more than anything else, was to spend the rest of his life at Ballinarin. Hearing words spoken in a soft, soothing brogue. Riding his horse across the green, verdant hills. But he had a duty. To his father. To his country. This was what he had trained for. What his mother had prayed for. What his father and brother had fought for.

He would do his best to turn away from his legacy as a warrior and become, instead, an advocate for peace. But if peace could not prevail, he would never submit to the oppressor. He touched a hand to the knife at his waist. A knife that had spilled too much English blood.

There was no turning his back on his destiny.

Clermont House, Outside London

"I grow weary of waiting for the throne." Henry, Earl of Huntington, paced back and forth. "Elizabeth grows more popular with her subjects every day."

His sister put a hand on his arm. "Queens have a way of dying."

He turned on her with a snarl. "Elizabeth is young and healthy. She could live for years."

"She need not die of…natural causes."

He studied her with new interest. "What are you planning?"

"What I have always planned. What we have always planned, brother. You will be king." She turned to the other man in the room, who had remained silent throughout their exchange. "You, Dunstan, will get richer. And I…" Her smile bloomed. "As the new Lady Vaughn, I hold power over a certain someone who will do exactly as I say."

Her brother Henry's frown deepened. "How can you be certain your stepdaughter will spy for us, Celestine?"

She walked to the window and pointed. "You see? Even now she rides up the lane. The girl is as predictable as the English rain. She thinks herself smart and strong. But I intend to prove her wrong." She touched a hand to his arm.

"Leave Emma Vaughn to me. And put your fears to rest. Prepare, instead, for your reign as King of England."

Huntington's voice was rough with impatience. "I am not prepared to wait forever."

"Nor am I," Dunstan said. "For I have a few plans of my own."

"Then see to them. But if your plans fail, mine will not." She left her brother and Lord Dunstan and went to her chambers to prepare herself for her performance. It was an art that she had perfected.

When she was ready she descended the stairs and made her grand entrance. "Foolish, defiant child. I ordered you to stay away. It is enough that I permit you use of your father's London townhouse." Celestine swept into the parlor with the polished air of a courtesan. Her gown had been artfully designed to show off her lush figure to its best advantage. Her eyes blazed as she confronted the young woman who was pacing before the fireplace. "Did you think the servants wouldn't tell me you were lurking about?"

"I am not lurking." Emma stopped her pacing and lifted her head to stare at the older woman. "I've come to see my father and little sister."

"I've told you before, Emma. You are forbidden to see them."

"You have no right, Celestine."

"I have every right. I'm your stepmother now. Yours and little Sarah's. And your father's wife. It is a wife's duty to look out for her husband."

"Husband." Emma's hands knotted into fists at her sides. "You care not a whit about being a wife to my father. All you care about is securing his wealth."

The woman gave a chilling smile. "It is my wealth now. I'll use it as I see fit. And you, my girl, will not see a farthing."

"I care not for my father's wealth."

"If that is true then leave."

"Oh, I shall. But first I will see my father and little sister."

"I forbid it."

"You cruel, wicked creature. If my father knew what you were doing, he would renounce this farce of a marriage and have you publicly flogged."

"Beware that idle tongue, my girl. For I am the mistress of Clermont House now. And I am telling you that your father and sister do not wish to see you."

"That's a lie. My father loves me. He would never turn away from me. Sarah adores me. I'm like a second mother to her." With an anguished cry Emma crossed the room and caught the older woman's arm. "What have you said to them? What have you done to turn them against me?"

She looked up into those narrowed eyes and saw a flicker of amusement. "They don't know, do they? You've never told them that you banished me from this home. Oh, how could they not know? Unless…" As a thought struck, she cried, "What have you done? Are they unwell? Dear heaven, are my father and little sister ill?"

Celestine stared at the offending fingers wrinkling her sleeve. "You will unhand me at once, or I'll see that you are physically removed from this house and never permitted to return."

When Emma released her, Celestine stiffened her spine and with a haughty gesture crossed to a side table. Pouring herself a goblet of wine she sipped, regarding her stepdaughter in silence.

She was pleased to see that all the anger had drained from the girl. In its place was fear. A terrible, palpable fear that her beloved father and sister had fallen under some horrible spell.

That must be the reason for this silence, Emma thought.

Her strong, handsome father had been duped into marriage and was now being betrayed by this woman. And her sweet little sister, who had already suffered the loss of their mother, was now being denied the only comfort she had ever known.

Just how far would this new bride go to insure that all the Vaughn wealth, all the power, all the titles, would be in her hands? Would she poison not only their minds but their bodies as well? At the very thought, Emma felt the terror begin to grow. A woman as ruthless as Celestine would be capable of anything.

"Just how much do you desire to see your father and sister, I wonder?"

"I wish it desperately." Emma felt a tiny flicker of hope. "Just to assure myself that they are not ill. And if, after seeing me, they should order me to leave, I will do so and never darken their door again. But please, I beg of you, I must hear it from their own lips. Let me speak with Sarah and my father."

"Sarah is no longer here."

"Not here? Where has she gone?"

"I had her sent to the country. To stay with friends."

"But why would you send her away? She's only six years old. Far too young to leave her father."

"Aye, young. Young enough to forget."

"Forget?"

"I wanted Sarah far away from you, Emma. You've had too much influence in her young life. Like you, she refused to accept my authority. But she will learn." A hint of a smile touched the corner of Celestine's lips. "I intend to keep Sarah away from you. But I might be persuaded to let you see your father."

"Oh, thank…"

She held up a hand. "Save your gratitude. Before I grant

this favor, you must do something for me, to prove that you deserve such kindness.''

''Anything. Anything,'' the girl said with a sob of relief.

''As you know, I am cousin to the queen. As such, I can arrange for you to live in the palace, and act as lady-in-waiting to Elizabeth.''

''But I...have had no training in such things. I wouldn't know what to do. And I would be all alone, for I know nobody at court.''

''All the better. You will get to know them. And one in particular.'' Celestine lowered her voice, to avoid being overheard by any of the servants who might be passing by. ''It is rumored that the queen is enamored of a certain Irishman, whose advice she values. I need to know what advice he gives the queen, and precisely how she intends to act upon that advice.''

The girl's hand flew to her mouth. ''You wish me to spy?''

''Don't be so melodramatic. There are no secrets at court. I merely wish to know what everyone else shall eventually learn. Only I wish to know it sooner.''

The girl was already shaking her head. ''I cannot do this. What you ask is wrong.''

''So be it, Emma. The choice is yours.'' Celestine turned to stare out the window. ''I have heard of so many...accidents in the country. A frail child falling from a hay wagon or from the back of a runaway steed.''

Emma sucked in a breath at the bold threat to her little sister.

Celestine turned to fix her with a steely look. ''Know this, my girl. You will never see your father or sister again. Until,'' she added with a sneer, ''they are laid in the ground.''

''Oh. How can you be so heartless?'' The girl turned away to hide her tears.

"Very well, you sniveling little coward." Her stepmother waved a hand. "Go. Leave me now. Put your own comfort and your lofty scruples above the safety of those you profess to love." She turned toward the door. "One of the servants will see you out. And the entire household staff will be instructed that you are forbidden to enter your father's house again."

"Wait." Emma began to pace.

Her stepmother counted to ten before saying aloud, "I grow weary of your foolish indecision."

"All right." Emma's shoulders sagged. "I'll do as you ask."

Celestine carefully composed herself to hide the glint of triumph in her eyes. It had all been so simple. She had correctly guessed Emma's one weakness. "I will send word to the palace at once." She looked the girl up and down and said sarcastically, "I would hope you can find something more fetching than those horrible rags you are wearing. And try to do something with that unfashionable hair. After all, your only purpose in serving my cousin is to snag the interest of the Irishman. See to it as quickly as possible. His name is Conor O'Neil."

Chapter Two

The Court of Elizabeth I of England

"**Y**our Majesty must, I beseech you, bring the power of your Throne upon these obstinate peasants." Lord Dunstan, trusted advisor to the queen, was charged with the "Irish problem." That was how everyone in England referred to the constant upheaval between their land and the tiny island across the sea. At the moment Dunstan was holding forth at a gathering of the queen and her council in a lavish suite of rooms at Greenwich Palace in London.

"Our control over these barbarians remains precarious, Majesty. They defy our laws. They betray our trust. Why, they even revile our religion. A religion, I might add, over which you are charged with supreme governorship. Why, I remember when your father..."

"Leave that." Elizabeth's voice had the sting of a scorpion. "I tire of this subject. Besides, I would greet my fine Irish orator."

Dunstan went deathly pale. Then he glowered at the handsome young man who bowed before the queen. At once she ordered her aged counselor Lord Humphrey to vacate his chair so that the newest arrival could be seated directly beside her.

"Here you are, Conor. You are late again."

"Aye, Majesty." More than a little out of breath, Conor bowed before the queen and brushed his lips over her outstretched hand. "I beg your forgiveness. I have no sense of time."

"You are forgiven, my rogue. Come. Sit beside your queen, Conor O'Neil."

Conor O'Neil. The very name curdled Dunstan's blood.

He turned to several advisors, who were watching in stony silence. "Ever since the Irishman has arrived at court, our young queen has been acting besotted."

"Aye." The florid-faced Lord Humphrey nodded. "Every day this past fortnight O'Neil has been invited to take the place of honor beside her at court. At dinner parties, she has insisted that he be her companion. Why, the Irishman has been included in every hunting party, every picnic, every dazzling ball, since his arrival."

Dunstan glowered. "Women are charmed by him. Men seem to find him both bright and witty. And to add insult to injury, Conor O'Neil makes no apologies for the behavior of his countrymen. Everyone knows his own brother, Rory, the infamous Blackhearted O'Neil, murdered dozens of the queen's own soldiers. Was he punished for such atrocities? Nay. Instead, he has been pardoned by the queen and allowed to return to his family estate, Ballinarin, where he lives this day like a free man."

Lord Humphrey gave a sly look. "I understand Rory O'Neil wed your woman."

Dunstan shrugged, denying the bitter taste of defeat. "I had no use for AnnaClaire Thompson. But I did covet her Irish estate, Clay Court."

"And now you have it."

"Aye." The boast rang hollow. The Irish servants who

had staffed Clay Court for generations had fled rather than
serve their new English master. He'd been forced to send
over his own loyal English servants, at considerable cost.
And still the estates were falling into disrepair.

But he would show her. He would show all of them. He
had already persuaded the queen to banish AnnaClaire's
father, Lord Thompson, to Spain. He would soon persuade
the queen to take similar action against the Irishman. Banishment back to his own miserable country would be the
sweetest revenge.

"Rory O'Neil lives like royalty while he incites other
Irish warriors to take up arms against England. And all the
while his brother, Conor, plays fast and loose with our vir-
gin queen. Why, she has even bestowed on him the title of
Lord Wyclow, and presented him with a manor house and
hunting lodge in Ireland."

That knowledge, more than any other, stuck like a stone
in Dunstan's throat. He hated any man who acquired what
he himself coveted. And he had long coveted Wyclow.
What was worse, the Irishman steadfastly refused to acknowledge the title, and it was rumored he'd turned over
the land around Wyclow to the villagers, along with a purse
of gold to maintain it.

There had been a time when Elizabeth would have bestowed the title and land on Dunstan, as she had bestowed
her friendship. Dunstan was a man who relished being part
of the queen's inner circle of advisors. He loved being the
center of attention, just as he loved the power which came
with it. But that had been before the arrival of the Irishman.

"I weary of this place." Elizabeth stood, and at once
every man in the room got to his feet and bowed, while
the women curtsied. "We will retire to a withdrawing
room."

They followed her from the suite and down the hall until
they reached a large formal parlor, where they were joined

by Elizabeth's ladies-in-waiting. Within minutes servants were passing among the assembled with trays of wine and ale.

"Come, Conor. Sit and amuse me." Elizabeth settled herself on a chaise and patted the place beside her.

"How do you wish to be amused today, Majesty?"

"Tell me more about your irreverent, misspent youth in Paris."

"Very well. There was the night..." Conor went into a lengthy description of a prank he and his fellow students had played on their very proper French tutor. The evening had involved a great deal of wine and a young woman of questionable morals, who agreed to hide herself in the tutor's bed after he'd fallen asleep.

Conor knew he was a gifted storyteller. It was an art he'd perfected. He accepted a goblet of ale and sat back, enjoying the amused laughter from the others. As he glanced around, he caught sight of a new face in the crowd.

She was young, no more than eighteen, and moved with coltish grace. In a sea of bright colors, her gown was conspicuous by its pale lemon hue and modest neckline, and by the fact that it was much too big for her. The bodice drooped. The waistline sagged. The skirts were so long, she was nearly tripping over them. While the others surrounding the queen flaunted their charms, this young woman apparently chose to keep hers hidden. Her hair, a nondescript shade of brown, was pulled back from her face in a simple knot. Several strands had slipped free to curve along one cheek. While Conor watched, she lifted a hand to brush at them. It was an awkward gesture that was both sweet and endearing. For a moment he was reminded of his little sister, Briana, who was much more comfortable in the stables than in the company of their parents' titled guests.

The queen sighed. "I envy you, Conor. If only my own

childhood could have been spent in like fashion. Alas, I was never permitted such frivolous behavior.''

"Aye, Majesty. We all know yours has been a dreary existence, locked away in sumptuous palaces, your every whim catered to by devoted servants, adored by your people wherever you go.''

Conor was rewarded by another round of laughter. The queen was clearly enjoying his wry humor. There were few in her company who would dare to ridicule her, no matter how gently. That only added to this Irishman's appeal.

"Majesty.'' Lord Dunstan set aside his goblet, determined to pursue the topic that had been abandoned at court. "I know you are weary of discussing the Irish problem. But all of England is talking about the recent attacks upon our soldiers. Attacks, I might add, that once only occurred in Ireland, but are now happening here on our very soil. A messenger brought news of one such attack this very morning, in a nearby village.''

"They are merely rumors.'' Elizabeth's eyes flashed. "What would you have me do, Dunstan? Imprison every man who wears the robes of a cleric?''

Dunstan shrugged. "Since I have little use for men of the cloth, I would have no problem whatever with such an edict. And it would remove this outlaw's disguise.''

"If this mysterious outlaw is as clever as everyone says, he will merely find another way to conceal his identity.'' Elizabeth turned to Conor. "What think you, my rogue?''

He gave her his famous smile. "I think, Majesty, 'twould would be simpler to imprison every soldier who is found forcing himself on an unwilling maiden.''

Dunstan sneered. "With such a law England would soon find itself without an army.''

The queen arched a brow. "I had no idea such behavior was so widespread.''

"The behavior of soldiers would surely offend Your

Majesty's delicate sensibilities." Dunstan shot a meaning-ful look at Conor. "As it would some of the less...stalwart gentlemen at court, it would seem. But such behavior is a fact of life. Our soldiers are trained to kill our enemies. They are accustomed to taking what they want, regardless of the cost to others."

Conor's voice was carefully controlled. "Are you sug-gesting that the virtue of innocents is the price Her Majesty must pay to maintain an army?"

Dunstan nodded. "It is the price every nation must pay. War changes men. They become akin to animals."

"Some do." Conor fought to keep the anger from his voice. "And some manage to retain the virtue of nobility while fighting for their rights as men."

"Are you saying you approve of what this so called Heaven's Avenger is doing to our soldiers, O'Neil?"

Conor's tone was dangerously soft. "I suggest you ask the maidens who have been spared by his knife."

The queen flashed a smile, thoroughly delighted by this skilled battle of words between these two.

A servant approached to whisper softly, "Your seam-stresses are here for the fittings for your new gowns, Maj-esty."

Elizabeth sighed. "You see how it is, Conor? A mon-arch's work is never done. And I was so enjoying this little discussion. Will I see you tonight?"

He kept his smile in place. "If you wish, Majesty."

"I do. We'll sup in my private dining room with Hum-phrey and Dunstan and a few friends."

"Aye, Majesty."

Elizabeth set aside her goblet and stood. At once the others in the room got to their feet and bowed as she fol-lowed her servant out the door.

Once they were alone, the crowd visibly relaxed. Without the pressure of the royal presence, they could be themselves.

"Wine, O'Neil?"

Conor looked up to find Lord Dunstan standing behind him.

"Thank you." Though he loathed the man, Conor was adept at playing the game. He kept a polite smile on his face as he lifted his goblet.

"I understand we'll both be dining with the queen tonight." Dunstan accepted a goblet from a passing servant.

"Aye." Out of the corner of his eye Conor saw the young woman talking with Lord Humphrey. She had a way of looking down, and then peering upward through her lashes, that was most appealing.

Seeing the way Conor watched her, Dunstan caught her arm as she passed. "Have you two met?"

She seemed startled, like a creature from the wild about to break free and run. She took one look at Conor and stared down at her feet. Instead of replying, she merely shook her head.

"Conor O'Neil, may I present Emma Vaughn."

"Vaughn?" Conor couldn't hide his surprise. "Are you related to Daniel Vaughn, from Dublin?"

"Aye." Her voice was low, breathy, with that lovely lyrical brogue that years of English tutoring couldn't erase. At that moment she lifted her head. Up close, Conor realized, her eyes were green, with little flecks of gold. Most unusual eyes, for a most unusual female. "Daniel Vaughn is my father. He lives outside London now."

"I'd heard. But he still keeps the estates in Ireland?"

She nodded while studying him with equal curiosity. So this was the man who had all of London talking. And no wonder. Thick black hair fell rakishly over a wide forehead. His lips, wide and full, were curved in an inviting smile. But it was his eyes that held her. Eyes as blue as the Irish

Sea. They remained steady on hers, holding her gaze even when she tried to look away. "There are tenant farmers to work the land and tend the flocks."

Before she could say more she looked up to see one of the women beckoning to her. "Excuse me. I must take my leave."

"So soon?" Dunstan kept his hand firmly on her arm.

"Aye." She looked almost terrified at the prospect of being touched in this manner. "I am at the queen's beck and call."

Dunstan looked from Emma to Conor and gave a smile. "Perhaps I'll arrange for you to attend the Queen's supper tonight. Would you like that?"

She shook her head. "It wouldn't be proper. I'm merely training..."

"Nonsense. There is nothing I would like more than to have such a lovely creature beside me during the long, tedious evening. I still hold considerable sway with Elizabeth. Consider it done."

When she walked away, Dunstan watched until she exited the room. Then he turned to Conor. "A bit shy for my taste. And then there's the matter of her clothes." He wrinkled his nose. "But she's a fresh enough face. I grow weary of the sport when the players are too eager." He drained his goblet and set it aside. "I'm sure you know what I mean, O'Neil. Since it's the same game you play with our queen."

Conor held his silence as Dunstan sauntered away. Let the others think what they would about his relationship with the queen. So far, though he had managed to stay out of her bed, he had her ear. He hoped it could remain that way.

He was weary of thinking about Elizabeth and struggling to read her many moods. Keeping his features carefully composed he turned to stare into the flames of the fire, and thought about the young woman in the ill-fitting clothes.

Emma Vaughn. Daughter of Daniel Vaughn, one of the most respected landowners in Ireland before his wife's ill health had forced him to seek out the healing waters of Spain. Vaughn's brother was bishop of Claire; his uncle one of Gavin O'Neil's best friends.

Conor thought again about the shy, demure young woman, unlike the other ladies-in-waiting who were so bold. There was something about her. Something almost familiar. As though he'd met her before.

He made up his mind instantly. Surely he owed it to his father's old friend to take her by the hand and lead her through the perils that could befall her at court. Especially at the mercy of one like Dunstan.

Dunstan. That animal would leave her honor besmirched and her dignity in tatters. The thought of thwarting Dunstan was instantly appealing.

Aye. He would do it. Not just because of Dunstan. And not only because her pretty little face had caught his eye. Nor because he'd admired her backside as she'd taken her leave. But because she was a fellow countryman.

Aware that Elizabeth was a jealous monarch, Conor knew he would have to be very careful not to incur the queen's wrath. He would keep his relationship with Emma Vaughn one of simple friendship. That would be best, especially in his line of work. Anyone who got too close stood a good chance of being burned, should the fires of war be fanned.

Still, it would be good to have someone with whom he could shed some pretense. A true Irish lass with whom he could simply relax and unburden himself.

In this den of vipers, both he and Emma Vaughn had need of at least one true friend.

Chapter Three

"**L**ord Dunstan has invited you to sup with the queen?" Amena, one of the queen's favorite ladies-in-waiting, arched a brow in surprise. Then she studied Emma with a knowing smile. "I must admit I'm more than a little surprised. He usually prefers…" She shrugged. "No matter. It is considered quite an honor. What will you wear?"

Emma picked through her meager wardrobe and chose one of her mother's old gowns, which she had brought along because her own seemed completely unsuitable. "I thought this would do."

"Hmm." Amena held it up to the girl and clucked her tongue. "It seems a bit…overlarge. But I suppose I could loan you a sash. And some decent slippers. I'll send my servant with them."

"Thank you." Emma watched as the older woman took her leave. Then she began pacing in front of the fireplace.

Lord Dunstan made her uncomfortable. In fact, the very touch of him made her skin crawl. There was something about his manner. Or perhaps it was the look in his eyes. Whatever the reason, she mistrusted the man. But she would do whatever necessary to see this task to its conclusion, no matter what danger or discomfort it entailed.

With a sigh she slipped out of her gown and into one of her mother's. Though it was no longer stylish, and far too big for her slender frame, it gave her a sense of peace to feel the fabric against her skin. She breathed deeply. She could still smell her mother. The very thought brought a sting of tears to her eyes.

At a knock on the door she blinked away her melancholy thoughts and opened the door to accept the sash from Amena's servant. Minutes later, when Dunstan arrived to escort her, she squared her shoulders and took a deep breath. *I do this for you, Father,* she thought. *And for little Sarah.*

"Well, Emma." Elizabeth glanced down the table at the young woman who was seated beside Lord Dunstan. "What do you think about partaking of such a splendid meal?"

Emma's face turned several shades of pink. She was clearly uncomfortable at having been singled out by the queen. "It is…as impressive as the company, Majesty."

"Well said." Elizabeth was enjoying herself away from the pomp that usually surrounded her at court. Though she reveled in her position as supreme monarch, there were times when the burden grew heavy. At such times, she withdrew, with only a few close friends and confidantes to relieve the tedium of public life.

The queen turned to Conor, who sat at her right side. "Have you met Emma Vaughn?"

He nodded. "Lord Dunstan introduced us this afternoon."

"Her stepmother, Celestine, is my cousin." Elizabeth pinned the girl with a steady look. "How is my cousin?"

Emma chose her words carefully. "She appears healthy, Majesty."

"Aye. Celestine is a very healthy woman." Elizabeth

gave a knowing smile. "With healthy appetites. As many of our young men will attest. And your father?"

"He is...not so well."

"Then it is fortunate that he has a strong young wife to see to his care. You have a sister, I believe?"

The young woman's eyes seemed to mist for a moment before she nodded. "Sarah. She is six years old."

"I am surprised that a woman like Celestine would take on the care of a child. Your father must be a man of extreme charm and wealth. You will give Celestine my regards when next you see her."

"Aye, Majesty." Emma stared at her plate.

In an aside, Elizabeth muttered, "I took this young dullard in as a favor to my cousin, but I feel my generosity has been abused. This simpleton would better serve me if she were a pot of pretty flowers."

There were snickers from several of those nearby who overheard. Conor coughed discreetly, hoping to muffle the sound of laughter from the poor girl's ears. If she knew what had been said about her, she would be humiliated.

He picked up his wine, determined to distract the queen from any further thought of insulting the shy young maiden who continued to hang her head.

"I hear you are recently returned from Ireland, Lord Dunstan."

"Aye." Dunstan rolled his eyes. "And grateful to be back on English soil. The peasants there live in hovels we wouldn't even use to shelter our livestock. They breed like field mice, surrounded by their dirty little offspring."

He glanced around the table, enjoying the laughter from the others.

Conor carefully controlled his temper. "If you feel so strongly about them, I wonder why you go there."

"As a loyal Englishman, I do it for my queen. Someone must deal with these savages."

Conor's tone was dry. "How lucky for England that you take such satisfaction in your work."

Dunstan's eyes flashed. "Aye. I do enjoy subduing those filthy animals. And why not? They plot and scheme against my queen." He turned to Elizabeth, his voice dripping honey. "Let no man ever question my love and loyalty to the throne of England."

Touched, Elizabeth squeezed his hand and glanced around the assembled at table. "Now you see why Lord Dunstan has known favor with me all these years." She pushed away and the others got to their feet. "I believe I'm now ready for some entertainment."

She placed her hand on Conor's sleeve and allowed him to lead her to the ballroom, where the musicians were already assembled.

When the others entered, Conor noticed Emma walking timidly beside Lord Dunstan. He felt a flash of annoyance, then dismissed it. After all, the lass could have refused Dunstan's invitation to sup with the queen. The fact that she was here must mean that she desired the man's company. Still, she had the appearance of a lamb tossed to the wolves.

"Will you dance, Majesty?" Conor asked gallantly.

"Aye, my fine rogue. For I'm feeling especially lively tonight."

They began to move through the intricate steps of the dance, while the others did the same. Across the room, Emma Vaughn was dancing with Dunstan. The gown she had chosen was pale pink, and was once again several sizes too large, making it extremely unattractive.

Elizabeth leaned close to whisper in Conor's ear. "Did you see how lovingly Dunstan leaps to my defense?"

"Aye, Majesty." He couldn't keep his eyes off Emma, awkwardly attempting to follow Dunstan's lead. Once or twice she actually stepped on the hem of her gown, nearly tripping both of them.

"I was truly moved by his words."

Conor tore his gaze away and forced his attention back to the queen. "Words cost little, Majesty."

"You would know that, wouldn't you, my silver-tongued rogue. But Dunstan's loyalty is unquestioned. It is for that reason that I reward him with gold and lavish estates."

Conor saw Dunstan lean close to whisper something against Emma's temple. Saw the girl pull back, as though stung. An icy chill raced along Conor's spine. The man was known to be coarse and crude. "And Your Majesty's largesse to Lord Dunstan will no doubt assure his loyalty through difficult times."

"Do you foresee storms in my future, Conor O'Neil?"

"Nay, madam." He forced himself to smile. "I foresee only blue skies and gentle weather during Your Majesty's reign."

She returned his smile. "I do believe, Conor O'Neil, that your presence here is a very good omen."

"I hope you will always think that, Majesty." He tried to keep his smile in place as he danced her around the room.

When they drew near Dunstan and Emma, Conor maneuvered the queen close enough that she brushed Dunstan's arm.

Dunstan looked up sharply. Then, spying the queen, he took the bait, as Conor had known he would. For Dunstan, it seemed the perfect opportunity to press for a dance with the most powerful woman in the kingdom, and to rid himself of his awkward companion.

Dunstan bowed smartly. "Would you care to change partners, Majesty?"

Elizabeth, glowing, gave him the benediction of her smile. "With pleasure, Lord Dunstan."

The two whirled away, leaving Conor and Emma facing each other. Conor paused for just a beat, so that the others in the room who might be watching would think he'd been caught by surprise. It was a seemingly insignificant victory, but a very sweet one.

He offered his hand. "Will you dance, my lady?"

"I… Yes." Emma placed her hand in his.

Conor felt a jolt as their bodies came together. Though she appeared even more slender in that ill-fitting gown, the curves brushing against him were those of a woman. A woman who, for some unknown reason, had his blood running hot.

For the space of a heartbeat he forgot to move. How odd that this shy, simple young woman should be the source of such unexpected feelings.

Knowing they were being observed, he forced himself into action. He led her in a slow, rhythmic circle. When the step was completed she turned to face him, and he absorbed another jolt as his lips hovered just above hers.

"Are you enjoying yourself, Emma?"

"Aye." She lifted her head a fraction, causing her lips to brush his throat. It was the merest touch of her mouth, and both of them pulled away instantly. But the damage had already been done. Her face flamed. His eyes narrowed slightly.

"In truth…" She swallowed, tried again. This flirting business was something so alien to her, it caused her great distress. "In truth, I feel quite out of my element. Everyone and everything seems so new and frightening."

Again that voice, low, breathless, as though she had been running across a meadow. It touched some long forgotten chord in him. He had an unreasonable desire to press his mouth to a tangle of hair at her temple and soothe all her fears.

"Soon enough you will know everyone here, and it will

all feel quite normal." Without realizing it he drew her fractionally closer. His hand at her waist opened, his fingers splaying across her lower back, and he marveled at how tiny, how delicate she was.

"And you, Conor O'Neil?" She lifted her head again, this time taking care to avoid brushing him with her lips, though she found the thought tempting. "Do you like it here at court?"

"Aye." He felt the whisper of her breath against his cheek and was suddenly too warm. "I would have to be a fool not to enjoy the luxury of such a life." Aye. A fool, he thought, as he slowly moved with her around the dance floor. A fool who could find all his carefully laid plans crumbling around his feet if he weren't careful.

She sighed. "Your words bring me comfort."

"Truly? How so?"

She gave him a tremulous smile. "If you can feel at home here, then perhaps, in time, I may do the same. I had feared, because of my father's name, that I would never feel truly at home anywhere but in Ireland."

He felt a quickening of his pulse at the mention of that dear land. "So, though your home is here in England, you still consider yourself Irish?"

She seemed shocked by his question. "Indeed. Don't you, Conor O'Neil?"

"Aye." He chuckled. "But I thought it might be different for you. Your father has taken an English wife, and has settled here."

At that, her nostrils flared. Her voice fairly trembled with passion. "Ireland is still my father's home. And mine, as well. Nothing will ever change that. Nothing. Least of all my father's new wife."

Conor looked up and realized that the music had ended. The dancers were laughing and chatting as servants moved among them offering goblets of ale and wine. The queen, with Lord Dunstan beside her, was even now bearing down on them.

"Here you are, Conor. I'd feared you had retired to the parlor, to join the gentlemen in a game of cards."

"And miss the chance to dance with you once more, Majesty?" He bowed grandly before Emma and lifted her hand to his lips. "I thank you for allowing me to be your partner, my lady."

She blushed, dimpled. "You are most welcome."

In a proprietary manner Dunstan took Emma's hand and turned away. She had an almost overpowering impulse to shrink from his touch. But, knowing there were others watching, Emma merely walked along beside him.

Conor led the queen to the dance floor, where they were soon laughing and chatting as they moved through the steps of another dance. And all the while, Conor was aware only of the shy young woman who was once again moving awkwardly in Dunstan's arms.

What was the matter with him? he wondered. Why was he allowing this newcomer to cause him to veer from his charted course? But as the night wore on, he found himself more and more distracted by the sight of Emma Vaughn in the arms of the lecher, Dunstan.

"Another dance, Majesty?" Conor plucked two goblets from the tray of a passing servant and offered one to the queen.

"No more, Conor." She took a single sip, then set the goblet aside. "If I do not soon retire to my bed you will have to carry me."

He shot her a dangerous smile. "A most pleasant chore, madam. I would be only too happy to oblige."

Elizabeth blushed like a girl. "You always know just the right thing to say, don't you?"

"It is why you keep me around."

"Aye. You amuse me, Conor O'Neil. And you also please me. Unlike so many of my advisors, you are honest. At times, a bit too honest."

He winced. If she but knew. "Can a man ever be too honest, Majesty?"

She studied him in silence. Then, turning to scan the others in the room she gave a shrewd smile. "Look at them, Conor. They all wish I would retire for the night."

He gave a glance around, then turned back to her. "They seem to be having such a grand time. Why would they wish that?"

"Because their blood grows hot, confined to this room where they must satisfy themselves with occasional touches while they dance. You see Lord Humphrey? As soon as they return to their suite of rooms in the castle, his elderly wife will go to her bed. But he will spend the night in the bed of my lady-in-waiting, Amena." Seeing Conor's look of surprise, she said, "Over there, the Earl of Danville is dancing with his wife, while his mistress, Brenna Lampley, watches from the balcony. And across the room, my advisor, Charles Malcolm, is fetching a pastry for his wife. But watch as he pauses to speak with the lovely Margaret Childon. Even now they are plotting their little tryst. But that cannot be accomplished until their queen takes her leave. Then they will suddenly disappear, to meet at some prearranged room where they can satisfy more…carnal hungers."

Conor turned to study the queen. "And how do you know all this?"

"There are no secrets at court. Remember that, my rogue." She gave a girlish laugh. "My spies are everywhere."

Conor coughed discreetly. "Madam, each time I think I know you, you reveal another fascinating side."

She got to her feet and placed a hand on his sleeve.

"There are many more sides to me, Conor O'Neil. And if you continue to please me, I may show you all of them. Now you will accompany your queen to her room."

"Aye, Majesty." He moved beside her, watching as the men bowed and the women curtsied.

When he saw Emma watching him, Conor felt a flash of annoyance. She would believe, as did all the others, that he was going to the queen's bed. Not that it should matter to him. But for some strange reason, it did.

With the queen's butler in attendance, they walked to her private suite. Inside, Conor took a seat, as he always did, while the queen was made ready for bed. Once her servants had completed that chore they were dismissed. Then the door to the queen's inner chambers was opened, and Conor was invited to approach the queen.

As always, Elizabeth, modestly attired, offered her hand.

Conor brought it to his lips. "I bid you good-night, Majesty. May your sleep be deep and dreamless."

"Thank you, Conor O'Neil. Perhaps, when next we dance, I shall share a few more of my ladies' secrets."

"I'm not at all certain I wish to hear them, madam."

"All the more reason I will share them. Now I must sleep. If anyone dares to disturb me, I shall have their head."

The queen was still laughing as Conor took his leave.

His own rooms were on the opposite side of the palace, and one floor above.

Candles flickered in sconces along the hallways. At this time of night, many of the servants had retired, except for those seeing to the needs of the guests who still remained awake.

Conor passed a small game room, where several of the queen's advisors were engaged in cards and chess. He thought briefly about joining them, then decided against it.

As he passed a closed door he heard what sounded like

a woman's cry. Almost at once it ended, as though abruptly cut off. Two lovers, he thought wryly. Snatching moments of pleasure where and when they could.

He was about to move on when he heard it again. Just a sound, really. Not quite a cry. But there was something familiar about it. A hint of fear. A trace of breathlessness.

He felt a prickling along the back of his scalp.

Retracing his steps, he paused outside the closed door and listened. At first he heard nothing. Then as he moved closer, he could hear the hiss of anger. And the whispered command, "Hold your tongue, woman. There is no one who would dare interfere. It is simply the way things are done at court."

Dunstan's voice. He was sure of it. Conor felt his blood freeze. Without taking time to consider, he turned the knob and thrust the door inward. With only the illumination of coals on the grate, the two figures across the room were in shadow. Both of them looked up when he entered. As he strode closer, Conor could see that Dunstan had pinned Emma against the wall. The bodice of her gown was open. Had it been torn? Her cheeks were moist. From kisses? Or tears?

His first instinct was to grab Dunstan by the throat and rip out his heart. His hand actually went to the knife at his waist. It would give him the sweetest of pleasures to slit Dunstan's throat and watch his lifeblood spill away. But years of training made him swallow back his black Irish temper. His voice, when he spoke, was almost casual.

"Ah. The very man I was looking for."

Dunstan glowered. "You can see I'm busy, O'Neil."

"Aye. And I do hate to interrupt such…pleasant business. But I was just told that the queen requests your presence."

Dunstan brows shot up. "The queen? Are you certain?"

Conor could barely conceal his glee at the way this fool

leapt at the bait. He wondered how Dunstan would feel when the queen flew into one of her famous rages. "That's what I was told. She awaits you impatiently in her private suite."

Everything was forgotten now except this rare opportunity. Dunstan turned away, straightening his coat, fumbling with the fasteners at his waist, completely ignoring the young woman who only moments earlier had been fighting for her virtue.

He brushed past Conor. "Apparently, when it comes to the queen's pleasure, she would prefer a loyal Englishman over an Irish peasant."

"Apparently."

Conor waited until the door closed behind Dunstan's retreating back. Then he turned to Emma. Her hands, he noted, were shaking as she struggled to draw the torn bodice of her gown over her breasts.

His casual tone was gone. In its place was a rough urgency. "Are you all right?"

She nodded, too ashamed to meet his eyes.

He caught her by the shoulders. It took all his self-control to keep from shaking her. He wasn't even aware that he was grasping her so painfully until she cried out. At once he softened his grip, though he continued to hold her. "Did he...hurt you?"

"Nay." She swallowed, fighting the sobs that were building inside, threatening to break free. "I couldn't free my knife from its place of concealment or the brute would now be nursing his wounds." She struggled with the sash at her waist, then managed to unloose the dirk hidden beneath.

He could barely hide his surprise that this shy, sweet Dublin lass carried a weapon on her person. Even while he marveled at that fact, he could feel the tremors that rocked her. It tore at his heart.

"Come." He caught her roughly by the elbow and began hauling her toward the door. "Show me to your chambers."

Neither of them spoke as they strode along the hall. When she stopped before the closed doors of her suite she pushed the door inward, glancing around before stepping aside and allowing her to enter. A fire burned on the grate. Through an open doorway could be seen the shadow of a servant, moving about the sleeping chamber, where the bed linens had already been turned down.

"You're safe now, my lady. Your servant will see to your needs." He turned away.

"Wait." She stopped him with a hand on his arm.

He turned to face her. Though she was struggling to hold back the tears, they were already wet upon her lashes.

"Thank you, Conor O'Neil. You saved me from... from..." She covered her face with her hands to muffle the sobs that threatened. "He was going to...I couldn't stop him."

"I know." He wanted, more than anything, to draw her into his arms and offer her comfort. But the servant had paused in the doorway of the sleeping chamber and was watching them. He knew there were no secrets here at Greenwich Palace. The servants gossiped as freely as the queen.

Taking care, he allowed himself to touch only a hand to her hair. It was as soft as silk. As lush as velvet.

He kept his tone deliberately harsh. "It's common knowledge that the privileged few who surround the queen consider themselves above the laws of common decency. The next time, you would be advised to know a man before you accept his favors."

She looked up, tears still glistening on her lashes. "Did Dunstan treat me this way because I am Irish?"

"Nay. Because you are female."

She blinked. "But how can I help that?"

"You can't. So you must learn to be more careful. Of the people you befriend. Of those you trust. Especially the men. Else, you can't hope to survive as lady-in-waiting to the queen. For there is much treachery among these people."

"And what of you, Conor O'Neil? Are you as treacherous as the rest?"

Out of the corner of his eye he saw the servant starting toward them. "I'll leave you to decide that for yourself, my lady." He stepped back, turned, then strode from the room.

As he made his way to his own suite, Conor thought about the warning he'd just given Emma Vaughn. He'd best take heed himself as well. There were so many secrets in this place. And so many devious people hoping to use the power of their standing with the queen for their own advantage. He was no exception. He was here for one reason. To manipulate the queen for the sake of Ireland. No one and nothing must get in his way. Especially one shy little maiden who, it would appear, would need an army of bodyguards to keep her safe in this den of vipers.

Chapter Four

"Thank you, Nola. You may leave me now." Emma waited until the servant closed the door before sinking to the edge of the mattress. Her legs were still trembling, her nerves still jittery from the ordeal.

Dear heaven, what had she gotten herself into?

She pressed her hands to her cheeks. She didn't belong here. These people were all mad. From the queen to her silly ladies-in-waiting. From the evil Lord Dunstan to the Irishman, Conor O'Neil. Especially Conor O'Neil. Why would a loyal son of Ireland pay homage to the Queen of England, unless he was a traitor or a complete fool?

And yet, had it not been for that fool, she had no doubt where she would be now. And in what condition. Still, though she was grateful, she wasn't about to be won over by his kindness. He'd only saved her because he'd stumbled upon her in his search for Dunstan.

Dunstan. Her eyes narrowed. How she hated the man. Too agitated to remain still, she stood and began to pace. The pompous, arrogant bully. She must see to it that she was never alone with him again. There was something in his eyes. Something dark and feral. The man had no conscience.

As for Conor O'Neil... She paused, staring into the flames of the fire. He frightened her in a very different way. When she'd been forced to dance with him, she'd felt strange stirrings. They were unlike anything she'd felt before. The mere touch of his hand at her back had left her with a prickly feeling along her spine, her blood heating, her mind suddenly going blank. Those deep midnight-blue eyes of his had pinned her, making her think he could see clear through her. And when her mouth had brushed him by mistake, she'd felt a strange yearning. Almost like a...a hunger for more.

Ridiculous.

She resumed her pacing. When she'd begun to weep, she had thought, for just a moment, that he intended to gather her into his arms and hold her. She'd foolishly wanted him to. Perhaps, she surmised, it was because she missed her father so. But even when the moment passed, and Conor had merely touched her hair, she'd felt a wave of trembling that left her weak.

Aye. She had a right to be frightened of Conor O'Neil. The man was a danger to her, unless she could ignore these strange new feelings he'd awakened. But she would have to put aside such things. For Conor was the key. It was plain that he was far dearer to the queen than her stepmother had suspected. A man like that could exert a great deal of influence. It would be no simple matter to keep one step ahead of such a man, but it would be necessary if she intended to get Celestine the information she desired.

No matter what her feelings or fears, Emma knew she was committed to this dangerous situation. For little Sarah's sake, for her father's sake, she would watch and listen and learn everything she could about the queen's intentions toward Ireland. And she would use anyone and anything she deemed necessary. Especially the proud peacock, Conor O'Neil. Of all the men surrounding the queen, he was by far the worst. If only because he was openly courting the avowed enemy of his own land.

One floor above, Conor, barefoot and shirtless, leaned a hip against the balcony and stared into the darkness. His tunic had been tossed angrily on a chaise. His boots had been kicked off in haste, landing against the far wall. In his hand was a silver chalice filled with ale. He downed half of it in one long swallow.

His hatred of Lynley Dunstan had been festering since he'd first heard of the man. It was no secret that Dunstan used his friendship with Elizabeth for his own benefit. Whenever an enemy of the queen had a fortune in gold and precious jewels confiscated, or a lavish estate in England or Ireland taken over by the Crown, Dunstan was the first in line to claim the spoils. At last count he was one of the wealthiest men in the realm. And greedy for more. He had even released Conor's sister-in-law from her betrothal, in exchange for her lovely Dublin estate, Clay Court.

But Dunstan's appetite didn't stop there. He had deflowered so many maidens, it had become something of a joke in the queen's inner circle. Sadly, that same friendship that earned his wealth and titles was the reason that no man lifted a hand to stop him. All feared Elizabeth's wrath. She was fiercely loyal to her friends. Like a wounded she-bear when one of them was threatened.

Conor's hand tightened on the stem of the chalice. Damn the man. He'd had no right to try to force himself on an innocent like Emma Vaughn. Anyone could tell by looking at her that she was as defenseless as a fawn at the mercy of the queen's bowmen.

Dunstan would try again. Especially when he found out that Conor had lied about the queen wanting to see him. One taste of her temper, and the man would retaliate in kind. With Emma bearing the brunt of his vengeance.

Conor swore and tipped back his head, draining the last of the ale, then flung the empty chalice against the wall before climbing into his bed.

Emma Vaughn wasn't his business. Ireland was. And he'd better not ever forget it.

"Ah. Here you are, sir." As the sunrise chased the mist from the land, the stable lad took the reins of Conor's mount. "Her Majesty's servants have been frantically seeking you. You are summoned to the queen's chambers at once."

"Thank you, Meade." Connor swung down from the saddle, relieved that, despite a lack of sleep, his early morning ride had helped to clear his mind. The queen would demand to know why he had sent Dunstan to her chambers last night. He would have to find a way to deflect her anger. It wouldn't be the first time. He was becoming a master of deception.

Deliberately taking his time, he strolled through the lovely formal gardens before entering through a rear door. Inside, the palace was swarming with activity. Cooks milled about, turning a pig roasting over a spit, stirring kettles of soup and gruel. The fragrance of freshly-baked bread wafted from the kitchens. In the hallways, servants bearing armloads of clean linens scurried from suite to suite. Ladies' maids rushed by, carrying exotic plumed hats or elegant gowns.

Conor made his way to the queen's quarters. A uniformed soldier stood at attention outside the closed doors. The moment he spotted Conor, he opened the doors and stood aside.

Inside, a liveried butler disappeared to announce his arrival, then reappeared, opening yet another set of doors.

Conor stepped into the queen's private suite. Elizabeth was seated at a round table set in front of the fireplace. She wore a robe of cut velvet, and beneath it a morning gown of lace with a high ruffled collar. Her hair had been carefully arranged in a coronet atop her head. In her hand was a steaming goblet of hot mulled wine.

She set it down and regarded him in silence.

He waited, knowing he could not speak until invited to do so.

Elizabeth knew it as well, and used it to her advantage, pinning him with an angry look.

Just then the door was opened again and the butler's voice broke the silence. "Majesty, your lady-in-training, Emma Vaughn."

"Show her in." The queen's words were clipped.

Emma stepped in, then, seeing Conor, stopped in her tracks.

It was clear that she had come running at the queen's summons. Though her face was pale, her cheeks wore two bright spots of color. Her hair, as yet uncombed, was a riot of chestnut curls that fell to her waist. Her gown was a hideous confection of dull rose, with a sagging neckline and drooping waist, at least two sizes too large.

Conor tried not to stare. But in truth, even the ill-fitting gown couldn't hide her youth and beauty. She was such a contrast to the queen, she nearly took his breath away. Elizabeth, despite her lavish trimmings, looked plain by comparison.

"Well." Elizabeth looked from Conor to Emma, then back again. "What do you two have to say for yourselves?"

"Majesty, I don't—" Emma began.

But Conor interrupted by stepping forward and holding up a perfect red rose. "On my way here I plucked this for you, Majesty."

Elizabeth was so startled she merely stared at it. Then she wrinkled her nose. "You smell of horses."

"Forgive me, Majesty. I was out riding on this splendid morning. But if I offend, I will go now and change my clothes."

"Nay." She placed a hand on his sleeve to stop him. "Being surrounded by so many women, I rather like the smell of a man. You will stay."

"As you wish." He pressed the flower to her hand.

She couldn't resist accepting it and lifting it to her nose, breathing deeply. On a sigh she asked, "How did you know I love roses?"

"I didn't. But since you are England's rose, I hoped it would appeal to Your Majesty."

She was smiling now, her earlier temper forgotten. "Sit with me. Both of you. We will break our fast together while we talk."

Conor held a chair for Emma, then settled himself beside her. A mistake, he quickly realized. He was far too aware of her. Of the way her knees were trembling beneath the table. Of the way her eyes kept darting to the queen's face, then away, to stare at a spot on her plate.

At a nod from the queen, her servants began circling the table, offering quail, pork, venison, as well as crusty rolls and goblets of wine or mead.

As she ate, the queen's spirits continued to rise. Her appetite was amazing. She ate slowly, deliberately, washing everything down with more wine.

When she was finished she turned to Conor. "So, you like to ride, do you, Conor?"

"Aye, Majesty. There is something about giving a steed its head and racing across a meadow. It allows the mind, the heart, the very soul to soar wild and free."

She was watching him, clearly enthralled. "Why is it that everything sounds so much better when you describe it?"

He shot her a wicked smile. "Perhaps because I believe

in what I say. Would you care to ride with me one morning, Majesty?"

She considered a moment, then nodded. "I believe I would." She turned to the timid young woman. "Do you ride, Emma?"

"Aye, Majesty." Emma was relieved to speak on a topic about which she was knowledgeable. "On my father's estate outside Dublin, we have some of the finest horses in all of Ireland."

"A woman after my own heart. Then you shall join us for an early morning ride. And we will see if our English horses measure up to yours."

Emma gave a shy smile. "I'd like that, Majesty, for I've missed the horses."

In the doorway the queen's butler cleared his throat. She looked toward him with annoyance.

"Majesty, your Keeper of the Treasury and your financial advisors have assembled for the meeting you requested with your Lord Chamberlain and your Lord Steward."

She gave a look of distaste. "Why can I never have enough time for my own pleasures?" She took a deep breath. "I must be about the business of England. A pity. There was much I wished to discuss. Such as why Dunstan came to me last night, disturbing my rest. After I'd finished my litany of insults, he told me a wild tale that you, Conor, were the one who had sent him to my chambers."

Instead of offering an explanation, Conor merely gave her his most charming smile.

Dazzled by him she turned to Emma. "And I'd hoped you would explain what Lord Dunstan told me about you."

"M…Majesty?" Emma paused with the goblet halfway to her lips.

"That you caught your heel and fell against the wall, tearing your gown. Then you fell into a fit of weeping for which you couldn't be comforted."

"Homesick, no doubt," Conor muttered aloud.

Some of the wine sloshed from Emma's glass, and she began to wipe at it.

Before she could speak the queen gave an exaggerated sigh. "Ah. No matter. I must attend to more important matters." She lifted the rose and inhaled its perfume, then got wearily to her feet.

At once both Emma and Conor stood.

"Stay," Elizabeth commanded sternly. "Finish your meal. And tomorrow, while the others are still abed, we shall ride. Do I have your word on it, Conor?"

"Aye, Majesty. I shall see to the arrangements myself."

She nodded. "A dawn ride then. I am eager to see if my mind and heart and soul will actually soar as you described."

With a swish of skirts she was gone.

While the servants began to clear the table, Conor picked up his goblet and drank. Emma did the same. Her hand, he noted, was trembling.

She turned to him. "What do you think...?"

He gave a firm shake of his head and the question she was about to ask died on her lips.

He waited until the servants were about to leave. Setting down his goblet he offered his arm to the young woman. "Perhaps you would care to take a walk in the gardens, my lady?"

"Aye."

Conor glanced at the back of a retreating servant, then added, "I believe the sunshine will be quite refreshing."

They moved stiffly out the door and down the long hallway to the stairs. Once outside Emma turned to him. "You don't trust the queen's servants?"

"I trust only myself. And you should do the same."

"Aye." Good advice, she knew. Especially in the game

she'd been forced into playing. She took a breath. "How am I to explain my tears to the queen?"

"With all that goes on in the palace, the question may never again come up. If it should, I think your safest explanation is that you are feeling adrift, so far from home."

"Aye. 'Twould not be a lie." For a moment her thoughts strayed, but to her credit she managed to compose herself. She hugged her arms about herself and lifted her face to the sun, breathing deeply. "Each time I step out of the palace, I feel as if I've been freed from a prison."

"If you feel so strongly, why are you here?"

She began to move beside him along the stone-paved walkway. "To please my stepmother."

"What about your father? Has he nothing to say about it?"

"He...also wishes to please her. Like her cousin, the queen, Celestine is a strong-willed woman."

Conor paused beside a curved bench and waited until Emma sat before seating himself beside her. "Will you ever return to Ireland?"

She looked away to hide the trembling of her lips. "It is my fondest wish. But I couldn't leave without my father and sister. And I fear they will never leave England."

"Because your father has made a new life for himself here in England with his bride?"

"Aye."

He stretched out his long legs, enjoying the sunshine. And the company. It occurred to him that there were few in England with whom he could converse. "Perhaps, if your stepmother could be persuaded to visit our island, she would learn to love it as we do, and your family could settle down in Ireland."

Emma shook her head. "Celestine is like so many in this land who have already hardened their hearts against Ireland.

They see no reason to ever visit its shores or get to know its people."

He nodded. "Aye. And the feelings against our land continue to grow. Dunstan is urging the queen to send more soldiers, to bring the Irish rebels to their knees."

She held her breath, wondering if what he had just revealed might be important to her stepmother. Gathering her courage she asked, "And what do you urge the queen to do?"

He shrugged. "What I always urge. Patience. Compassion. But Elizabeth is not a patient woman. And her closest advisors agree with Dunstan. I stand alone in this battle of wills."

"Oh, you're hardly alone, Conor O'Neil." Emma turned to him, and he was aware that all her shyness had somehow disappeared. In its place was a strange mix of emotions. Anger seemed the strongest, along with a strength he hadn't noticed before.

"And what is that supposed to mean?"

She had no idea why she was experiencing this sudden rush of temper. This man was nothing more to her than a means to an end. But just thinking about his relationship with Elizabeth of England had her blood boiling. It wasn't jealousy, she told herself. It was righteousness. He was a son of Ireland, openly courting the Queen of England.

She stood, shaking down her skirts. "From what I've heard, you have the queen eating out of your hand like a favorite pet. And, if what I witnessed this morrow in the queen's chambers was typical, I'd say you've found many ways to win her with your charm."

Though he was annoyed, he hid his feelings behind a lazy smile as he got to his feet, towering over her. "Haven't you heard? Women can't resist me."

She turned on her heel and started back along the path. "You're very sure of yourself, Conor O'Neil."

He merely chuckled as he kept pace beside her. "Does that annoy you?"

"I care not one way or the other about you. But I am grateful that you managed to deflect the queen's questions."

"Aye. I thought the rose was an especially nice touch."

"It was all an act?" Stunned, she suddenly stopped and turned to him.

When he said nothing in his own behalf she studied him more closely. "What arrogance, that you would use even the queen in this fashion. What favors do you hope to obtain for yourself, I wonder?"

Without thinking he caught her roughly by the shoulders. "Beware my temper, Emma. Though I keep it on a tether, it breaks free from time to time. And when it does, it is a most unpleasant sight."

She lifted her chin, refusing to back down, though the mere touch of him caused her heart to stutter. "And you avoid all unpleasantness, don't you, Conor O'Neil?"

"Aye." He hadn't meant to touch her, but now that he had, he couldn't think of any good reason to release her. Up close she smelled as fresh as the flowers in the garden. Her hair gave off a fragrance of rose water. "You might consider doing the same, Emma Vaughn, if you know what's good for you."

"Is that a threat?" Her eyes narrowed. Gone was all pretense of the shy, timid young woman she showed to the rest of the world. And though her blood was pounding in her temples, she refused to back away.

"Call it whatever you wish. If you're wise you'll take care not to make enemies among the queen's friends at court. There may come a time when you're in need of a friend.'' He found himself staring at her pouting lips. Lips that were made for kissing. That thought had the blood rushing from his brain.

''Are you suggesting that I should allow an animal like Lord Dunstan to do with me as he pleases?''

''Of course not.'' At the moment, there were any number of things he would be pleased to do with her himself. None of them polite. All of them far too tempting. ''But you would be well-advised to find a way to hold him at arm's length while not incurring his wrath. Dunstan is much favored by Elizabeth. Should you arouse his ire, you arouse the queen's as well. And those who are not favored by this monarch sometimes find themselves and their families in grave danger.''

''Then you need not worry, Conor, since you are obviously much in Elizabeth's favor. Everyone at court whispers about her strange alliance with her...'' Emma's tone lowered in scorn ''...her charming rogue.''

She saw the sudden change in his eyes. She knew she had said too much, had gone too far. Alarmed, she tried to push free of his hands. But it was too late. The last thread of his frayed temper snapped.

''Do you know how weary I am of that name?'' He dragged her close and saw her eyes widen.

Ignoring her little cry of distress, he lowered his head and covered her mouth with his.

Heat flowed between them. Heat that softened her lips, and tightened his hands on her arms.

She tried to pull back, but her strength was no match for his. And then, as his mouth moved over hers, she was caught up in something so new, so powerful, she lost the will to fight.

She had been kissed before, but never like this. At first, the kiss was harsh, demanding. Filled with anger and impatience. But even as she absorbed the first jolt, the kiss suddenly softened, gentled, causing her even greater distress.

Conor lifted his head for a moment, staring at her as if seeing her for the first time. And then he lowered his head and kissed her again, almost hesitantly. The lips moving over hers seemed to be tasting, sipping, absorbing. The hands at her back were holding her as carefully as if she were made of glass. And though she could have easily pulled away, she felt frozen to the spot, mesmerized by the feel of his clever mouth on hers.

He hadn't meant for any of this to happen. Like all in his family, he'd always known that his temper was a source of trouble, and so he always kept it under tight control. But once loose, it took over his will, taking him places better left untraveled.

At the first touch of her, everything had speeded up. His pulse. His mouth on hers, tasting, devouring. His hands on her body, wanting to touch her everywhere, needing to feel her in every part of himself.

One small section of his mind was shouting a warning. It was midmorning in the queen's own garden. Any number of people might see them. All his plans could be spoiled by this one foolish act. But another part of his mind ignored the warning. He didn't want to stop holding her, kissing her. He would pay any price, forfeit any success, to go on like this forever.

He took the kiss deeper and was rewarded by her sigh. Her hands, which had been pushing against his chest, were now clutching him to her. Her body was pressed to his, imprinting itself on his flesh. Her full pouty lips were as eager as his to taste, to feast, to devour.

He was, in the space of a heartbeat, fully aroused. He

wanted more. Wanted all. A most dangerous situation, he knew. He needed to step back. To think. To breathe.

Sweet heaven, to breathe.

One last touch, he promised himself as his hands moved along her back, stroking, soothing, exciting. One last kiss, he vowed, as his mouth moved over hers.

At last, drawing on all his control, he managed to lift his head.

Filling his lungs with air he took a step back, breaking contact. "Let that be a lesson to you, Emma. Even the most charming of rogues has a limit to his patience."

"Aye. A rogue. An arrogant, pigheaded...." Her words came out in a rush, threatening to choke her. She would never let him know how difficult it was to speak. "But there is nothing charming about you, Conor O'Neil. And I'll remind you that I am not one of those brainless little butterflies who flit around the men at court, hoping to play at love. If I were, it would be with a heroic figure, like...like Heaven's Avenger, who saves helpless maidens, and certainly not with the likes of you."

She drew back her hand to slap his face. Reading her intention, he caught it and dragged her close.

His breath was hot against her cheek as he whispered, "Aye. That's why you refused to cooperate in that kiss, isn't it, Emma?"

She was stung by his jibe. It hit too close to the mark. She knew she'd wanted what he'd offered, and had made no move to stop him. But now that she had her wits about her once more, she was feeling shamed and embarrassed. It was one thing to pretend to be interested in him, in order to learn his secrets. It was quite another to allow herself to get caught up in any real emotion for this man.

In order to cover her rush of feelings she said, "You're no better than Dunstan. Like him, you think all women will fall at your feet. Well, I'm not the queen, blushing and giggling at your every word, Conor O'Neil. I intend to save myself for a real man, not some pompous peacock.''

She turned and caught at her skirts, racing as fast as she could toward the palace. Leaving him standing alone in the sun-drenched garden. With the taste of her still on his lips. And the scent of her filling his lungs.

Chapter Five

"Good morrow, sir." The stable lad had seen Conor coming and was already leading his mount from the stall.

"Good morrow, Meade. I hope you haven't forgotten that the queen will be joining me."

"Nay, sir. I've forgotten nothing." The boy's smile was dazzling. It was a rare opportunity to serve his monarch. "I have Her Majesty's mount saddled and ready. And a third horse suitable for the young lady you mentioned." He looked beyond Conor. "I believe this must be your young lady now."

Conor turned. Emma was striding toward him, looking slightly uncomfortable in a heavy riding gown the color of green leaves. As with all her clothing, it was obviously borrowed from one of the other ladies-in-waiting, since it was as ill-fitting as the others. Her long hair was tied back with matching ribbons. Perched on her head was a most fetching bonnet, adorned with feathers and lace.

When she drew close he called, "Good morrow, Emma."

"Good morrow, Conor." She avoided his eyes, feeling the old shyness take hold. She had managed to avoid him since that scene in the garden yesterday. But this morning she had awakened with a sense of excitement. It wasn't the knowledge that she would be spending time in this man's company that had her pulse racing. After all, she could hardly tolerate Conor O'Neil. She was convinced that her eagerness was really caused by the opportunity to ride in the open air.

The stable boy led a spirited mare from its stall, and Conor studied the horse with suspicion. "Are you certain you want such a headstrong animal, Emma?"

"I've told you I'm an accomplished rider."

"Very well." He offered his hands, and she placed one dainty foot in them. She was boosted into the sidesaddle, where she quickly arranged her skirts. The heat she'd felt at his touch was merely generated by the excitement of the ride, she assured herself.

As for Conor, he took a moment to enjoy the sight of shapely ankles and legs, before her skirts tumbled down to hide the view. When he heard the sounds signalling the arrival of the queen, he turned.

Elizabeth bustled along the walkway, accompanied by a maid, a footman, a butler and several ladies-in-waiting, who were all talking at once.

"Good morrow, Majesty." Conor bowed. "Will we saddle more horses for the others?"

"Conor. Emma." Elizabeth, in high spirits, lifted a hand in greeting. "Nay, these others have merely come to see me off on my little adventure." She studied Conor and added, "How is it that you manage to look so handsome this early in the morning?"

"The same way you manage to look so regal, Majesty." Conor cast an admiring glance at her scarlet riding gown with matching jacket and hat.

"Ah. I see." Elizabeth gave him a knowing smile. "You were born to it?"

From her position in the saddle, Emma gritted her teeth. The queen and her Irishman were equally adept at flattery.

Conor merely laughed and turned to the stable lad. "Fetch the queen's mount, Meade."

When the horse was led from its stall Conor said, "I hope the chestnut mare meets with your approval."

"Aye. And well she should. She was a gift from Philip of Spain. He was hoping to win favor so that he might press for a betrothal." She gave Conor a sideways glance as he helped her into the saddle. "Does that bother you, my Irish rogue?"

"That the King of Spain desired you? Nay, madam. All the world desires Elizabeth of England."

She laughed as he stepped back and her maid arranged her skirts and petticoats. "As always, you know just the right thing to say. Come. Let us be on our way. I wish to ride." She waved to the others, then wheeled her mount and led the way toward a distant meadow.

Conor pulled himself into the saddle and followed.

The horses moved in single file, following a well-traveled path, with Elizabeth in the lead, Emma in the middle, and Conor trailing behind.

It was a perfect summer morning, with the grass damp with dew, and a misty haze hanging over the edges of the forest that ringed the meadow.

As the path gradually widened, Elizabeth slowed her mount until the other two drew abreast. They rode up a steep incline, then came to an abrupt halt. Ahead of them was a small herd of deer grazing. For the space of a heartbeat the entire herd seemed to freeze. Then, as several does and their young took off at a run toward the shelter of the forest, the buck stood his ground. Only when his herd was safe did the buck follow.

"Magnificent." Elizabeth watched as they disappeared

into the underbrush. "How I long for my bow and arrows. But I have ordered no hunting in this forest today."

"A wise move. You shall hunt another time, Majesty. For today, it is enough that we are free to ride." Conor pointed to a falcon riding the breeze high above them. "As free as the birds."

"Aye." Elizabeth gave a little laugh. "I've always wished I could fly. Come then, my friends. Let us fly across the meadow to the far side where the forest begins." Without waiting for their agreement, she urged her mount into a gallop.

Emma's mare, eager to run, took off at a thunderous pace. For a moment Conor held his mount steady, enjoying the sight of her astride her horse. The fact that she was a skilled rider made the sight all the more pleasurable. Her hair streamed out from beneath her hat as she bent low over her steed's head. Her laughter filled the morning air.

At last, feeling the tug on the reins, he gave his horse its head. Halfway across the meadow he caught up with her. As he rode alongside, he felt a jolt of pleasure at the sight that greeted him. Emma's cheeks were a becoming shade of pink; her eyes were warm with excitement.

A peal of delighted laughter rose up from her throat. "Oh, how I've missed this. I hadn't realized just how much until now. I do thank you, Conor."

"You're welcome, my lady. It pleases me to see you so happy."

Gone was the awkwardness that always seemed to set her apart from the others at court. Here, astride a sleek animal, she was definitely in her element. There was such grace and poise in this young woman who turned to him with a smile of pure pleasure before she spurred her mare into a gallop.

Seeing her, the queen followed suit.

Conor watched, then urged his horse to follow. Just ahead of him the two horses remained neck and neck.

Emma called over her shoulder, "Look at me, Conor. I'm flying."

Emma's horse began to inch ahead. Conor urged his steed into a last burst of speed. But even that effort couldn't overtake the lively mare. She fairly flew across the meadow, slowing only when Emma reined her in. As soon as Conor and Elizabeth joined her, they began congratulating one another on an excellent ride.

"Oh, Conor." Emma's eyes were shining. "It was as you said. I felt as though I were flying."

"I do believe that was as close to it as you'll ever be." He turned to include the queen. "Both of you looked as though your steeds had sprouted wings."

Emma leaned down to run a hand affectionately over her mare's neck. "It has been too long since I've enjoyed this pleasure."

"Is this how you spent your childhood?" Elizabeth asked.

Emma nodded. "Riding wild and free across the green meadows outside Dublin. Oh, Majesty. If you could but see the wild beauty of my homeland. It truly takes the breath away."

"I've not heard much about the beauty of Ireland from Lord Dunstan," Elizabeth said dryly. "Most of what he has relayed is about the savagery of its people. Especially this Heaven's Avenger who seems to have spawned a twin on our shores." The queen glanced upward, watching the path of a falcon as it glided across the sky. "Come. I wish to fly again." She wheeled her mount and took off at a brisk pace, leaving Emma and Conor to follow.

As they started off Conor held his horse to a more gentle trot.

Emma, keeping pace beside him, turned to him with a

worried frown. "Do you think I offended the queen by mentioning my home?"

Hearing the concern in her voice he shook his head. "I've learned that this queen is accustomed to saying exactly what's on her mind. If she had been offended by your words, she would have told you. At the moment, the only thing that concerns Elizabeth is the feel of sunshine warm on her face, and a strong, solid horse beneath her." He reached over and placed his hand on Emma's. At once he felt the jolt and was startled by it. Why did the touch of this simple young woman arouse him so? "Let's do the same, Emma. We'll put away our worries, and enjoy the day."

Her smile faltered. Just the feel of his hand on hers brought a strange ripple of pleasure. What sort of power did this man have? Whatever it was, she wanted none of it. She had to remember that all she wanted from him was his secrets.

With an impish grin, Emma nudged her horse into a gallop, determined to escape his charm. Over her shoulder she called, "I do believe my mare can outrun your mount, my lord."

For a moment he was so surprised, he could only stare after her. Then, he threw back his head and roared with pleasure as he spurred his horse into a gallop. Halfway across the meadow Emma's horse passed the queen's. A few moments later Conor's mount did the same. By the time he reached the far side of the meadow, Emma was standing beside her horse, watching his arrival.

"I knew I could beat you." Her voice, still breathless, rang with pride.

"That was fine horsemanship, my lady." Conor remained in the saddle, enjoying the color that suffused her cheeks.

The queen rode up, clearly pouting at having been left

out. "Had I known this was to be a race, I would have won it easily. I demand another. And this time I must be included."

Conor nodded. "Fair enough, Majesty. But a race is not a race unless there is a prize to be won. What will we race for?"

"Gold always works," the queen said regally.

"Alas, I have none." Emma's cheeks reddened.

"I see." Elizabeth pondered for a moment, then said, "I have it. The winner shall choose an article of clothing from each of the losers."

"An article of clothing?" Emma looked perplexed.

"Aye. For instance, if I should win," Elizabeth said with a glint of teasing laughter in her eyes, "I should require of you that delightful riding hat, for it is far more fashionable than mine. And no one should look more fetching than the queen."

Emma blushed. "The hat isn't mine, Majesty. It belongs to Amena."

"I thought I recognized it." The queen's laughter grew. "All the more reason why I desire it. Amena owes me a gold sovereign from an earlier wager." She turned to Conor. "And from you, my dashing companion, I would require those riding gloves."

He bowed gallantly. "Then I shall have to lose, just so you can claim them, madam. But they will prove to be far too big for your delicate hands."

"Ever the gentleman. So." Elizabeth glanced from Conor to Emma. "Are we agreed that the winner will demand an article of clothing from the losers?"

Connor couldn't help laughing. "I doubt that either of you ladies would have anything I might care to wear. But, since I intend to win, I will give it some thought." He turned to Emma. "Do you agree?"

She nodded as she pulled herself into the saddle. "I quite

agree, since I intend to be the winner. Am I allowed to claim the queen's riding gown?''

"If you win, Emma Vaughn, you may claim whatever you please.'' Elizabeth's tone was haughty enough to assure she had no intention of losing this race.

The three positioned their horses while the queen outlined the course that they would take.

"We will ride across the meadow to those tall trees, circle them and return to the starting point. The first one back here shall be declared the winner.''

As soon as the others nodded their agreement, Elizabeth gave a shout, spurred her horse into a gallop, and the race was on.

The horses were evenly matched. Though Elizabeth's mount was slightly ahead, the other two kept up an even pace. As they rounded the trees and headed back across the meadow, Conor's horse managed to take the lead. Conor glanced over his shoulder and could see that Elizabeth and Emma were gaining on him. It was Elizabeth's horse that passed him first. She gave a shout of laughter as she raced ahead. Moments later Emma's mare streaked by, and she was soon straining to catch the queen's horse.

In spite of the fact that he was losing, Conor couldn't help grinning at the sight of the two women. It was a grand sight, watching the queen and the Irish lass pouring heart and soul into a simple horse race.

It appeared that Elizabeth's mount would win. But at the last moment Emma's mare gave a final burst of speed and began to overtake the queen's horse.

As he watched, Conor caught sight of a glint of sunlight reflecting off something shiny just beyond the finish line. Though the flash of light was too blinding to make out anything more, he thought he saw a blur of movement beside a tree. Could it be an animal? A deer, perhaps? Or a man?

Suddenly his attention shifted as he heard a cry, and saw Emma tumble from her horse.

He spurred his mount into a frantic run. By the time he was leaping from the saddle, Emma's crumpled form lay in the grass, as still as death. Out of the corner of his eye Conor could see Elizabeth sliding from her saddle and rushing forward. But all Conor's attention was focused on Emma. So pale. So fragile. So motionless.

"By heaven." He was beside her in the blink of an eye. And as he gathered her still body against his chest, his heart forgot to beat while he pressed a finger to the pulse at her throat.

"Is she...?" Elizabeth dropped to her knees beside him. "Conor, is she all right?"

"She's alive." As he began to examine her, he stared in dismay at her arm, where an arrow had pierced the flesh.

"How can this be?" Elizabeth reacted with first shock, then slow, simmering anger. "My soldiers knew that I would be riding here today. They were ordered to see that no hunters were allowed in this forest or meadow." She glanced around. Except for the nervous pawing and stomping of their horses, there was no other sign of life. But just beyond them loomed the forest, thick with trees and underbrush. Any number of hunters could take cover there and never be spotted. Her tone was strangled with fury. "Heads will roll for this."

"Aye, Majesty. As well they should. But for now, our most immediate concern must be for Emma."

In softest tones Conor crooned to her. "Emma. Can you hear me, my lady?"

"Aye." Her lids fluttered, and she managed to look at him through a blur of pain.

"We must get you back to the palace as quickly as possible. It will mean a very long and painful ride. Can you manage the discomfort?"

She nodded weakly. "I...I think so."

Elizabeth got to her feet and stood watching as Conor draped his cloak around the young woman. Then, as gently as if he were handling a newborn, he lifted her in his arms and pulled himself into the saddle before nudging his mount into a slow, easy walk.

Even that gentle pace caused Emma pain, and she moaned softly.

"Forgive me, Emma." Conor pressed his lips to her cheek as he cradled her against his chest. Every movement, he knew, was a source of agony for this sweet young woman.

The queen rode beside him, leading Emma's mount.

The ride, which only that morning had seemed so easy and carefree, now seemed the longest of their lives. For Emma, each jarring motion had her setting her teeth against the pain.

For Elizabeth, the hardest part of the journey was watching this young woman's courage as she was forced to endure her suffering in silence.

For Conor, the worst was not knowing what had actually happened. As he rode toward the palace, he pondered the painful end to this delightful morning. His thoughts were dark and ominous, weighing him down as he struggled to sort through the events that had led to this.

Had Emma been struck by accident, the result of a careless hunter? Or had she taken an arrow that had been shot deliberately? If that were the case, was Emma the intended victim? Or had the arrow, in fact, been aimed at the queen?

The closer he came to the palace, the darker Conor's thoughts became. Just what sort of sinister plot had they stumbled upon? And what part, if any, did he and Elizabeth and this young innocent play in it?

"The young lady is in no danger." The queen's own physician had been summoned to Emma's room, where the arrow had been removed and her wound carefully bound. "She was indeed fortunate. The arrow managed to avoid shattering any bones. It pierced only the fleshy part of her arm. There will be some lingering pain, but the wound is clean, and the bleeding has been stopped."

"Praise heaven. Do you hear that, Emma?" Elizabeth had insisted upon remaining, along with the other ladies-in-waiting who had gathered around the bedside, until the physician could render a verdict.

The young woman nodded, trying to smile through the haze of confusion brought on by the opiates that had been administered. But the attempt only added to her discomfort.

"Now." The queen headed toward the door, trailed by the other women. "I will speak with the captain of arms about this unfortunate accident." She turned to Conor who continued to stand beside Emma's bedside. "Will you join me?"

"Nay, Majesty. With your permission I'll linger awhile and see to Emma's needs."

"She has maids for that, Conor." Elizabeth saw the darkening of his eyes and sighed. "Very well. Stay, if you wish. But only for a short while." She turned to the young woman in the bed. "If you should desire anything at all, Emma, you need only ask."

"I am most grateful, Majesty."

When the room had emptied of all the clucking, chattering hens, Emma closed her eyes with a sigh. She heard the sound of a chair being dragged close to the bed, but it required too much effort to open her eyes. When she felt her hand engulfed in warmth and strength, she forced her lids open. Conor was seated beside her, his hand gently stroking hers. His eyes were so filled with concern, she felt her heart contract.

"You look as wounded as I feel. Is there something the queen's physician hasn't told me?"

"Nay, my lady. You'll mend quickly. But it pains me to see you like this."

"It's my own fault, Conor. I took a foolish risk, attempting to win a silly race. And this is the price I must pay for my vanity."

His voice roughened with emotion. "This has nothing to do with vanity. And it wasn't your fault, Emma. You were struck by an arrow."

"Aye. Pity the poor hunter who will be severely punished for his error. And all because I gave him no warning that I was approaching at such breakneck speed."

He shook his head in amazement. "Even now you try to excuse another's error, and lay the blame on yourself." He lifted her hand to his lips. "Can I bring you anything to ease your pain?"

"No...pain." Her words had begun to slur as the opiates dragged her further into a mist. Or was it the touch of his lips that brought this strange, floating sensation? Why was he here, when he ought to be attending to the queen? Still, the fact that he was beside her brought her a measure of comfort. Her lids opened slowly. "Will you...stay?"

"For as long as you wish, Emma."

"I wish...wish..." The words trailed off as she struggled with so many conflicting feelings. She wanted to stay just like this, with her hand held firmly in Conor O'Neil's. Wanted to know that when she awoke, he would still be here, watching out for her. For some unexplained reason, she felt as she once had in the arms of another. Warm and safe. She wished...wished... Such strange, unsettling wishes. Surely they were far beyond her reach.

Her eyes closed. She drifted into sleep.

Conor continued to hold her hand in his. Such a small

hand. As smooth as an infant's. And yet, there was such strength in this tiny female.

There was nowhere else he wanted to be at this moment, except right here beside her. Holding her hand. Watching her sleep. And hoping desperately that this was all some simple accident.

Still, all his instincts led him to believe that this had been something far more sinister. He couldn't help but feel that he had somehow stumbled into some dark, evil plot. And this innocent female had become entangled in the web, as well.

There was a tavern wench in the nearby village of Prestwyck who often overheard snatches of conversation that had proven valuable in the past. He thought perhaps he might pay her a quick visit while Emma slept.

Chapter Six

"**F**ool!" Celestine rounded on Dunstan as he entered the parlor. Henry, her brother, paced in front of the hearth, his eyes as hot with temper as those of his sister. "Whatever were you thinking?"

"That I could do what you don't seem capable of doing. Eliminating the one who occupies the throne. And laying the blame on the Irish for good measure."

"And instead you've put my little spy out of commission."

"Only temporarily. She merely sustained an arrow to the shoulder."

"You could have killed her."

"It would have been precious little loss. Your stepdaughter is nothing more than an ineffective, bumbling fool."

Celestine's oath split the air. "Your assassin was no better."

Dunstan's own temper flashed. "I hired no assassin. The arrow was my own."

Celestine's jaw dropped. "You fired the arrow meant for the queen?"

He nodded, and glanced toward Huntington, who had

gone as still and pale as death. "I trust no one but myself to see to a deed as vital to our future as this."

"Then you trusted a fool. All you managed to do was arouse the queen's suspicion. From now on she'll probably insist upon being surrounded by a full complement of armed guards."

Dunstan merely smiled. "I've just begun to ply my tricks. By the time I'm finished, Elizabeth won't trust anyone except me. Even her precious Conor O'Neil will be treated with disdain. And she'll be ready to send her own regiment to Ireland to seek vengeance." He cackled. "And I will be her most trusted companion. And the one who will finally see to her untimely death."

"Well." Elizabeth slanted a look at Conor as he strolled casually across the great hall and made his way to her side. "Once again, my charming rogue, you have made your queen wait. Do you do this deliberately, to test my patience?"

"Forgive me, Majesty." Conor took the hand she offered and lifted it to his lips.

When he offered no explanation for his tardiness, she patted the chair beside hers. "Sit. And tell me why you have kept me waiting."

"I have no good reason, madam. I was simply careless with my time."

"Beware I do not find you careless with my affection as well, Conor O'Neil." She indicated Lord Dunstan, seated on her left. "Dunstan was just telling us about the latest attack by Heaven's Avenger. It seems he came to the defense of a wench in a nearby village. Prestwyck, I believe?" She turned to Dunstan, who nodded his assent. "The wench was being abused by several drunken soldiers."

"Another mysterious warrior?" Conor accepted a goblet of ale from one of the servants.

"Aye. As he has in the past, he spoke not a word, but left all the soldiers dead. Their throats slit. When the wench burst into tears, this avenger dried them with his cloak, then handed her a gold coin and departed as quickly as he had appeared."

"How romantic," one of the ladies-in-waiting said with a sigh, while the others nodded.

"Some peasant, out to make a name for himself," Dunstan scoffed. "Majesty, do not forget the ill treatment our soldiers received at the hands of O'Neil's countrymen."

"My countrymen?" Conor arched a brow.

"Aye." Dunstan's voice rose with righteous anger. "Three of them killed. Six more wounded by swordsmen who attacked them while they slept."

Conor could feel all his muscles contract as he kept his gaze fastened on the goblet of ale in his hand. "Where did this occur?"

"In a forest just across the Boyne River. A place your people call Drogheda, I believe."

Conor was careful to keep all trace of emotion from his tone as he glanced around the table. "I know the place. Serene countryside. A swift current runs through the Boyne as it curves through County Louth."

"Then the scenery is deceptive." Dunstan's voice grew louder. "For your countrymen can surely not lay claim to serenity. In truth, they are all troublemakers." He turned to the queen. "I fear, Majesty, that unless you soon give them a taste of English justice, these peasants will band together. If that should occur, the rebellion could get out of control. And England will find itself at war."

Elizabeth remained silent, lost in thought.

Taking advantage of her mood, Dunstan's shrill voice carried the length of the room, causing heads to turn.

"Your Majesty has seen with her own eyes how persuasive the Irish peasants can be. There is one of them seated at your right hand at this very table."

Feeling the stares of the curious, Conor decided to deflect Dunstan's anger with humor. "Aye. And if this Irish peasant may speak for his countrymen, may I say that it is an honor to be allowed to sup in such august company. Most often we are found supping with the sheep and the swine."

That brought a roar of laughter around the table.

Elizabeth signalled for the meal to begin. As the servants circled the table, Conor asked, "What did your sergeant at arms have to say about Emma's unfortunate accident, Majesty?"

"He assured me that if there is even one hunter hidden in the forest, my soldiers will find him. Thankfully, Dunstan accompanied me to the stables and suggested that they scour the woods on foot and horseback in search of the fool who dared encroach on my security."

It occurred to Conor that such an army of men and horses would also serve to obliterate any tracks left behind by the attacker. "That is indeed comforting, Majesty."

"Aye." Dunstan leaned close to inject himself into the conversation. "And if the poacher should turn out to be one of your Irish peasants, O'Neil, he will surely feel the sting of English anger. For we do not take lightly our queen's safety. Especially here on her own soil."

Seeing that the queen had sunk into thoughtful silence, her ladies-in-waiting turned the table talk to gossip about several titled gentlemen and their mistresses, in order to amuse her.

"Did you hear that the Earl of Greyton actually commissioned the same diamond-and-ruby pendant for his mistress that he'd bought earlier for his wife." Amena glanced toward several of the other ladies-in-waiting, who nodded and giggled.

"Aye." Dunstan caught the eye of a serving wench and lifted his goblet for more wine. "When his mistress admired it, he had no choice but to buy it for her."

Amena's laughter bubbled. "He added ear bobs as well. And when his wife found out, she removed her pendant and tossed it out of the carriage into the roadside. The earl sent his servants to comb the area in hopes of retrieving it. Alas, so far nary a glimmer of rubies or diamonds has been spotted."

"Serves him right." Dunstan drank deeply, enjoying himself. "Jewels are wasted on wives. They ought to be showered upon mistresses. And then only when they have proven themselves to be...deserving of such treasures."

"You are a wicked soul." Despite her earlier melancholy, Elizabeth laughed. "Now I know why you aren't wed, Dunstan."

"Not wicked, Majesty." He bowed grandly. "Merely honest. I think we are of like minds where marriage is concerned."

"Ah. If I were a man..." She sighed, then turned to Conor, who had remained silent throughout the exchange. "I'd be a rogue like this one." She patted his hand before scraping back her chair. At once, everyone got to their feet. "Come. We will take our sweets and spirits by the fire."

Elizabeth led the way, with the others following.

While a servant moved among them, offering pastries and goblets of ale, the talk turned to the aging Lord Humphrey, who was absent.

"It's been long known that one of his earlier mistresses gave him an illness." Dunstan stretched his legs toward the fire. "Now it's beginning to affect his mind."

Seeing the look of surprise on the queen's face, he couldn't help boasting. "You didn't know, Majesty?"

"Nay." She glanced at Amena, who had fallen silent. "His servant told me that he suffered from gout."

Dunstan roared with laughter, and the others soon joined in. "That may be. But the old man's mind is fading. If you desire his advice, you had best seek it quickly, for he will soon be leaving this world."

Conor felt a flash of annoyance. "A pity Lord Humphrey can't be here to defend his good name."

"Perhaps you'd care to become his defender, O'Neil?" Dunstan glanced from the queen to the others. "It isn't bad enough the old fool is dying of the dreaded French disease. Now he is to be protected by an Irish peasant whose only strength seems to be his ability to lift a goblet of ale to his lips."

Conor's hand went to the sword at his side. His blood was still hot from the scene he'd stumbled upon in Prestwyck. A few minutes more and the poor wench would have been brutalized. Still, no matter how many times he managed to come to the aid of one such innocent, there were hundreds of others who had no one to champion their cause.

Dunstan saw the flash of anger in Conor's eyes. "Careful, O'Neil. Everyone at court is aware that you wear that sword for mere adornment."

Conor struggled to keep his anger carefully in check. Now was not the time. But there would come a day when he would exact revenge. Not just for himself, but for all his countrymen as well.

Dunstan was still laughing when he turned to see the queen's sergeant at arms standing in the doorway. A cluster of soldiers entered, hauling with them two men in tattered hooded cloaks. Everyone in the room fell silent.

"Forgive me, Majesty," called her sergeant at arms. "But you asked to be notified immediately should we find the hunter who fired the arrow."

"It was one of these?" Elizabeth strode forward.

"Aye, Majesty."

At the sight of the queen the men fell to their knees sobbing.

"Were you not warned that hunting in that forest was forbidden?"

Unable to find their voices, the men shook their heads and continued to sob.

Elizabeth's voice grew haughty. "It will go much harder on you if you do not tell the truth. Look at your queen and speak. What were you doing in the forest?"

"Please." The younger of the two was trembling so violently, he could barely be heard. Those in the queen's court gathered around, eager to watch and to listen.

"So. You can speak." Elizabeth lifted a hand. "Go on. Tell me."

"I have a good wife and five children. All are hungry."

"And so you thought you could poach game in the queen's own forest."

"Nay, Majesty." He was wringing his hands and weeping. "I would never steal. But a man must feed his family. I couldn't pay what was due my lord." The man stared hard at the floor. "When I was brought here from Ireland…"

"Ireland." She seized on the word. "You were brought here from Ireland? Who brought you?"

"It was…" In his confusion the man dared to lift a hand to the hem of the queen's skirt.

With a snarl of rage Dunstan pulled his sword and ran the man through. It happened so quickly, there was no time to react. As the others looked on with a mixture of shock and amazement, the man clutched his chest, then fell forward in a pool of his own blood.

The queen and her ladies, unaccustomed to such violence, recoiled with horror.

"Dunstan." The queen's voice rang with authority. "How could you do such a thing in my presence?"

"A beggar such as he is not worthy to touch his queen. I had no choice but to put a sword through his filthy, lying heart."

Elizabeth put a hand on Dunstan's arm. "I am deeply moved by your concern, my friend. But I desired to hear his story." She turned to the other man. "You will tell me what your friend was about to say."

The man's trembling increased until his entire body was consumed with tremors. He couldn't seem to tear his gaze from Dunstan's bloody sword. "I know not. Brady never revealed the name of the man who offered him gold."

Elizabeth's voice swelled with anger. "For what purpose was your friend offered this gold?"

"We were told to hide ourselves in the forest and wait until we were found."

"That's it? To hide and to wait?"

"Aye, Majesty. And now I'm told I will go to Fleet Prison, where I will surely die. And my family will surely starve." He was sobbing again. Great, wracking sobs that shook his whole body.

"You should have thought of that before you committed this hideous act." Dunstan took aim with his sword. "Your queen was riding nearby. That same arrow could have struck her royal person."

The man turned to the queen. "I shot no arrow, Majesty. I merely hid in the forest."

"Liar." Dunstan's tone rang through the room.

But before he could run the second man through, Conor unsheathed his sword with such speed, everyone gasped in surprise. "Do you now declare yourself judge and executioner, Dunstan?"

Dunstan's eyes narrowed with fury. "Do you dare to challenge me, O'Neil?"

"Aye. If that's what it takes to save this man's life until he can tell us all he knows."

"He has told us." Dunstan took a step closer. His hand holding the sword fairly quivered with eagerness. It was well known throughout the realm that he was a skilled swordsman. "He has no more right to live than you do, O'Neil. But perhaps you plead for this assassin's cause because he is from your homeland."

"The cause I plead is the chance to hear the truth. Or do you fear that, Dunstan?"

Dunstan's blade flashed as he lifted it, intent upon thrusting it through the heart of the sobbing captive. But before he could, Conor moved with lightning speed. In one swift motion he sent the tip of his sword slashing through the air to pierce Dunstan's hand. With a yelp of pain and fury Dunstan released his hold on his weapon, and it clattered to the floor between them.

A low murmur of surprise rippled through the crowd as Dunstan, in a rage, bent to retrieve his sword. When he straightened, he found the point of Conor's blade pressed to his tunic, directly over his heart.

"Yield, Dunstan. Or prepare to die."

For the space of a heartbeat, all who were watching forgot to breathe. These two men, whose hostilities had long simmered, made no secret of the hatred that had now reached a boiling point.

"I'll not permit this in my presence." The queen's voice quivered with indignation. "Dunstan, you will yield at once."

As if in a daze he looked up, seeing the queen's regiment prepared to take up their own weapons if he should disobey the royal command. Though he seethed with hatred, he knew he had no choice. He lifted his hands, then took a step backward.

Conor continued to stand, sword aloft, while he fought his own black temper.

"You will sheathe your weapon, Conor O'Neil," the queen commanded imperiously.

For a moment longer he hesitated, before bending and retrieving Dunstan's sword.

In the silence that followed, Elizabeth averted her head to avoid seeing the body of the one man lying in his own blood. Taking a deep breath she commanded, "Take this wretched liar and see that he never again has the chance to breathe the air of freedom."

"Please, Majesty. Have pity. Please." The man's cries continued to echo as he was hauled from the room and down the long hallway.

When the dead man's body was dragged from the room, servants scurried about to clean his blood from the floor.

Taking advantage of the commotion, Dunstan leaned close to whisper to Conor, "This thing is not over between us, O'Neil. One day soon you will taste the sting of my sword."

"As you wish." Conor handed over his sword, then sheathed his own. "Any time. Any place."

With a shrewd smile, Dunstan handed the queen a goblet of wine. "You showed considerable restraint, Majesty. If you had but given the word, I would have run the scoundrel through."

"Let him rot in prison." Elizabeth lifted the goblet to her lips and took a long slow drink. Then, squaring her shoulders, she turned toward Conor. "So, my fine, clever companion. You appear to be as skilled a swordsman as your brother. But I much prefer your charm to your...more base instincts. Amuse me, so that I do not dwell on all this unpleasantness."

It took all Conor's resolve to put aside the feelings that still seethed. The O'Neil temper had always been a curse. It was temper that had him playing into Dunstan's hand

and revealing a skill he would have much preferred to hide from these people.

With supreme effort he managed to summon an array of stories that soon had the queen and the others smiling and nodding. But as the ale flowed and the evening wore on, he found himself thinking more and more about the poor man's tale, and the fate of his friend. And wondering why the man's words nagged at the edges of his mind.

"I must take my leave." Elizabeth put a hand to her lips to stifle her yawn. "I have enjoyed your entertaining company. And your many naughty stories."

There was a smattering of laughter. But instead of motioning to Conor, the queen pointed to Dunstan. "Come, my dear friend. Escort me to my chambers."

"Aye, Majesty." He shot a look of triumph toward Conor, then offered his arm to the queen.

As soon as they were gone, Conor took his leave of the others. Instead of making his way to his own rooms, he moved quickly along the hallway until he reached Emma's door. He stepped inside, closing the door softly behind him.

The sun had long ago set. The sky outside the windows of Emma's room was dark as midnight. It was evident that servants had come and gone all through the evening, lighting candles, laying a fire on the hearth, fetching water and ale, and finally, a tray of food that was as yet untouched.

Conor sat beside the bed, watching as Emma slept.

She was a vision. The bed linens had slipped, revealing a good deal of pale, creamy skin. Apparently the servants had cut away her clothes and left her in nothing but a chemise, which revealed as much as it concealed. And though he knew he ought to look away, at the sight of that dark cleft between high firm breasts, his breath backed up in his throat.

Her hair, long and unbound, spilled in wild tangles across

her pillow. In the candlelight it seemed more red than brown. An errant curl dipped over her eye in a most appealing manner, and he itched to touch it.

She sighed in her sleep, and he ignored the warning echoing through his mind as he reached over to smooth the hair from her forehead. Her lids flickered, then opened.

"I'm sorry I woke you."

"I'm not sorry. Have you been here long?"

He shook his head. "I've only just arrived. I had to first sup with the queen."

Emma studied him by the light of the candles. "You look weary, Conor. Far worse than I feel. Perhaps you should go to your bed."

He shook his head. "I doubt I'll sleep this night. I have too much on my mind."

She gave him a long, steady look. "What is it that troubles you?"

"It isn't your concern. I'll not burden you with my dark thoughts."

"So serious. What happened to the queen's charming rogue?"

"Perhaps he grows weary of the role for which he has been cast."

"A pity. The queen will surely miss him."

He gave her a gentle smile. "And she shall have him back. But for tonight, I wish to put aside everything and just be myself." He touched a hand to her forehead and found it cool. "Are you in any pain?"

"Nay. None." Nor would she feel any, she thought, as long as his gentle touch was upon her like this. "Tell me about this evening, Conor. What did you and the others talk about at supper?"

"Things better left unsaid. Gossip. Innuendo. The latest court scandals. Crude jokes. They grate on my nerves."

"Aye. I know the feeling. When I am in the company

of the other ladies-in-waiting, they pass the hours with such silliness. There are apparently no secrets among the titled people who call themselves friends of the queen.''

"Their lives seem empty. Meaningless. They actually seem to enjoy each other's misfortunes.''

"I found that to be true of my stepmother, as well. She seemed never truly happy unless someone else was unhappy.''

"Your stepmother is cousin to the queen?''

"Aye." Emma's smile faded. "She's the reason I am here.''

"Then I'll have to remember to thank her." At her questioning look he smiled. "If you're strong enough to sit up, I could help you with some of the food on that tray.''

She glanced over, then nodded. "Perhaps some broth would restore my spirits.''

He stood and mounded the pillows behind her, then helped her to sit. When the bed linens slipped even lower, he had a quick glimpse of shapely thigh and knee before she pulled the covers up.

He set a small table beside the bed and placed the tray upon it, then poured her a cup of steaming broth. As she lifted it to her lips he noticed that she used only her right arm.

"Is your wounded arm paining you?''

"Aye. There's some pain." She saw the dark, angry look that came into his eyes as he poured water from a pitcher and sprinkled a powdered opiate into it before holding it to her lips. It was a look she'd seen before. But, in her confused state, she couldn't seem to place it.

"Drink this, my lady.''

She did as she was told. "From that scowl on your face, I suppose you're probably planning to scold me for my carelessness. But I assure you, I'd have won that race had it not been for our mysterious hunter.''

"He's a mystery no longer." Conor described briefly the scene in the great hall as the two men were dragged before the queen. And though he told her of the death of one of the men at Dunstan's hands, and the imprisonment of the other, he left out the rest of the events, saying only, "The remaining man insisted that he and his friend had been given gold, not to fire an arrow, but merely to hide in the forest and wait until they were found."

Emma wrinkled her forehead. "Why would he make such a foolish claim? Doesn't he know that lying will only bring him a stronger punishment?"

Conor had thought the same thing. "Enough of this talk." He leaned over her and held the broth to her lips. "Drink. You need to restore your strength."

When his fingers brushed her mouth she felt a curious heat deep inside. She peered at him from beneath her lashes. "Do you do this for all the ladies at the palace, my lord?"

"Only the truly beautiful ones, who share my love for my homeland."

She felt a warm glow at his words. He thought her beautiful. No one had ever said such a thing to her before. It made her heart soar, even while she was cautioning herself to pay no heed to this charmer.

"Now." He sat down on the edge of the bed and began to cut small portions of meat and cheese. "I think you should eat a bit more."

She ate several bites before refusing the rest. "I can eat no more, Conor."

He set the tray aside, then stood beside the bed. "Would you like me to go? Perhaps you'd care to sleep now."

She touched a hand to his, enjoying the quick flash of fire through her veins. "Stay awhile longer. Unless you're eager to go."

"I'll stay." In fact, he couldn't think of anywhere he'd

rather be. But instead of taking the chair, he eased off his boots and sat down on the bed beside her. Plumping a pillow beneath his head, he turned to her. "Now, tell me about your life in Ireland before your father took a new bride."

"Oh, it was such a grand life." Just thinking about it had a light dancing in her eyes. "My mother was a saint. Sweet and loving and so patient. Best of all, she adored my father and my sister and me."

"How old is your sister?"

"Six." Emma's voice grew soft with the memories.

"Is she as beautiful as her big sister?"

Emma laughed. "She's stunning. Father used to say when Sarah gets older, she'll break hearts."

As she told of her family, and their horses, and the life she'd once lived in Ireland, she found herself relaxing for the first time since she'd arrived at the palace. Odd, that it could be this man who would bring her such comfort.

Beside her, Conor closed his eyes and let her voice wash over him. Just hearing that sweet brogue seemed to soothe away the troubles that had nagged at him all day.

Gradually her voice faded, and he realized the opiates were taking effect. When he started to get up she rolled toward him, clutching his arm. "Don't...go, Conor...want you near."

"Then I'll stay." He drew her into the curve of his arm and pressed his lips to a tangle of hair at her temple. "I think, Emma Vaughn, you may be my only true friend in England. With you I can be myself. I need not pretend to be silly and charming."

"You are...always charming." In her befuddled state, she looked up at him and saw another. A hooded man, whose blue eyes had flashed with danger and compassion. Who, unlike this famed orator, had spoken not a word, but who had held her and made her feel safe and warm. "And I would like...very much to be...friend."

Those were her last words before drifting into a deep, dreamless sleep.

While she slept in his arms, Conor leaned his head back, relaxed, content. It wasn't the feeling he'd expected to find in a woman's bed. And this certainly wasn't the woman with whom he'd expected to share a bed.

Of all the people he'd met since his arrival in England, Emma Vaughn was his most unlikely ally. She was as clumsy as he was smooth. As rough as he was polished. But this strange, awkward little woman put him at ease. Even while she caused an unsettling yearning in his heart.

What he was feeling was extremely dangerous. If Elizabeth were to sense that he had eyes for another, she could make his life miserable. To say nothing of what she might do to this young innocent beside him.

Whatever friendship he and Emma might enjoy, they would have to be extremely careful. And no matter what his feelings for her, he would have to continue to remind himself that she could never be anything more than a friend.

Chapter Seven

Conor awoke with a start. For a moment he was puzzled by the unfamiliar warmth in the bed beside him. The room was in darkness except for the faint light from the glowing coals in the fireplace. He turned to see Emma curled up like a kitten, with her small hand tucked into his.

How long had he been here, asleep in her bed? Too long, judging by the sounds of muted footsteps and swishing petticoats in the hallway outside her door. Very soon now a servant would be coming to stoke the fire and light the candles as the household awoke to another day. If the queen's favorite companion should be found asleep with one of the young ladies-in-waiting, the palace would be alive with the scandal by the end of the day.

He studied the spill of silken curls against the pillow, wishing he could take a minute more to watch her. How sweet she was. How innocent. Aye. Innocent. His smile faded. He would do well to remember that in the days and weeks to come.

There had been more than a few heated moments during the night, when she'd pressed her cheek to his, or touched her lips to his throat, that he'd been nearly swamped with need. Perhaps, if she had been a different kind of woman…he shook his head. Emma wasn't the kind a man could casually enjoy and then leave. He sensed that Emma Vaughn was a woman who would become a fever in a man's blood. Once would only whet the appetite for more. Emma was the kind who deserved the promise of a lifetime. And that was something he could never give. For his life was already pledged to this dirty business he did for his country.

He lifted her hand to his lips and pressed the softest of kisses to her delicate flesh. Then he slid from the bed and made his way across the room. With his ear to the door he waited until the footsteps receded. Then he slipped quietly away and hurried to his own suite.

A ride, he decided, would be the best way to shake loose the fog that seemed to have enveloped his brain this morning. He was in a strange, almost melancholy mood.

He pulled on his tunic and made his way to the stables. And all the while he found himself brooding about the scene at dinner the previous night. It wasn't just the poor beggars, one who was now dead, the other rotting in Fleet. Or the fact that their tale of intrigue made no sense at all. Or that he had, in a fit of temper, revealed a part of himself better left concealed. It was also Dunstan and the others surrounding the queen at court. They had actually laughed and jeered as those poor fellows were dealt with in such a harsh manner. The more time Conor spent with these people, the more shallow they revealed themselves to be.

"Good morrow, sir." The stable boy led his mount from the stall and held the reins while Conor pulled himself into the saddle.

"Good morrow, Meade."

"You've a fine day for a ride, sir."

"Aye."

"You'll be riding alone?"

Conor nodded. And as he guided his mount along a

wooded path toward the distant meadow, he found himself brooding again. Alone. Sometimes, in this opulent pleasure-palace, surrounded by wealthy titled ladies and gentlemen, he felt completely alone. He looked like them. Dressed and talked like them. Made them laugh. Charmed them. And yet there were times when he felt as though a wall had been built between himself and them. For he could never think like them. Nor did he want to. And so he remained alone. He kept his own counsel. He shared his thoughts, his hopes, his dreams with no one.

He gave his horse its head and felt the breeze fill his lungs and toss his hair. He was so weary of the game. But there was no turning back. He'd given his word. He did this for family, for friends, for country.

For Emma.

The thought startled him. But as he digested it, he found himself smiling despite the darkness of his thoughts. Aye. For Emma. The innocent Irish lass who, like him, found herself alone.

"Wake up, my lady." The servant touched a hand to Emma's shoulder.

"Umm. Not yet." Emma smiled and reached a hand to the pillow beside hers. It was still warm. She traced the imprint of the head that had rested there.

Suddenly she sat bolt upright. She had fallen asleep in Conor's arms. And through the night, whenever the pain had awakened her, she had been soothed by his presence beside her in the bed. Her eyes widened as she glanced around. She sighed with relief when she realized he'd managed to slip away before they'd been found together.

"What is it, Nola? Why do you disturb my sleep?" Emma demanded of the servant.

"My lady, you must let me help you dress at once. Her

Majesty sent word that she will be visiting your chambers as soon as she has broken her fast.''

"The queen? Here?'' Emma glanced around the room in consternation. Had Conor left any of his belongings behind? Would the queen notice the disarray of bed linens and guess that she'd had a visitor through the night?

"Aye, my lady. Her Majesty ordered a tray sent to your room, and said I was to see to your toilette at once.''

"Did the queen say why she would deign to come to my humble chambers?''

"Nay, my lady.'' The servant filled a basin with warm, rose-scented water. "Shall I help you wash?''

Emma shook her head, struggling to clear the cobwebs of sleep. "I can manage it by myself. But first I need an opiate for the pain.''

The servant filled a glass and sprinkled a packet of powder in it. Emma drank gratefully, hoping it would take effect quickly. As she washed and dressed, she fretted over the reason for the queen's visit. A monarch such as Elizabeth never humbled herself to set foot in the lowly chambers of others. It had to be because of Conor's nighttime visit. Someone must have seen him come in. And now a jealous Elizabeth was about to order her to leave. Sweet heaven. She would be banished in disgrace. And the blood of her father and sister would be on her hands.

"Hold still, my lady. Why, this gown's so big on you, it's apt to fall clear off if you walk too fast.''

"No matter. Just tighten the sash.'' Emma was so distracted, she didn't even bother to look in the mirror.

What would happen to Sarah and her father now? She would never see them again. She would be alone. And penniless.

"Here, my lady. Sit and I'll brush your hair.''

Like a sleepwalker, Emma sat, her mind awhirl. She was

so agitated, she could hardly sit still as the servant combed and brushed and pinned.

"That's the best I can do, my lady. You've lovely hair. But with that gown..."

"Thank you, Nola. You may leave me now."

"Aye, my lady."

The servant scurried out just as several other serving wenches entered. While one carried a tray to the small round table set in front of the fire, another servant began to make up the bed and fold the bed linens.

"Did you hear that Her Majesty is coming?" The servant's tone was hushed with awe.

Emma nodded as she picked at a biscuit. "Aye. Do you know why?"

"Nay, my lady." The servant bustled about, opening draperies, seeing that the door to the wardrobe was neatly closed.

When the room was spotless, the serving wenches hurried away, leaving Emma alone.

Perhaps it wasn't Conor's nocturnal visit that was bringing the queen to her suite. She began to pace. Perhaps Elizabeth wanted to see for herself how the wound was healing. Still, if that be her reason, she could have satisfied her curiosity with a simple question of the servants.

Even the pain in her arm was dull in comparison to the fear that was beginning to wrap itself around her heart.

By the time the chirping of female voices announced the arrival of the queen, Emma had worked herself into a state of pure panic.

"Did you have a good ride, sir?" Meade caught the reins as Conor slid from the saddle.

"Aye, lad. I'm feeling much improved." Indeed he was, he thought, as he sauntered toward the palace. The fresh air had cleared his mind. The sunshine, warm upon his face, had brightened his outlook considerably.

He squared his shoulders, ready for another day of political intrigue. If the queen called upon him to play the fool, he would do it with ease. If he had to listen to Dunstan's ramblings about the Irish peasants, he would manage it without allowing any hint of the anger that simmered just beneath the surface.

"Good morrow, my lord." As he strode into his chambers a little servant blushed and bowed before emptying a pitcher of water into a basin. "Her Majesty's maid left word that you are to join Her Majesty as soon as you are presentable."

"I suppose that means she expects me to see that I don't smell of horses." He laughed at his little joke. "Send word that I will join Her Majesty in her chambers as soon as I've washed and changed."

"Aye, my lord." The servant bowed again before adding, "But Her Majesty will not be in her chambers."

"Where then?"

"I was given to say that she would meet you when she left the chambers of Emma Vaughn, my lord."

Conor turned away to hide his surprise. The queen had gone to Emma's room? This didn't bode well for either of them. He musn't have been as cautious as he'd thought. Someone must have spotted him leaving the lass's chambers.

They were in for it now.

Conor's stride was swift and impatient as he hurried along the hallway. Drops of water still glistened in his hair. He'd barely taken time to dry himself and dress in a clean tunic before going in search of the queen.

This was all his fault. Emma hadn't invited him into her chambers. He'd invited himself. And though she'd asked him to stay, he'd needed no coaxing. If truth be told, it had been the most pleasant night he'd spent since his arrival in England. And now his head would roll. And Emma's too, unless he found the right words. He didn't mind for himself. But Emma was the innocent party in all this. He would have to make Elizabeth understand that.

He was still rehearsing his words when he skidded to a halt outside the door to Emma's suite. From inside he could hear the sound of…laughter.

Laughter? Was Elizabeth heaping ridicule upon poor Emma? In front of all her ladies-in-waiting?

He felt a surge of righteous indignation and rapped loudly on the door.

A serving wench opened the door a crack and peered out. "Yes, my lord?"

"Tell Her Majesty that Conor O'Neil is here."

"Aye, my lord."

The door closed. He heard another round of laughter and was about to shove the door open and leap to Emma's defense when the door was suddenly opened from within. He nearly fell forward before he managed to regain his balance.

"Her Majesty says you cannot come in just yet."

He pressed a palm to the door before she could close it. "But I am here at Her Majesty's bidding."

The girl glanced over her shoulder, then back at Conor. "You cannot come in just yet, sir."

Desperation made him bold. The girl's strength was no match for his. It was an easy matter to push the door inward. "I'll not be turned away until I see for myself what is going on here."

The queen and her ladies-in-waiting were sitting in a circle around Emma, who was standing on a stool, wearing nothing but her chemise and petticoats. Several women knelt on the floor, holding up bits of fabric, ribbon and lace.

Several others stood around Emma, holding what appeared to be bolts of colorful silks and satins.

The moment Emma spotted Conor she let out a shriek and the others followed suit.

"Oh, no." Emma crossed her arms over her bosom and, for the space of several moments, seemed unable to move. Like the deer they had spotted in the meadow, she simply froze.

The scene seemed frozen in Conor's mind as well. The sight of her, in scanty undergarments, made the blood pound in his temples.

Then, as Emma gathered her wits, she leapt from the stool, knocking it over in her haste. Her voice was high-pitched in distress. "Conor O'Neil. Whatever are you doing in here?"

"I came to see…"

Before he could explain, more shrieks followed. "I'll die of shame. I'll simply die." With that she dashed into her sleeping chamber and slammed the door shut.

The queen and her ladies remained where they were, clearly enjoying the spectacle.

Especially enjoyable was the look on Conor's face. What in heaven's name had he walked into?

He glanced from the queen to the others. "What's going on here?"

Elizabeth's tone was haughty. "I might ask you the same, Conor O'Neil. Didn't my servant tell you that you were not welcome in here?"

"I thought…" He bit back the words that sprang to his lips. A little warning bell went off in his mind. Emma had not been weeping when he'd entered. She'd been laughing. As loudly as the others. Whatever this was, it was not a scene of the queen's vengeance.

If he were to do as he'd originally planned, pleading Emma's cause with the queen, he would simply do more harm than had already been done. He managed to assume the air of a man who knew a secret, and wasn't about to share it. Crossing his arms over his chest, he fixed the queen with a dangerous arch of his brow. "I thought I would just enter without invitation."

"Oh, you wicked, wicked rogue. I should have guessed." Elizabeth walked to him and placed a hand upon his arm. "You knew all along what we were doing in here. And you just wanted to embarrass our little innocent."

He gave her what he hoped was a knowing smile. "And did I? Embarrass our little Emma?"

"You did indeed. Why, it's the fastest she's ever moved." Elizabeth put a hand to her mouth and giggled like a girl. "Did you hear her say she'd die of shame? She had better get accustomed to being looked at by men. When we've finished with her, everyone at court will see a great deal more of her than they have in the past."

"Finished with her?" Conor caught himself and added, "You haven't finished yet, Majesty?"

"Nay. But that was to be the last fitting. Now the seamstresses will ply their needle and thread until our poor little Emma has a wardrobe fit for the queen's lady-in-waiting."

Conor caught himself before he could sigh in relief. "A wardrobe?"

"Aye." She gave him a flirtatious smile. "As if you didn't know. Who told you?"

His mind raced. "I believe it was the whispering of some servants."

"I should have known. I suppose by now it's all over the palace."

"Aye, madam. There are no secrets here, as you well know."

"Ah, well." The queen turned to the others. "Come. You will join us for a stroll in the garden. We'll leave the seamstresses to their work with dear little Emma."

As she walked from Emma's room and headed toward the door Conor prompted, "About this wardrobe?"

"Aye. The wardrobe. I thought it was the least I could do to make it up to Emma for that horrid incident. After all, it was I who insisted that she accompany us on our ride, Conor. I feel responsible for what happened to her. And then that race. All for the sake of an article of clothing. Nasty business, that. She was forced to endure a great deal of pain on my behalf. And you must admit, she does need clothes that fit."

He paused and turned to her. "You're very kind, Majesty."

"Indeed I am." She threw back her head and laughed. "Of course, I had my own reasons. The child is an embarrassment. After all, how does it look for one of the queen's ladies-in-waiting to dress like a beggar's wife?"

As they stepped into the garden, Conor glanced up. Emma was standing at her window, bathed in a pool of sunlight. Her neck and shoulders were bare, her hair spilling around her face like a veil. For one brief moment she stood perfectly still, staring down at him. Then several women circled around her, holding up their bolts of fabric.

She turned away, and the curtain fluttered down to cover the window.

It occurred to Conor that all the fine clothes in the world couldn't change the simple young woman. What beauty Emma possessed came from within. She had no need of satin gowns and fancy adornments. Nothing could improve upon what nature had already given her. She was, in his humble opinion, as perfect as a female could be.

As he slowly circled the gardens with the queen and her retinue of laughing females, his thoughts kept drifting back to Emma. The way she had looked asleep in his arms. All soft and dreamy. And the way his blood had heated at the sight of her in that state of undress.

In both instances, he'd reacted in a purely male fashion. Though Emma deserved to be shielded from such instincts, there was no denying that he was far more attracted to her than he cared to admit.

"I wish to be amused, Conor." The queen's words brought him out of his reverie.

"Then you have chosen the perfect companion, madam. I'm happy to see you in such high spirits."

"Aye. Though the thoughts shared by Lord Dunstan gave me a most unpleasant night. But I've decided to put aside such gloom today. Tell me something amusing, Conor."

"Have I told you about the time my brother and I found a jug of Friar Malone's wine beside the altar, and decided to have just a wee taste?"

"You young devil."

"Aye. A very foolish young devil. For I paid a dear price for my foolishness. I wasn't able to keep any food down for days."

Conor soon had Elizabeth and her ladies laughing with delight as he relayed yet another tale from his misspent youth. And all the while, as they hung on his words, he found himself glancing toward the upper window of the palace, hoping for one more fleeting glance of a certain sweet young colleen.

Chapter Eight

"How do you like the wine, my handsome rogue?" Elizabeth lifted her goblet aloft, touching it to the one in Conor's hand.

They had gathered in the great hall before supper. The queen was seated on a slightly raised platform, so that the others could see her. Conor stood, one step below, while the rest of the guests mingled around the room.

Fires blazed on the hearths at either end of the room, filling the air with the cheery scent of woodsmoke. Servants moved among the crowd, filling goblets with wine and ale.

"It is excellent, Majesty. Is it new?"

"Aye. Several barrels of wine were just unloaded from a boat sent by the Archduke Charles. He hopes to win my interest and possibly court me."

"And has he won your interest, Majesty?"

She merely smiled. It pleased her to toss out the names of men who wished to pursue her, even though it was widely speculated that the queen had no intention of sharing the throne with any man.

While she flirted with him, Conor tasted the wine again. After the tension of the morning, he was feeling extremely mellow. All his fears had been for naught. Instead of the ugly scene he'd envisioned, he had been delighted to find a benevolent queen rewarding her newest lady-in-waiting.

He glanced around. "The dining hall is more crowded than I've ever seen before. Are you planning a special entertainment, madam?"

Her smile was smug. "Aye. A very special entertainment."

"What are you celebrating?"

"The arrival of the Earl of Blystone, for one. He is an old and dear friend." She gave a negligent shrug of her shoulders. "But I need no reason to celebrate. I merely crave excitement. Life here at court can be rather dull. Don't you agree?"

"I'd hardly call mingling with titled nobles from every corner of England dull, Majesty."

"But that's only because you haven't grown up with them, Conor. I find them to be rather vapid. And so I must devise ways to amuse myself."

"I gather you have no intention of telling me what you're planning for tonight's entertainment."

She sipped her wine. "Quite correct. Why should I tell you and spoil the surprise?"

"Why, indeed, Majesty." He sipped again, enjoying the wine and the chorus of voices filling the great hall. Soon enough Elizabeth would reveal her secret. Whatever it was, he had no doubt it would be a pleasant diversion.

He found himself thinking about Emma. If she were to learn how he'd fretted and worked himself into a frenzy of worry this morning on her behalf, she would be amused. It was just as well, he thought, that she would never know. At least he'd managed to avoid another storm of Elizabeth's wrath.

"Where have you gone, my handsome rogue?" Elizabeth touched a hand to Conor's sleeve before accepting another goblet of wine.

"Forgive me, Majesty. My mind wandered."

"I should be insulted. I always thought men were incapable of thought while in my sparkling presence."

"That's true." He gave her his most charming smile. "As you well know, power and beauty are a potent combination in a woman."

It was the perfect remark, guaranteed to make Elizabeth smile. "If I had to choose but one, Conor, it would be power. Even a commoner can be beautiful. But few women in this world ever know true power."

"Beautiful."

Amena and the others stood around as the servants finished dressing Emma.

"I'll have to take your word for it, since you won't let me see myself in the looking glass."

"You'll see soon enough." Amena waved away one of the servants and picked up a comb, turning Emma's hair into a cascade of burnished curls. "You missed all the excitement last night," she said absently.

"What excitement?" Emma smoothed down the skirt of her gown and cast a quick glance at the toes of her slippers.

"Conor O'Neil." Amena spoke his name on a sigh, and the other women began to nod and giggle. "It seems the queen's sly rogue is also an accomplished swordsman."

"Conor?" Emma's hands went still.

"Aye. When it looked as though Lord Dunstan would run through the second scoundrel, Conor moved so quickly, we saw little more than the flash of his blade."

Another lady-in-waiting interrupted with excitement. "It was the most amazing display. One moment Conor's sword was sheathed. The next, his blade was at Dunstan's heart, and he had ordered Dunstan to yield."

Amena glanced toward the others. "I would never have believed it, had I not seen it with my own eyes." She propelled Emma toward the tall, oval looking glass. "There now. What do you think?"

Emma stared at her reflection without really seeing herself. In her mind's eye she was seeing Conor, blade flashing, blue eyes challenging. "I think," she muttered, "that we are in for all manner of surprises this night."

Conor heard a growing murmur of voices throughout the hall, and found himself wondering what caused it. Beside him the queen broke into a wide smile.

The crowd seemed to press closer, watching the arrival of one who was hidden from Conor's view. But from the murmurs, which seemed to grow until they filled the room, he surmised that it must be someone of great importance.

Curious, he continued to watch as the crowd began to part.

Striding toward the queen was no duke or count or bishop. No foreign emissary. It was merely Emma. But this was an Emma such as Conor could have never imagined. Her gown was a shimmering sparkle of white satin, shot with gold and silver threads that caught and reflected the light of hundreds of candles blazing in chandeliers overhead. Unlike her borrowed gowns, this one fit her slender body perfectly, emphasizing her tiny waist and hips. But it was the neckline that caught his attention. A neckline so low, it revealed more of her high, firm breasts than it covered. Because she owned no jewelry, she wore a simple white ribbon tied at her throat. The pure simplicity of it only added to her allure. Dainty kid slippers peeked out from the lace-edged hem of her gown.

It was plain that great care had been taken with the lady's toilette. Her hair had been pulled back into a mass of curls that spilled over one breast.

She walked toward the queen with eyes downcast, which only added to her appeal. Her cheeks bright pink, the only indication of her discomfort at the pressure of so much scrutiny.

She stopped in front of the queen's chair and dropped an awkward curtsy. "Majesty, forgive my late arrival. Your seamstresses only now finished this, the first of the gowns you commissioned."

"You are forgiven, Emma Vaughn. I would say the gown was well worth waiting for. What say you, Conor?"

Conor's hand closed on the stem of his goblet until, aware that it might snap from the pressure, he forced his fingers to relax their grip. He managed a smile, though his throat was as dry as dust. "Very nice work, Majesty."

Emma refused to look at him. It was just as well. He was afraid to meet her eyes. Afraid that all he was feeling this moment would be revealed in a single look.

"Judging by the admiration on the faces of the men in the room, and the jealousy on their ladies', I'd say this gown is a smashing success. Come." Elizabeth rose and swept down the steps of the dais. "You will sup at my table, Emma."

"As you wish, Majesty." Emma followed as the queen led the way toward the dining hall.

When they reached the queen's table, Elizabeth said haughtily, "Emma, you will sit beside me, and Conor will sit on my other side."

Again Emma evaded his glance. Conor stood until the two women were seated, then took his place beside the queen.

Within moments Lord Dunstan approached. "Majesty, I would be honored to sit at table with you and this lovely creature."

"Of course you would, Dunstan." Elizabeth laughed. "As would every man in this room. But since you have been so bold, I agree. You shall join us, as will my friend James Blystone.''

Flushed with pleasure, the two men took their places on either side of Emma. Seeing the look on their faces, Conor gritted his teeth. ''I had thought you would invite Lord Humphrey to sit with you this night, Majesty.''

''Humphrey?'' Elizabeth put a hand to her mouth to stifle her giggles. ''A fresh young face like Emma's deserves handsome young men beside her, not that old bag of bones.''

But that was exactly what Conor wanted beside Emma. Someone old and dull, with failing eyesight. Not a lecher like Dunstan. Nor a wealthy widower like James Blystone.

He tried not to listen as Dunstan began talking about himself in an attempt to smooth things over with Emma. But Conor couldn't help himself. With every word out of Dunstan's mouth, his own anger grew.

''Every year I give a sumptuous midsummer ball at my estate in Surrey.'' Dunstan's tone was as haughty as the queen's. ''Perhaps you can attend this year.''

''You'd love it, Emma.'' Elizabeth's eyes danced with pleasure. ''It's a costume ball. Oh, I do so love the masque. Last year Dunstan dressed as Apollo and I was his Diana.''

''And you were the loveliest lady at the ball, Majesty.'' Dunstan sipped his ale, obviously pleased with himself. Everyone in the room was watching the queen's table, and he did so love being the center of attention.

''Last year we stayed over as I recall.'' Elizabeth signalled for Sterling to give the command. At once the servants began circling the tables, offering trays of succulent roasted pig, platters of doves and plates of salmon.

''Perhaps Your Majesty will consider staying on for a fortnight or more this year.''

Elizabeth gave him a measured look. ''Is this because

you find my company so enchanting, Dunstan? Or could it
be because of this vision beside me?''

Dunstan merely smiled and chose his words carefully.
''No beauty compares with yours, my queen. But I must
say the transformation in our young Emma leaves me quite
breathless.''

Beside her, Conor muttered something under his breath.
Elizabeth turned. ''What was that, Conor?''

''Nothing, Majesty.''

''I thought I heard you say something about the fires of
damnation.''

''Nay, madam. I was merely commenting on fare that
brings such satisfaction.''

''Ah. I see.'' She patted his hand. ''Do not fear, my
handsome rogue. You may be invited to Dunstan's ball as
well. That is, if you continue to please and amuse me.''

''That gives me great comfort, Majesty.'' He spoke each
word through gritted teeth.

When Elizabeth turned her attention to Emma, Conor
pushed aside his plate. He had lost his appetite. Instead, he
emptied his goblet and held it up to a passing servant, who
poured more wine from a flask.

Throughout the interminable meal, he was forced to
watch in silence while Dunstan and Blystone did their best
to impress Emma. And every other man in the hall craned
his neck to study the stunning creature.

When the meal finally drew to a close, Elizabeth led the
way back to the great hall. As soon as she arrived, musicians burst into song.

''Come, Conor. We must dance,'' she called gaily.

''Aye, Majesty.'' With a forced smile he led her to the
floor and began to move with her through the intricate steps
of the dance.

He was still managing to smile when he glanced up and

saw a line form in front of Emma. Every gentleman, young and old, seemed determined to snag the attention of the fascinating new lady.

"Look." Elizabeth was clearly enjoying herself. "Our Emma has just been transformed into a swan. Isn't she delightful, Conor?"

"Aye, Majesty. Delightful." His smile faltered, and he had to struggle to keep it in place.

Six dances later, when Elizabeth finally decided to take a seat and watch from the sidelines, Emma was still dancing.

"I believe I'll have some ale."

At Elizabeth's words, Conor signalled for a servant. He offered a goblet to the queen, and snagged a second for himself, drinking it down in several long swallows.

"Oh, look." Elizabeth pointed, and Conor turned in time to see Dunstan pushing his way through the crowd of men toward Emma. "I do believe Lord Dunstan is feeling a bit peevish at having been ignored so long by our Emma."

Conor watched as Emma put her hand in Dunstan's and began to dance. "Perhaps she is not amused by arrogance."

The queen gave Conor a sharp look. "If I didn't know better, I'd think you were suffering the pangs of jealousy."

"Jealous? Of a twit like Dunstan?" He felt a swift, unreasonable rush of an emotion that had to be anger. "What nonsense."

"You must admit they make a handsome couple." Elizabeth sipped her ale while Conor drained his goblet a second time. The queen put a hand on his arm. "Almost as handsome as you and I, my charmer."

"Aye." He kept his smile on his lips while he signalled for a serving wench and helped himself to another goblet of ale.

"Though I must admit," Elizabeth added dryly, "Dunstan does have a look of hunger in his eyes."

Her remark only added to Conor's misery.

As soon as the dance ended, the Earl of Blystone, tall, aristocratic, bowed before Emma and took her hand in his.

"Now, this is even better. We'll pit Dunstan and Blystone against one another as they vie for the lady's affection." Elizabeth nodded and motioned to several ladies-in-waiting who hovered nearby. "Ten gold sovereigns that Dunstan will come out the winner."

There was a flurry of wagering as the others cast their votes.

"The earl has been a widower now for over a year, Majesty." Amena put a hand to her mouth and whispered, "He will not waste any time if the lady appeals to him. I'll put my money on him."

"Aye," said another lady-in-waiting, "but Lord Dunstan has a reputation for moving quickly, once a female catches his eye. I cast my gold, with the queen, on Dunstan."

Elizabeth turned to Conor, who had remained ominously silent. "What say you? Who will win the right to see the lady to her room tonight?"

He could feel the effects of the ale, and knew that he was already drunk. But not drunk enough to forget to smile. Assuming a look of boredom he shook his head. "I care not who accompanies the lady to her room. As long as I am still permitted to see you to yours, madam."

Elizabeth was so pleased, she actually blushed, while the others smiled behind their hands.

"Come then, my rogue. Dance with me." Elizabeth offered her hand and Conor swung her around the dance floor. At one point he actually lifted her off her feet, and she gave a gasp, before falling into a fit of laughter.

"Conor O'Neil, I have never known a man quite like you."

"Nor have I ever known another like you, madam."

"We are a pair." She laughed, then pressed a hand to her heaving bosom. "I do believe I may need another goblet of ale."

"With pleasure." He led her to her chair, then signalled to a passing servant. And managed to empty two more goblets of ale, while Emma danced past in the arms of the Earl of Blystone.

Elizabeth gathered her ladies around her. "I must take my leave now. You are all sworn to discover which lucky gentleman will see our Emma to her room. On the morrow, you will bring me the news while I break my fast."

The women giggled and nodded.

"Come, Conor O'Neil. See your queen to her chambers," Elizabeth called imperiously.

The musicians ceased playing. With bows and curtsies, the crowd fell silent as the queen and her escort walked from the room. Behind them, Dunstan scowled.

In the queen's chambers Conor was once more left to cool his heels while Elizabeth was prepared for her bed. When he was summoned to her inner chambers, Elizabeth turned to Conor with childish glee. "You may join me on the morrow, Conor. We will break our fast together. And learn the name of Emma's suitor."

"Aye, Majesty. It would be my pleasure." He kissed her hand, then walked away.

He sauntered along the hallway until he rounded a corner. At once his smile fled.

The night was still young, but he had no desire to return to the dancers. The thought of watching Emma Vaughn make a fool of herself with those lechers held no appeal for him. Nor did he wish to join those who were busy playing cards. A stroll in the garden might cool his fevered flesh and clear his ale-fogged brain, but he had no interest in it.

He thought about taking himself off to his room and sleeping, but just as quickly discarded the idea. What he wanted was the one thing he couldn't possibly have.

He paused outside Emma's door. And muttered every rich ripe curse he could remember.

Chapter Nine

"**A**nother dance, Emma?" The Earl of Blystone was having a marvelous time. And the fact that his old adversary, Lord Dunstan, was watching from the sidelines with a hideous scowl on his face only added to his enjoyment. He couldn't imagine why this lovely little female wasn't betrothed to someone by now. But he was most grateful for the oversight. "Please. I beg of you, Emma. Just one more dance."

She shook her head. "No more. My poor head is spinning."

"A glass of wine then?"

Emma laughed. "That would only make it spin faster. If you please, I must retire to my chambers."

Blystone offered his arm. "Then I shall accompany you."

Dunstan overheard and stepped between them. "If anyone is going to accompany the lady to her chambers, it should be me."

"You, Dunstan?" Blystone's smile faded. "And why is that?"

"Because..." Dunstan's mind raced. "Because I have

known Emma longer. Why, we're practically family. I've known her stepmother for years.''

"You have?" Emma swiveled her head. "Celestine never told..."

"And I've likewise known her father for many years." Blystone placed Emma's hand on his sleeve, intending to steer her toward the door.

She gave him a quick smile. "I didn't know."

"Aye. I bought my last stallion from Daniel Vaughn. You remember, Dunstan. The one that beat yours in the queen's hurdles last year?"

Dunstan's scowl deepened at the memory. "Aye." He strode along beside them, and tucked Emma's hand through the crook of his arm. "Since I'm heading to my chambers now, I'll just walk along with you."

"That isn't necessary, my friend." Blystone's teeth were clenched tightly.

"Not at all. I insist." Dunstan patted Emma's hand and forced a smile as he nodded to the parting crowd.

Outside the great hall the two men continued their attempts to impress the young woman, who walked between them in silence.

Her thoughts were disquieting. All evening she had waited for one kind word from Conor O'Neil. But he had been too busy charming the queen to even look her way. And when he did, all he'd done was frown.

She had thought, when she'd caught sight of herself in the looking glass, that Conor would take notice. This had to be what her stepmother had in mind when she'd sent her here. Though the neckline of this new gown was rather immodest for her taste, revealing a bit too much flesh, there was no denying that it was the most luxurious piece of finery she'd ever owned. The feel of the lush fabric against her flesh was heavenly. Like the underside of a rose petal. And, though she'd never spent any time admiring herself in the past, she had to admit that she'd never looked like this before. Thanks to the talent of the queen's seamstresses, her waist had never appeared so small; her bosom and hips so...so round and feminine. She'd looked more like a woman and less like the Irish lass who still lived inside her mind.

A woman. Aye. Even Amena had taken great pains to arrange her curls in the latest fashion, like the other women who surrounded the queen.

And all to no avail.

Conor O'Neil hadn't even seen her. He had eyes only for the queen. And why not? How could she ever hope to compete with the Queen of England?

She felt a welling of shame for her jealousy. If it weren't for the queen's generosity she wouldn't be here, living this opulent life. Wearing this fashionable gown. Dancing with titled gentlemen, and having them vie for the privilege of seeing her to her chambers.

But if the queen had any idea what she was really about...

"Here you are, my lady." Blystone and Dunstan paused outside her door.

"Perhaps," Blystone cleared his throat. "I could have a maid bring some wine to your sitting chamber, my lady. We could sit and sip and...visit a while."

Emma touched a hand to his. "That's most kind, my lord. But I couldn't drink another drop of spirits."

"Of course you can't." Dunstan refused to be left out. "I could send for some tea, my lady. I'm told it aids the digestion, and enhances sleep. Why, I'd even be willing to stay until you're resting comfortably."

"That is so very kind of you, my lord." Emma kept her smile in place while she gave a little sigh. "But I have no need of sleep aids. If I don't soon retire, I shall fall asleep right here."

He stepped closer, keeping a firm grip on her shoulder. "I can think of no more pleasant thing than that, my lady."

The touch of him curdled her blood.

Both men reached for the door handle. Blystone got there first and opened the door. Emma stepped inside, then quickly turned to face the two men, effectively blocking their entrance.

"I thank you both for your kind attention. You have made this a most enjoyable evening."

Blystone caught her hand and bowed over it grandly. "It is I who thank you, my lady. Just being in your company has lifted me from my sadness of the past year."

"I've heard about your loss, my lord. I know how lonely you must be. I'm truly sorry."

"You are too kind, my dear."

Not to be outdone, Dunstan caught her hand between both of his and brought it to his lips. "I would be honored if you would consent to a walk in the garden on the morrow, my lady. It would greatly ease my loneliness, as well."

Emma's first inclination was to slap his face. What gall. Did he think she had forgotten that ugly incident on her first night here in the palace? Still, she managed to keep her tone even while she withdrew her hand. "I fear my morning hours have already been filled, my lord."

"Then perhaps another time?"

"Perhaps. Good night." Emma flicked a glance over both men before closing the door. With a sigh she leaned her forehead against it and listened to the sound of their retreating footsteps.

When they were gone she turned. And froze.

There was a figure seated across the room, hidden in the shadows. The figure of a man. Her hand flew to her mouth and a scream leapt to her throat and seemed to lodge there.

The man stood and started toward her. In that instant she recognized him and let out a long hiss of breath.

"Conor O'Neil. What are you doing here? You frightened me half to death." On legs that were still shaking she stepped closer. "Just how did you get in here without my maid's permission?"

He steadied himself with a hand on the mantel. His mind was reeling. But it couldn't be caused by the vision of loveliness standing before him. It had to be the ale he'd drunk. That, and the fact that his anger had grown with every minute he'd been forced to wait for her, imagining her in the arms of all those men in the great hall. His temper and his unsteadiness hadn't been helped by overhearing the exchange between Emma and her two suitors. Blystone and Dunstan had been falling all over themselves to win her approval.

"Nola was only too eager to leave when I told her that the stable lad, Meade, was awaiting her belowstairs with growing impatience."

She stopped in front of him. Studied him. Sniffed the air. Her eyes narrowed. "You're drunk."

"Not nearly drunk enough." He knew he had no business here, especially in his condition. But he was beyond caring. He had spent the past hours watching her flaunt herself in the arms of every man in the hall. Laughing with them. Flirting with them. Each time, it had been like an arrow to his heart. Though he hated to admit it, this infuriating little woman endangered his sanity.

Still, he had a need to justify himself. "I came here to see that you didn't do something foolish and dangerous."

"I don't need the queen's drunken companion to tell me what to do."

"Don't you?" He shot her a fierce look. "I can see that ale isn't the only thing that clouds good judgment. Now that you've been transformed into a butterfly, you think everything changes. Let me remind you, there are even more predators out there now, my lady. If you aren't careful, I may have to protect your virtue…again.''

At that her temper rose another notch. He had no right to remind her about that scene with Dunstan. It was callous and cruel. And besides, he had merely stumbled upon them. It wasn't as though he had actually been her protector. ''How very thoughtful of you, Conor O'Neil. But as you can see, your help is not needed.''

''Is that so? From the false flattery I overheard outside your door, you've managed to turn more than a few heads, my lady.''

''False flattery indeed. It would appear that there are some at Court who still know how to behave as gentlemen.''

''Gentlemen?'' He gave a sneer. ''How quickly you forget how such gentlemen treat their ladies.''

She felt the quick flash of anger, and the sting of shame. ''I forget nothing, Conor O'Neil.''

''So you say. But I distinctly heard Dunstan's voice outside the door. And I heard you teasing him.''

''I wasn't teasing him. I was refusing his invitation with as much care as I could manage. If you'll recall, it was you who told me, in the queen's own garden, that I should take care not to offend Dunstan.''

He was too angry to see the truth in her statement. ''But I didn't advise you to flirt. To lead him on like a…little temptress.''

Her temper fled. In its place was pure feminine pride and pleasure. ''Is that how you saw me tonight?''

''Aye.'' His gaze raked her. ''With your bosom bared for all men to admire. Letting them hold you and dance with you.'' His voice lowered. Without even realizing it, he caught her roughly by the arms. ''Gazing up into their eyes. Laughing at their little jokes. It would take a man with a heart of stone not to be tempted by a vision such as you.''

"A...vision?'' She blinked, afraid to believe it yet. "You thought me a vision, Conor?''

"Yes, damn you.'' He hadn't meant to touch her. But now that he had, he couldn't help drawing her closer. Another miscalculation. Up close she smelled of a summer garden. Sweet. Delicate. With a hint of wildflowers.

He had a sudden irrational need to press his lips to her hair. "God in heaven, you're so lovely.'' He breathed her in, filling his lungs with her scent. His tone roughened. "I couldn't keep my eyes off you. All night I watched you in the arms of other men. And I hated them. All of them.''

"You...hated them?'' She could barely manage to speak over the sudden pressure in her throat.

"Aye. I wanted you for myself.''

At his unexpected admission, her eyes widened. "You're only saying that because you're drunk.''

"Perhaps. Too drunk to guard my words. But not so drunk I don't know what I want.''

"You want me.'' She said the words with a trace of awe and wonder. "You want me.''

"Aye.'' He lowered his head and covered her mouth with his. The kiss was so hot, so hungry, it rocked her, nearly bringing her to her knees. She brought her hands to his chest, holding on firmly. But, as he took the kiss deeper, her fingers curled into the front of his tunic, clinging to him, drawing him nearer.

All she could do was hold on as the most amazing feelings swept through her. Delicious tingles of fire and ice curled along her spine. And then a sudden tightening deep inside, as pleasure seeped through her veins.

"All night I've wanted this. Just this.'' He nibbled her lips. The words were spoken against her mouth, then inside her mouth as he changed the angle and kissed her again, long and slow and deep. "I wanted to be the one holding you." He brought his hands along her spine and felt her trembling response. "Moving with you." He backed her up until she was pressed against the wall. "Watching your eyes as they looked into mine."

He stared down and saw the smoldering look. A look that told him she was feeling the same things he was feeling.

"I was jealous." He nibbled his way from the corner of her mouth to her ear. "Jealous." He spoke the word harshly, with a trace of wonder. "A new emotion for me. I've never known it before. Nor would I have believed myself capable of such a thing."

She shivered. He tugged and nibbled on her lobe, sending even more delicious tremors through her. She gasped and pushed against him, but that only seemed to inflame him more.

Now that he was holding her, kissing her, he was beyond stopping. He covered her mouth with his, kissing her until she made a sound that could have been a whimper or a sigh. It mattered not to him. He brought his lips to the little hollow of her throat. He drank her in like a man starved for the taste of her, filling himself with her sweetness. And still he didn't have enough. He would never have enough.

"Conor. Conor." She was so confused. It was one thing to flirt. To lead him on, in order to gain information. But now, she was feeling things that had her trembling with new awareness. She wanted him. Wanted him so much it frightened her. "Oh, yes. Kiss me again."

From some distant place in his mind he heard the first warning. But still he resisted as he gave himself up to the passion.

He framed her face between his hands and muttered thickly, "I look in the queen's eyes and see yours, Emma. I make her laugh, and hear your voice. She squeezes my arm, and I long for your touch. God in heaven. What's happening to me? I want you, Emma. Only you.''

She felt her heart soar. Did he have any idea how desperately she'd longed to hear those words? All night, while she had despaired of catching his attention, he had been aware of her, the way a man was aware of a woman.

Emma had never known such happiness. Or such despair. Should she encourage him? Discourage him? Oh, if only she knew what to do. Perhaps she should simply let her heart rule. For right now, her heart was soaring.

In her innocence she lifted herself on tiptoe, offering her lips again. Her voice was a breathless whisper. ''I want you too, Conor. Desperately.''

Too weak to stand, they dropped to their knees, all the while locked in an intimate embrace. With a muttered oath Conor dragged her to the floor and brought his lips to the swell of her breast, nibbling and suckling, until she was dazed with need.

Never had she known such feelings. Pleasure that bordered on pain. And still his clever mouth took her higher, then higher still. When he could no longer tolerate even the thin barrier of fabric between them, he tugged on the bodice of her gown, freeing her breasts.

She wrapped herself around him, drawing him in. Her body seemed to melt into his, slim and eager and boneless.

Though he fought to ignore it, the alarm sounded louder in his mind. Even while he drew out the kiss, he began the impossible struggle to pull back.

''Wait, Emma.'' He pressed his forehead to hers. Shuddered out a breath. ''This isn't right. You're much too sweet.''

''I'm a temptress.'' She laughed up at him, so trusting. So innocent. ''You said so yourself.''

''Aye. You are that. But you have no idea what this leads to.'' Even while he fought his own emotions, he was cursing himself. She was his for the taking. All his. And he was about to refuse her precious gift.

"I know that it leads to loving." She offered her lips again. "Love me, Conor."

I already do, he thought. That was the problem. Somehow, without even knowing how or when, he had begun to care too much for this strange little female. And now that he did, he felt responsible for her as well.

"I can't. We can't." With exquisite tenderness, he began to withdraw from her arms, even as he rained kisses over her face, her eyes, the tip of her nose. That was when he tasted the salt of her tears.

Tears?

The shock of it sobered him more effectively than a dash of cold water.

"Sweet heaven, what have I done?" With his thumbs he brushed away her tears. "Oh, Emma. Forgive me, my lady. I never meant to make you cry."

"Conor. I'm not... You didn't..." Horrified at the enormity of her emotions, she took in a deep breath, struggling to find the words. How could she tell him of her joy? Of her sorrow? Of her fears for what they were experiencing?

But he was beyond consolation. Filled with self-loathing, he closed his eyes and thought about all the helpless women and children whose honor he'd fought for. Thought of all the blood that stained his knife. His soul. "I'm no better than the English. Than Dunstan. Forcing myself on a helpless maiden. And all in the name of..."

He caught himself in time. He wouldn't make a mockery of the word he'd been about to speak. Love was far too precious an emotion. "I've had too much ale, Emma. I've behaved in a despicable manner."

He got to his feet and reached down, helping her to stand. Then he took a step back, determined to break contact.

She felt bereft. But when she tried to reach for him, he lifted his hands, palms up, and backed away.

"I'll not touch you again. It was never my intention to force you. To make you weep. I hope in time you'll forgive me, my lady."

"Conor, you didn't force me. I want you…"

"I'll leave you now. And I'll order you to bar your door."

"That isn't necessary, Conor. I want…"

The look he gave her was so smoldering, she felt her breath hitch in her throat. In that moment she saw something dark and dangerous in his eyes. Something that frightened her. And she had a fleeting sensation that she had seen it before. In another's eyes.

"Aye. It's necessary. You'll bar the door. And you'll think no more about me, do you hear?" He crossed the room, then paused at the door. "I hope in time you can forgive me."

"Conor. There's no need to forgive…"

Emma watched as he let himself out. On trembling legs she walked to the door and listened to his footsteps recede. Then, as he had requested, she set the bar on her door and made her way slowly to the sleeping chamber.

Though the candles had long ago burned down, there was enough light by the glow of the fire to see that the seamstress had completed her new nightshift, and had left it lying on the bed. The sight of it mocked her. The fabric was so delicate, it looked like some gossamer web shimmering with starlight. She found herself wishing that Conor could see her in this.

She held it up to herself and turned to look at her reflection in the looking glass. The image looking back at her was different somehow. Was it because of Conor that she saw a beautiful, desirable woman looking back at her? Was it Conor's kisses that had made her lips seem fuller, her eyes softer, her color higher?

What a strange day this had been.

She had been in absolute terror of the queen's wrath and had experienced delight at the queen's offer of friendship. Had entered the great hall quivering with fear at the thought of being stared at, and had discovered, much to her surprise, that she could not only survive, but thrive, under the scrutiny of nobles. She had managed to gently rebuff two attempts at seduction, and had nearly drowned in a whirlpool of emotions at the hands of Conor O'Neil.

But of all she had endured this day, this last had been the most astonishing. She lowered the nightshift and touched a finger to her lips. The taste of Conor was still there. Teasing her. Taunting her. Arousing her as nothing else ever had.

She pressed a hand to her heart. Dear heaven. Despite the fact that he had been drunk, and would probably regret this in the morning, she would have no such regrets. His words, his kisses, had moved her as nothing else ever had.

She sank down on the edge of the bed and allowed the tears to fall. Great sobbing tears that shook her slender body.

Oh, what was wrong with her? She was falling in love with this man. The man she'd been sent here to use for Celestine's vile purposes. And there was nothing in the world she could do about it. For the rules of the game had already been set into motion. If she wanted to save her father and little sister, she would do what she had come here to do. She would seduce Conor. Would learn all she could about his advice to the queen and what the queen's intentions were. And when she had learned all she could, she would leave as quickly as she had come.

But when she left, though Conor O'Neil's heart would remain intact, hers would surely be broken.

Chapter Ten

"My lord, the queen bids you to join her at once in her chambers while she breaks her fast."

"Aye." The word was more a snarl than a response. Conor, barefoot, shirtless, remained at the balcony, staring off into the distance, as morning sunlight glinted off the dew-covered meadows. The beauty of the scene was lost on him. Without turning around, he called, "Tell Her Majesty I'll be there shortly."

When the maid left his chambers, Conor stayed where he was. His dawn ride had done nothing to clear his mind or ease his black mood.

He'd put in a night of misery, torturing himself with thoughts of Emma's laughter turning to copious tears. And all because of him. He'd behaved like a brute. A drunken lecher.

When he thought about that scene in her chambers, he was revolted by his behavior. What had happened to that charming Irish lad, who had always enjoyed his harmless, pleasant flirtations? When had he decided to take himself so seriously? It would seem that he'd become like all the others at Court. Jaded, shallow, unfeeling.

He ran a hand through his hair in frustration. There was

no excuse for what he had done. He'd been jealous. Jealous. And he'd let that jealousy and anger and too much ale turn him into someone he neither knew nor liked.

Now, somehow, he would have to find a way to make it up to the lass. Emma Vaughn deserved so much better.

Emma. He could hardly bear to think about her. She had been a vision of loveliness last night. Relaxed and happy for the first time since she'd come to court. And he had reduced her to tears with his jealousy and rage and passion.

Aye. Passion. That was the problem. He'd let passion cloud his mind. In his position, he couldn't afford to feel passion for anything except duty and country.

Damn the fates that had condemned him to this. He slammed a fist down on the edge of the balcony with such force a covey of quail took wing, startling him. With a muttered oath he turned away and finished dressing. Then he made his way to the queen's chambers.

"Ah. My fine Irish rogue. You've kept your queen waiting. You know how I dislike that in a man."

He gritted his teeth as he bowed over her hand. "Aye, Majesty. I hope you can find it in your heart to forgive me."

"With charm like yours, how could I not?" She patted the chair to her right. "Sit here beside me. My ladies are on their way. I'm eager to learn if I won my wager."

As the ladies-in-waiting were ushered into the chambers, Conor was stunned to see Emma among them, looking fresh as a spring flower in a pale blue gown. From the looks of her, she had no idea what the queen was about to do.

He glanced at Elizabeth, who seemed to be thoroughly enjoying herself and her little game.

"Ah. Emma." Elizabeth's smile was radiant. "You caused quite a stir among the gentlemen last night."

Emma paused in the doorway. For one brief moment she stared at the man beside the queen, and felt the heat rise to her cheeks before forcing herself to look away. She hadn't expected to see Conor here. It was too soon. The emotions he had stirred up last night were still too close to the surface. But she would have to put on a brave face and find a way to endure it.

"The gown of silver-and-gold cloth was truly lovely, Majesty. As is this morning gown." Emma ran sweating palms along the skirt, then laced her fingers together, hoping she hadn't left streaks on the new fabric. "I thank you for your generosity."

"You are most welcome." Elizabeth pointed to the chair beside Conor's. "Sit, Emma. We have much to ask you this morrow."

"Ask me, Majesty?" Emma's legs trembled slightly as she walked to her designated place.

A servant held her chair and she sat. When her thigh brushed Conor's, she jerked away quickly. The nearness of him turned her mind to mush. Oh, why did her heart have to betray her this way? And why he have to look so handsome and virile this morning? "What do you wish to ask me?"

"Why, how your night ended, of course."

"Ended?" Emma felt the stares of the others and studiously avoided looking at them. Or at the man beside her. Instead she stared at her plate, tracing the lines and colors, while she struggled to make her mind work.

How much did the queen know? Was she aware of Conor's nighttime visit to her chambers? Was this why she had been summoned to break fast with the queen and her ladies? Was she about to be publicly humiliated for entertaining the queen's companion? Oh, how would she get out of this trap? If only she knew how much Conor had already revealed.

"As the belle of the ball, you were the object of much speculation last night, Emma." Elizabeth's words brought her out of her troubled thoughts. "It was obvious that both the Earl of Blystone and Lord Dunstan were engaged in a duel for your heart. And so my ladies and I made wagers."

"Wagers?" Emma tensed.

"Aye." With a roar of laughter Elizabeth pointed. "There were those, Amena among them, who wagered that Blystone, the lonely widower, would touch your heart with his sad tale and manage to invite himself into your chambers. As for me, I put my gold on Dunstan. When he wants something, or someone, he is like a beast with the scent of fresh blood. Dunstan made it plain last night that he wanted you." The queen paused while a servant offered her a goblet of hot mulled wine. "Now you must tell us who won."

Emma glanced around the table at the smiling women. "I'm sorry to be the bearer of unhappy tidings. But nobody won. I permitted neither man to enter my chambers."

"How unfortunate." The queen gave a knowing smile. "Not only for us, but for the two gentlemen who were so eager to…sample your charms, Emma. Ah, well." Elizabeth shook her head in defeat. "I hadn't counted on the fact that you would be a woman of such high virtue."

Emma flushed at the queen's blunt language. But just as she began to relax, thinking she had managed to elude danger yet again, she was stunned to hear Amena burst into laughter.

"If our little Emma is so virtuous, how does she explain the mysterious man she entertained in her chambers after the others had retired?"

Around the table, the women made little noises of surprise.

Emma gave a gasp of shock.

Beside her, Conor went very still.

Elizabeth's head came up sharply. "A mysterious man? What are you saying, Amena? How would you know that?"

"As everyone knows, I do not take my wagers lightly, Majesty." Amena gave a smug smile. "I had my servant hide herself in the hallway just beyond Emma's door, to watch and listen. I had hoped, of course, that Blystone would charm his way inside, so that I would be the winner of your gold. To my disappointment, he was turned away, as was Dunstan, just as our Emma said."

The others began to nod and smile.

Amena was flushed with pride at her little secret. "But after the gentlemen left, my servant listened at the door and, hearing sounds, peered inside."

Elizabeth caught sight of the horror on Emma's face and clapped her hands in delight. "Tell me, Amena. What did your servant see?"

"It was too dark to make out their faces. But she saw a man and a woman engaged in a passionate embrace. Alas, like all serving wenches, she did not have the good sense to wait around and see who he was. Instead she came hurrying back to my chambers to relate what she had seen and heard. By the time she told me of this secret tryst, it was too late to catch him. When I arrived at Emma's chambers the door was barred. But from what I could hear, she was alone."

With a gasp of outrage Emma got to her feet. "I cannot believe what I am hearing. I was spied upon in the queen's own palace? In the privacy of my own chambers?"

"It would appear so. How clever you are, Amena." Elizabeth giggled like a girl. "Now tell us, Emma. Who is your secret lover?"

Emma's shock was evident. "I have no secret lover. What Amena's servant saw was not what it appeared."

The queen's tone grew sarcastic. "Come now. How can one mistake the intentions of a man and woman locked in an embrace? If not love, what then?"

"You must believe me. The man's intent was not..."
Her lip quivered. "...love."

Elizabeth's tone hardened. "Are you implying that a
gentleman in my household forced himself on you?"

Caught in a lie, Emma's face flamed. "Nay, Majesty. I
mean... That is not what I meant to say at all." Her words
faltered. "I know not what his intentions were. But I do
not wish to speak of this. It would seem that all of you are
enjoying my humiliation."

"Nonsense. We have no wish to embarrass you." Elizabeth leaned across Conor to place a hand on Emma's arm.
"My young friend, we are all sisters here. We share our
secrets. Why, some even share lovers. There is no shame
among us."

"Perhaps that is so." Emma's shock and anger made her
careless with her words. "But you ought to be ashamed."
Feeling the sting of tears she turned her head. "Please,
Majesty. By your leave, I would go to my chambers now."

Elizabeth's tone grew haughty. "The cheek of you, my
girl. Nay, Emma. You do not have my leave." She watched
as the young woman sank down in her chair and stared
morosely at a spot on the table, avoiding everyone's eyes.
"But while we break our fast, we will speak of this no
more. Later, when you are ready, we will speak." The
queen smiled knowingly at the other women around the
table. "For we intend to learn the name of this mysterious
man, Emma Vaughn. Whether he be lover or lecher, it isn't
fair to keep such a secret."

Elizabeth signalled for the servants to begin. Those
seated around the table fell silent. A serving wench handed
Conor a chalice of hot mulled wine. He drained it quickly,
hoping it might ease the throbbing in his temples.

More than anything, he longed to take Emma into his
arms and soothe her troubles. Watching her struggle with
these callous women tore the very heart from him. The

thought of her so close, and yet so far away, was the greatest pain he could endure. And still he sat, his voice silent, his true feelings carefully hidden behind a mask.

"Did you enjoy yourself last night, Majesty?" Amena glanced from the queen to the silent, somber man beside her.

"Aye. I did indeed. And this handsome rogue is the reason."

"Should we take wagers on whether or not he was refused entrance to your chambers?"

Elizabeth pretended to be shocked by her lady-in-waiting's meaning. Then, laying a hand over Conor's, she merely smiled, giving the impression that theirs had been a night of passion.

The women exchanged smiles and nudged one another as they ate.

And all the while, forced to sit silently beside Conor, Emma watched and listened. The queen's words had planted a seed of doubt. How could she be certain that Conor, prodded by anger and ale, had not made his way to the queen's chambers after leaving hers? The very thought of it made her want to weep.

She struggled to pay closer attention, cautioning herself to learn all she could about this cruel, heartless game of truth and lie that was being played. For it was one she must master and play to win. The stakes were too high to allow for any errors.

"Majesty, Lord Dunstan wishes to speak with you."

Elizabeth looked up from her meal with a frown. "More of that Irish business, I'll wager."

When Dunstan entered the chambers and saw the laughing, chattering group of women, as well as his rival, Conor, with the queen, he managed a thin smile. "Forgive me,

Majesty. I did not wish to disturb your morning repast. But I must relay urgent news.''

Elizabeth pushed away from the table, and the others scrambled to their feet. "We will walk in the gardens." She motioned for Conor to join her. "Come. I could use some sunshine."

"Aye, Majesty." Conor was careful to keep any inflection from his tone. But he could tell, by the look on Dunstan's face, that the news he carried was important.

Elizabeth turned to the women. "I will expect you by my side when I hold court this afternoon."

Without waiting for their reply, she led the way out of her chambers, with Conor and Dunstan following.

Outside, as they walked along the tree-lined pathways, Dunstan's tone was low and urgent. "What I have to tell you was relayed to me by the captain of Her Majesty's Ship *Meridian,* Madam. There are said to be several leaders in Ulster who have been raising vast sums of gold. A messenger from Philip of Spain has assured them of arms and supplies."

"Philip." Elizabeth's eyes were narrowed in thought. "Even while he claims to pursue my hand in marriage, he schemes with my enemies to do me harm. Will they never give me peace?" Her head came up. "What about soldiers? Did Philip promise men, as well, to these Ulster leaders?"

"I know not, madam. Captain Whitten said only that rumor is rife in Ireland that a revolt is being planned."

Elizabeth turned to Conor. "Surely you have heard of these rumors."

He shook his head. "Nay, Majesty. This is the first news I have of it."

Dunstan gave a sneer. "Nor would he tell you if he knew, madam. These are his people who plot against you. They own his loyalty."

Conor managed a laugh over the anger that simmered.

"You forget, Dunstan, that I am here, far from my home, at the queen's invitation. It is difficult to hear the rumors of home while living in seclusion in the palace."

"That could be remedied, O'Neil." Dunstan leaned close, his eyes burning into Conor's. "I would be only too happy to put you on the next ship heading to Ireland."

"Beware, my friend." Elizabeth put a hand on Dunstan's arm. "If my two advisors cannot be civil, how can I expect civility from that barbaric little island?"

Dunstan, watching Conor's eyes, saw the quick flare of anger before he managed to bank it. So, the Irish charmer was not quite as unfeeling as he pretended. Seeing a weakness, he attacked. "Majesty, I urge you to defy Philip and show these Ulster leaders the power of England. Send over enough troops to subdue these rebels and end all thought of rebellion once and for all."

Seeing the queen's sudden interest in the suggestion, Conor was quick to ask, "And if Philip should make good his threat?"

Dunstan shrugged. "I don't believe he'll risk his soldiers for such an insignificant country as Ireland."

Elizabeth's tone was thoughtful. "You may be right. But if you are wrong, Dunstan, we will find ourselves involved in a war that would drain our coffers."

"Then you simply tax the people. Especially the Irish peasants, who are the cause of this drain."

"Do you think to get blood from a stone, Dunstan?" Conor kept his tone even, but his hands were tightly clenched at his sides. "My countrymen are already being burdened by unfair taxes, so that men like you can live in luxury."

"I urge you to be careful, Conor O'Neil." Elizabeth's words were spoken softly, but there was a thread of steel beneath. "Such words are considered treasonous."

"Then consider this, Majesty. If you burden the people

with another tax to support a war in Ireland, a great many of your citizens will be uttering such treasonous words.''

Dunstan could barely contain his fury. "Will you allow this man to say such a thing in your presence, madam?''

"I permit it for the same reason I permit you to speak your mind, Dunstan. You and Conor O'Neil are my advisors on this Irish problem. I will think on what you have told me, and what Conor has said, as well. When I have made my decision, I will summon you both.''

Dunstan lowered his head to hide the flare of anger. As always, his rival had reminded the queen of the one thing she most feared—the loss of the love and devotion of her people. "As you wish, Majesty. I pray you consider my words carefully.''

When the queen's chief usher arrived to escort her to court, Elizabeth beckoned. "Come, Dunstan. Conor. I desire your presence at court. Your smile always manages to ease my tensions.''

"Aye, Majesty. It will be my pleasure.'' Conor held back. "But I would take a moment.''

"You won't be late?''

He gave her his most charming smile. "I'll do my best to be on time.''

As soon as he was alone, he left in search of Emma. Without the ale to cloud his mind, he intended to beg her forgiveness.

He prayed his words wouldn't fail him. Both the words he intended to speak to Emma, and the words he would use later to persuade the queen to resist war.

Chapter Eleven

Emma paced her chambers, grateful that the seamstresses had finally departed. In her hand was a rolled parchment. The missive had been delivered by a rider from Clermont House. The cruel, cutting words were etched indelibly in her mind.

> You have kept me waiting too long. I warned
> you of the consequences of such a delay.
> Sarah was tossed from a pony cart. She is
> unharmed except for a broken leg. Do not
> attempt to see her unless you bring the
> information requested.
>
> Celestine

This was exactly what Celestine had promised, if the terms of her scheme were not met with all possible speed.

Sarah. Little Sarah was paying the price. For her sister's scruples. For her hesitation to do as she'd been instructed. Emma wouldn't have minded for herself. But the thought of her little sister, wounded and grieving and alone, was almost more than she could bear.

She would do anything for Sarah. She clenched a fist.

Anything. But she had waited too long to summon the necessary courage. She could wait no longer.

At the knock at her door, she hurried forward. When she opened it to find Conor O'Neil, she was so startled, she couldn't think of a thing to say. She turned away to hide her confusion.

Mistaking her silence for anger, Conor stepped inside and closed the door, leaning against it. He stared at the rigid line of her back for several moments before saying, "Forgive me, my lady. I know I have no right to disturb you. I came to apologize for my behavior last night."

"Last night…" Words failed her.

"Aye. Last night was a mistake. An inexcusable mistake, my lady. I had too much ale. And I…"

"Nay, Conor…." She turned, hoping to silence him.

When he spotted the anguished look in her eyes he forgot what he'd been about to say. In quick strides he crossed to her. "What is this? Am I the one who causes you such pain?"

She shook her head, embarrassed at having been caught in such turmoil. "Nay. It is this missive. My little sister has been hurt. A broken leg from a spill from her pony cart."

"Then you must see her."

"I cannot." She backed away, sinking down on the edge of a chaise. "I cannot leave the palace."

"But why? Surely the queen would not hold you here if she heard your reason for leaving."

"The missive assured me that Sarah is fine."

He dropped to his knees beside her and took her hand in his. "I have a little sister, too. Her name is Briana. She is a fiery little vixen with the heart of a warrior and the quick temper of a thundercloud. She can stir up trouble and make me angrier than a nest of hornets." He smiled at the image. His tone softened with affection. "But she is dearer to me than my own life. And if she were hurt, I would move heaven and earth to be with her.''

Emma was so touched by his words she could do nothing but stare at him. The tenderness with which he spoke of his sister struck a chord in her as nothing else ever could.

''I can order a carriage and have you out of London at once, Emma. We could visit your father's estate and still be back at the palace in time to sup tonight with the queen.''

''You would do that for me, Conor?''

''Aye. It's the least I can do to atone for last night.''

Her mind was working feverishly. If Celestine were to meet Conor O'Neil, she might believe that he and Emma had already become lovers. And that would lead her step-mother to be patient, in the hopes that, in time, the information she desired would be forthcoming.

Would it be enough to fool Celestine and warrant a visit with Sarah? And perhaps with her father, as well? Her heart pounded at the very thought.

''Last night is already forgotten, Conor.'' A lie, she knew. She would never be able to erase the memory of his fervent kisses. But right now, it wasn't love she needed, it was friendship. She desperately needed him to be her friend.

''If it isn't too much trouble, Conor, I would dearly love to visit my father's home.''

He seized the opportunity to make amends. ''Order your servant to fetch your cloak and help you prepare for travel, my lady. I'll have a carriage brought around to the court-yard immediately.''

When he was gone Emma rang for Nola. Then she walked to the fireplace and tossed the parchment on the flames, watching until it had burned to ash. She needed no reminder of Celestine's threat. She had already committed the hated words to memory.

* * *

"Oh, Conor." As the carriage rolled along, Emma spread her arms wide, as if to hug the day. "It feels so good to be away from the palace."

"Aye." Conor studied her, enjoying the way she seemed to open like a flower the moment she escaped the stuffy formality of the palace. There was such joy in her it seemed contagious.

He held the team to an easy gait as they moved along a wide, tree-lined road.

"Have you ever seen the sky so blue?" Emma lifted her head and Conor followed suit.

"Only in Ireland."

"Aye. There's a special way the sun comes through the clouds, turning the land to softest green."

He nodded. "And a smell to the turf as it's dug. And a taste to the air just before the rain."

She glanced at him. "Do you miss it as much as I?"

He nodded. "I miss it every day."

She was stunned by his admission. "Then why do you stay here in England, Conor?"

"Because this is where I must be, until my task is completed."

She turned to him. "What task?"

He shot her a smile that had her heart doing somersaults. "You ask too many questions, my lady."

"Forgive me."

When she turned away he placed a hand over hers. At once they both felt the jolt.

"I was only teasing you. I enjoy your questions. You may ask anything you please, Emma."

She felt her heart flutter. Did she dare? But she had to have something to offer Celestine. Else she would be turned away at the door and forced to return to the palace without seeing Sarah.

How to begin? Slowly. Carefully. "There are those who say you are the most influential man in England."

He gave a sound that could have been a laugh or a sneer.

"Do you deny that you have the queen's ear, Conor?"

"Nay. I do not deny it. But Elizabeth is a singularly independent woman. She may listen to many people, but the decisions she makes are her own."

"You cannot deny that she listens when you speak."

"I hope so. With the queen, one never knows. But I like to think my words have some small effect on her decisions."

"There. You see?" She gave him a bright smile. "So, we are back to the beginning. You are a very influential man. What influence did you bring to bear on her discussion with Lord Dunstan this morrow?"

"Dunstan?" He turned to study her.

"When he came to the queen's chambers this morrow, Dunstan claimed to have important information."

"Aye. Rumors. Speculation. Nothing more."

"How fascinating. Are these rumors something you can repeat?"

Conor shrugged. "By now it is probably being angrily debated in Council." A Council meeting he'd been expected to attend. He felt a flash of guilt, then shrugged it aside. Emma was far more important than any Council meeting. "There is talk of a rebellion among the Ulster leaders."

Her heartbeat quickened. She couldn't believe her good fortune. Even if it were no longer a secret within the palace walls, it wouldn't be well-known throughout the rest of England. This would be something Celestine wouldn't have heard yet. "Rumors of a rebellion? Do you think it's true?"

"According to the captain of Her Majesty's ship the *Meridian,* Philip of Spain has offered to assist Ireland in a rebellion against England."

"What has the queen decided?"

Again that careless shrug as he turned the team from the road into a narrow, hedge-shrouded lane that smelled of primrose and lavender. "Elizabeth agreed to weigh carefully all that I said, and all that Dunstan said. I suppose, when she announces her decision, we will know whether I have any influence with her, or whether Dunstan's words carry the day."

"What did you tell her, Conor?"

When he gave her a quizzical look, she blushed and added, "All this talk of rebellion and the King of Spain makes me rather dizzy. But I'm certain whatever you said was very wise. And the queen will take your words to heart."

"I hope so." He drew back the reins, slowing the team to a walk as they labored up a hill. "I reminded Elizabeth that England can hardly bear the expense of a war at this time."

She couldn't mask the censure in her tone. "Is that all that concerns you about a war between England and Ireland? The gold it would take?"

His tone was patient. "What concerns me is the cost to my family. My father. My brother, Rory. My friends and neighbors, who would gladly give their lives in defense of their homes and families. But such things matter not to the queen. And so I reminded her of the gold it will take, for that is something that does matter. Gold, and her place in her people's hearts, are always uppermost in Elizabeth's mind."

Emma looked at him with new respect. "So, it would seem that you know what to say, and what not to say, to impress the queen. You must understand her very well."

"I've made it my job to know her better than I know myself. The fate of my people depends upon it."

At his words, spoken so forcefully, she glanced at him

in surprise. "Do you put the fate of Ireland above your standing with the queen?"

He shot her a dangerous look. "What do you think?"

Instead of replying, she fell silent. Was there more to this man than merely the queen's charming rogue? Or was she reading too much into his words? Before she could give it more thought they came to a fork in the road.

He turned to her. "Which way, my lady?"

"This way." She pointed and he flicked the reins.

It occurred to Conor that this had been one of the most pleasant days that he could ever recall. There was something so easy about being in Emma's company. After all this time in England, being with her made him feel as if he'd come home. Perhaps it was the soft brogue that was so musical after the shrill voices at Court. Or perhaps it was the young woman herself. She was as modest, as unassuming, as the nobles were haughty and overbearing. Whatever the reason, being with her had a soothing effect on him.

The team followed along the road until they came to a lovely, curving driveway that led to an elegant manor house.

At the sight of it, all Emma's thoughts centered on her father and little sister. Finally, she would be given her chance to see them, to touch them, to assure herself that they were truly well. Celestine wouldn't be so cruel as to keep them apart this time.

"This is Clermont House." She said it with such reverence, Conor turned to study her. "My father bought it for my mother, in the hope that English physicians might be able to help her, when the Spanish physicians failed. This is where she died. And afterward, my father couldn't find the heart to leave it and return to Ireland. I think he believed that he would somehow feel closer to her here."

"And then he met his new wife."

"Aye." Her tone hardened. "Celestine." She spoke the name as though speaking of a serpent.

As they pulled up to the courtyard, a servant helped Emma from the carriage.

"Welcome, my lady."

"Thank you, Charles."

Another servant took the reins from Conor.

At the door, Emma's way was barred by the butler. She stopped, puzzled.

"Edward, is my stepmother here?"

He glanced from Emma to the man beside her. "Lady Vaughn is entertaining friends in the parlor."

"It isn't necessary to disturb her. I came to see my sister and father. Will you fetch them please?"

He seemed to hesitate, then stepped back. "Follow me." The butler led them along the hallway to a large, fashionably appointed room that looked out over the formal gardens. Without a word he left, closing the double doors as he did.

Emma was too agitated to sit. While Conor watched in silence, she began to pace from the fireplace to the windows, then back again. With each tick of the clock on the mantel her nerves seemed to stretch and tighten, as she continued glancing toward the doors.

At last the doors opened and she spun around. Her bright smile faded. "Celestine. I was told you were entertaining friends. I didn't wish to bother you."

"I'm certain you did not." A satisfied little cat-smile touched the corner of Celestine's lips. "I have given Edward orders that I am to be informed of everyone who passes through these doors." She flicked a glance over the young woman, then turned to study her companion. "Who might this be?"

"This is Conor O'Neil."

"O'Neil?" Celestine's eyes widened before she caught herself.

Emma kept her tone cool. "Conor, this is my father's wife, Celestine."

"Lady Vaughn." Wearing his most charming smile Conor crossed the room and lifted her outstretched hand to his lips. "What a delightful surprise. I must admit, I was expecting someone older."

Emma could see the subtle change that came over her stepmother. Her eyes softened. Her lips curved in a most inviting smile. "Conor O'Neil. I can see why the queen is so taken with you."

"And I can see how you managed to capture Lord Vaughn's attention and heal his broken heart. You must be an extraordinary woman."

"Why, thank you." It was plain that she was dazzled by Conor's charm.

"I've brought..." Emma cleared her throat and tried again. Her annoyance at feeling shut out by these two made her tone sharper than she'd intended. "I hoped I might have a chance to see Sarah and my father."

Celestine barely flicked a glance in her direction. "That isn't possible."

"Why?" Emma had to grip the back of the chair to keep from crumpling. "Where are they? What have you done with them?"

"What have I done with them?" Celestine smiled broadly at Conor. "What a silly child our Emma is. Do you see what I must tolerate from this stepdaughter?" She turned to Emma and her eyes narrowed. "They are asleep."

"In the middle of the day?"

"I had to see that Sarah was given a potion for pain. As for your father, he was given a potion to settle his nerves. Else I would have no respite from the constant whining and complaining from the two of them. But have no fear. When the potions wear off, they will be refreshed and renewed by sleep. There are servants looking after them who will notify me when they have awakened.''

''The same servants who were looking out for Sarah when she fell from a pony cart and broke a leg?''

Celestine shot her a calculating look. ''That happened in the country, where there are less restrictions. The child has learned her lesson, I expect. Next time, she'll take better care.''

''She's just a baby, Celestine. She needs comfort. She needs me. And her father.''

''Your father isn't strong enough to even see to himself. How can he care for a six year old? That's what servants are for. As for you, your place is with the queen. Why, I would have given anything to have the opportunity I've given you.''

She turned to Conor and her smile was back. ''Daniel's two daughters are so ungrateful. I've brought order into their lives. And dignity and nobility. The sort of nobility that only a member of the royal family can bring. And all they can do is complain.''

Conor returned her smile. He'd been listening intently. Not only to what was said but also to what was left unsaid.

With a look of dogged determination Emma started toward the door.

''Where are you going?'' Celestine demanded.

''To see my father and sister. Whether awake or asleep, I need to see for myself that they are truly well.''

''That isn't possible.'' Celestine reached the door first and stood in front of it, barring Emma's way. ''As I explained, they've been given potions to help them sleep. I'll not allow you to disturb them.''

''Please, Celestine. I'll be very quiet.'' Emma's voice was close to pleading. ''What more do you want?''

''I desire the same as you, Emma.'' Celestine's tone became patient, soothing. "We both want your father and sister to grow strong and healthy. That is why I must forbid you to disrupt my schedule at this time. I know, better than anyone, what is best for them. But, since it is my nature to be generous…" She managed a benevolent smile. "And since you have come all this way, I must insist that you and your handsome guest take tea with me before you leave."

Emma started to shake her head.

"I insist. And then you and I will talk, Emma. Alone." Celestine looped one arm through Emma's, then placed her hand on Conor's sleeve. "Come. I'm entertaining Lady Bolton and the Duchess of Trent. They'll be so delighted to meet Daniel's daughter and Queen Elizabeth's much-admired advisor." She fluttered her lashes. "Why, all of England has heard of the handsome, charming Conor O'Neil."

"Here you are, my lord."

Conor accepted the reins from the servant and climbed to the seat of the carriage. He turned to watch Emma, standing in the doorway of Clermont House, head bent in earnest conversation with her stepmother. It was the first time the two women had taken a moment to speak privately. Emma stood with her back to him, her hands clenched tightly at her sides. Celestine, facing Emma, was wagging a finger as she spoke. Though he couldn't hear the words, he could see the look on her face that said she would tolerate no nonsense.

Within minutes Emma turned away and nearly ran to the carriage. When she was seated beside Conor, he lifted the reins and the team broke into a trot. He glanced over her head and noted that the door was already closed.

"No fond farewells from your devoted stepmother?"

Emma didn't bother to respond. Instead she clutched her hands tightly in her lap.

"Your father's home is beautiful, Emma."

"There was a time when I thought so." Her voice was drawn, tired. "Now I consider it merely big and cold and empty."

"Like the woman who presides over it." He urged the horses faster, as eager to escape as the young woman beside him.

"I hadn't thought you'd noticed." She looked at him angrily.

"What is that supposed to mean?"

"You know exactly what it means. You were so busy charming Celestine and her friends, I nearly choked on my tea."

"It cost me nothing to be charming."

"It never seems to cost you, does it, Conor?" Her throat grew clogged, and she knew she was close to tears. "Whether it's the queen or a stranger you've just met, you're always the same. Smiling. Captivating. Completely irresistible. Why, you had those women practically feeding you their cakes, while you told those enchanting stories that everyone finds so endearing."

He bowed his head and smiled wickedly at her. "Thank you, my lady. From your reaction, I thought you hadn't noticed."

"Oh, I noticed." To her embarrassment her eyes filled, and she had to blink furiously to keep them from spilling over. It wasn't jealousy, she consoled herself. It was simply the emotions of the day.

She wiped at her eyes with the back of her hand. "I was forced to sit there listening to you prattle on while all I wanted was the chance to see my father and sister. And I...I fear I'll never see them again."

He brought the team to a sudden halt and turned to her. "You'll see them, Emma."

She shook her head and buried her face in her hands. "Nay. Celestine will never allow it. She's a vile, evil woman."

"I know." He gathered her into his arms.

She lifted her head. "You...know?"

"Aye. The lady is so sure of herself, she doesn't even bother to hide her feelings." He felt the dampness of her tears against his chest and pressed a clean handkerchief to her hands. "But while I was busy being charming and amusing, I had a chance to notice several things."

She hiccuped and blew her nose. "Things?"

"Aye. Such as the burly servant she has posted at the foot of the stairs."

"To keep everyone from going above stairs." Emma's tone was filled with sadness.

"Aye. And I noticed something else. The rose arbor."

She blinked, not at all understanding. "You made a great show of admiring it."

"So that your stepmother would allow me to go into the garden for a better look. I tested it for strength. It rises to the second story of the house. And it's sturdy enough to take my weight."

She looked up. "Your...weight?"

He nodded. "I thought I might bring you back at some time when your stepmother is gone."

"How would you know when she's gone?"

"I gave the butler, Edward, a gold sovereign to send me a message the next time Lady Vaughn goes into London. I've found that most servants are willing to perform a great many...extra services, for the sake of gold."

She stared at him in stunned silence, unaware of where this was leading.

"And while Celestine is in London, and we arrive at

Clermont House, you will keep the servants occupied, Emma, while I climb that rose arbor and take a look at your father and sister.''

She started to shake her head. ''What you're suggesting could be very dangerous.''

''It could be. Are you afraid?''

She stiffened her spine. ''Of course not. I'd risk any danger to see my father and sister. But what about you? Why would you risk such a thing?''

''Let's just say…'' He winked, and she felt her heart do a series of flips. ''…that I have a need to do something nice for a lovely lass from my homeland.''

''Oh, Conor. I don't know what to say.'' She was weeping again. But these were tears of happiness.

As he gathered her into his strong arms and sought to comfort her, she clung to him. And then, without giving a thought to what she was doing, she lifted her mouth to his, pouring out all her feelings of fear, of confusion, of hope.

He was caught by surprise. And deeply moved. There was no time to be clever. No time to prepare himself for the flood of feelings. He returned her kisses with a passion that left them both breathless.

She gave a little gasp, and he swallowed the sound with another long, slow kiss that had both their heads spinning.

He poured all his hunger into the kiss. Needs, so long denied, began to pulse and throb. With every touch of his hands along her spine, with every press of her soft body against his, the need grew.

All around them the air was perfumed with the fragrance of primrose and lavender. It taunted him with thoughts of lying with her in the cool grass, and loving her until they were both sated.

He knew this was madness. Knew that he had no right to want her. But he did. Desperately.

Emma was shaken to the core. His kisses were no longer

easy or gentle. His mouth moved over hers with a savageness that shook them both. His hands moved up her spine, igniting fires everywhere as he pressed and kneaded. When his thumbs encountered the swell of her breasts, he stroked until she moaned and moved against him.

They were both thoroughly aroused, and struggling for breath.

It was Conor who came to his senses first. He drew back, determined to bank the fire, for her sake. He pressed his forehead to hers, hoping in vain to clear his mind. But the touch of her, the warmth of her body against his, had him fighting for control. And losing.

His touch gentled as he held her a little away. His thumbs made lazy circles along her shoulders. "My mind knows that I have no right to this, Emma. But I'm not certain my heart is listening."

She gave a shaky laugh. But when she looked into his eyes, her laughter died in her throat. "Perhaps we could linger here."

Stunned, he lowered his mouth to hers for another drugging kiss.

Emma felt a series of tremors that rocked her.

Against her lips Conor whispered, "If I could have but one wish, it would be to stay here and lie with you in this meadow, and make slow, lazy love with you all through the night."

As his mouth moved over hers, she sighed and gave herself up to the pleasure that curled along her spine. In truth, it was what she wanted, as well. Above all else, she wanted this man. And this slow, sensuous passion that was building a fire deep inside. A fire that was threatening to become an inferno.

When at last he lifted his head, he took in a deep draught of air. "But we must beware. By now the queen will have scoured the palace in search of us. If we value our heads, we must go. Now.''

He lifted the reins and the team started with a jolt.

As they headed toward the palace, Emma struggled to ignore the twinge of guilt over the information she had just given Celestine.

It was true that she loved Conor O'Neil. And wanted him as she had never wanted any man. But she couldn't put her own pleasure above that of her father and Sarah. It was for their sake that she had betrayed Conor's confidence.

But even that knowledge couldn't stop the ache around her heart. For she knew that the man beside her would never be able to understand, if he should learn of her betrayal. Nor would he ever be able to forgive.

Chapter Twelve

"My lord, O'Neil."

At the sound of the servant's voice, Conor looked up from the basin where he was washing himself.

"Her Majesty bids you to come to her chambers at once."

"Aye. Thank you." With a sigh of resignation he pulled on a clean tunic and prepared himself for what was to come.

Elizabeth would be peevish. She was, after all, a royal accustomed to having those around her bowing and scraping, and seeing to her every whim. She would not lightly forgive the fact that he had deliberately disobeyed her command to be with her at court.

As he made his way to her chambers, his frown turned into a smile as he began to warm to the challenge. He would find a way to charm her. Didn't he always?

"So." The queen was standing in front of a tall looking glass while several servants finished dressing her for dinner. She peered at Conor's reflection as he made his way toward her. "My absent rogue suddenly reappears after keeping himself hidden from my sight the entire day." She waved the servants away and turned to glower at him imperiously.

"You were seen leaving the palace grounds in a carriage with Emma Vaughn. What have you to say for yourself, Conor O'Neil?"

"I must first say that I have never seen you looking lovelier, Majesty." He bowed and brushed his lips over her hand.

"All those sweet words just fall like pearls from your lips, don't they? But flattery will not deflect my temper this time."

"Nor should it, madam. You are the Queen of England. Entire nations bow to your will. I am but a mere man. And a most unworthy one at that." He knelt at her feet and lowered his head. "It would serve me right if you should banish me from your sight."

"Aye. Banishment would be a fitting punishment." Elizabeth touched a hand to his hair. Her touch lingered, and she gave a sigh that seemed to come from the depths of her soul. "Except that I would be the one to suffer your absence. Stand, my rogue. I would look into those laughing blue eyes. For I need you to lift me out of this strange mood that has befallen me."

He got to his feet and met her look. "And what mood is that, Majesty?"

"Sadness. A great welling of sadness seems to have taken hold of me. First my handsome companion seeks the company of a mere slip of a girl who has neither beauty nor wealth enough to compete with her queen. And then Dunstan and the others urge me to send soldiers to Ireland to put a stop to this latest insurrection before it gains favor with the Irish peasants."

To his credit Conor managed to keep his expression bland. But his spirit plummeted. "To the first I say simply that you need have no fears. No lady compares with Your Majesty." Not a lie. But definitely not the truth where he was concerned. That mere slip of a girl had stolen his heart and was robbing him of his senses. "As to the second, tell me what you have decided, Madam, now that your advisors have spoken."

"I am still mulling over all that I have been told. A part of me yearns for a chance to send a message to Philip of Spain. He thinks to punish me for spurning his proposal of marriage. And so he meddles in my problems with Ireland."

"Would Your Majesty allow herself to be dragged into a war by an unhappy suitor?"

She arched a brow. "However you choose to define it, wars have been fought for worse reasons, Conor."

"Aye, Majesty. And what of my countrymen? Do you have any feelings for them?"

"Your countrymen are, like the Scots Highlanders, nothing more than barbarians."

"Perhaps, Majesty, we are all barbarians. If so, we are not worth a war. What your advisors fail to warn you is that France watches and waits for a chance to find you distracted, so that she might intervene in your Scottish problems. Can you afford to divide your energies and your fortune on two fronts?"

He saw the way her lips pressed together into a hard, tight line and knew that he'd hit a nerve.

"You see? It is another reason why I must keep you by my side, Conor O'Neil. You are more worldly, more knowledgeable, than a score of my advisors put together. I had forgotten that you studied abroad, and have intimate knowledge of both France and Spain. So. Tell me. Would you have me reject the advice of my own Council?"

"As queen you must consider what is most important, not only for yourself, but for your people."

She nodded, thinking aloud. "Will I risk soldiers for the sake of a few unhappy peasants? Or will I simply wait, and hope that these Ulster barbarians end up fighting among themselves the way the Highlanders have?''

She was watching his eyes as she spoke. And, he realized, hoping to catch some glimmer of his thoughts. But he had managed to suppress his emotions. Every day he learned to play the game as cunningly as those who surrounded Elizabeth at court. It wasn't a fact of which he was proud. In truth it would have shamed him, except for the knowledge that with every lie, he was keeping his father, his brother, his people free of English domination for another day.

The queen's butler entered her chambers and stood at attention. Elizabeth nodded toward Conor. ''Come. It is time we joined the others.''

At the entrance to the hall they paused while the queen's butler announced her to the crowd. Elizabeth swept imperiously into the room and made her way to the head table.

As Conor took his place beside her he saw Emma making her way toward them. She was accompanied by the other ladies-in-waiting, as well as Dunstan and Blystone and the other nobles.

This night Emma wore a gown of buttercup yellow, with lace inserts at the bodice, sleeves and hem. The neckline was daringly low, like all the gowns commissioned by the queen.

The moment Emma took her place at table, Elizabeth pinned her with a look. ''Conor tells me you and he went for a carriage ride. Where did this rogue take you?''

Emma looked with panic at Conor, and was stunned to see him wearing a lazy smile. A smile? What did that mean? She hoped to heaven it meant that she should tell the truth. For she was simply incapable of lying to the queen, while all around her were watching and listening.

''He found me grieving over the news that my little sister had fallen from a pony cart and had broken a leg, Majesty.

Conor insisted that I should see her, in order to calm my fears. And so he took me to my father's estate outside London."

Elizabeth's eyes narrowed. "That was a most thoughtful gesture."

"Not nearly thoughtful enough, Majesty, for I caused you unnecessary concern." Conor managed to look contrite. "I should have sent word of my intentions through one of your servants. It would have spared you unnecessary worry."

"Aye. It would indeed." Elizabeth picked up her goblet and sipped the wine.

Emma did the same.

Dunstan's dark gaze locked on Emma's. "Had you but asked, my dear lady, I would have been only too happy to drive you to your father's estate."

"Thank you, Lord Dunstan." Emma gave him a half-hearted smile. "That is most generous of you."

Not to be outdone, Blystone touched a hand to hers. "Perhaps you wish to visit again tomorrow, my lady. If so, I would be pleased to take you in my carriage."

"You are too kind, sir."

Across the table Conor found himself thinking again of the passionate encounter of a few hours ago. Even from this distance, he could taste her lips, and feel the press of her body on his. Just thinking about it brought a rush of heat. He drained his goblet in the hopes of putting out the fire.

"You're quiet tonight, Conor." Elizabeth leaned close. "Are your thoughts on a possible war?"

"Aye, Majesty." Making war was the farthest thing from his mind. But the thought of making love with Emma Vaughn had him sweating. And wishing with all his might that this interminable evening would end.

* * *

"I will leave you now." Elizabeth stood, and the entire assembly got to their feet.

Instead of asking Conor to accompany her, she turned to Dunstan. "Come, my friend. Since you have requested a private audience, you may accompany me to my chambers."

Conor tore his thoughts from Emma. He'd been far too distracted this night. A dangerous miscalculation. "Perhaps you would like me to attend you as well, Majesty."

She waved him away. "It isn't necessary. You've had your say. It seems only fair that I give Lord Dunstan a chance to speak his mind."

As Dunstan brushed past he muttered, "You think you have persuaded Elizabeth in your favor, don't you, O'Neil?"

"I think the queen is capable of making wise decisions without my influence, Dunstan."

"So you say." Over his shoulder he whispered fiercely, "Perhaps, before this night is over, we will see if I still have any influence with my queen."

Agitated, Conor waited with the others until the queen had exited the hall, followed by Dunstan and the ladies-in-waiting. Then feigning a yawn, he casually took his leave, and made his way to his own chambers. Minutes later, dressed all in black, he slipped out his balcony and made his way to the queen's chambers.

He had made it a point to go over every room in the palace, seeking out places where he might conceal himself. With so many soldiers and attendants surrounding the queen, it was imperative that he learn as many hiding places as possible.

In a musty storage room he pressed his hand to a panel and watched as it slipped open soundlessly, revealing a small enclosure just beyond the queen's sitting chamber. When he had stepped inside, the panel closed behind him.

He waited a moment to give his eyes time to adjust to the darkness, then turned toward the door. But before he could pull it open, he realized he wasn't alone. Someone was beside him in the darkness.

With a muttered oath he pinned the shadowy intruder's arms to prevent an attack, then clapped a hand over the mouth. It was then that he recognized Emma.

"Are you mad?" he demanded harshly.

All she could do was shake her head.

"I'm going to let you go," he muttered against her ear. "If you make a sound, we'll both be discovered. Not a word. Do you understand?"

She nodded.

He released her. But before he could demand an explanation, the sound of the queen's voice caused both their heads to jerk up.

"...suggesting we go to war at once?"

Conor slipped the door open just a crack, enough to see Dunstan pacing in front of the fireplace.

"It is our only hope of suppressing these savages, Majesty."

"And what if, as Conor O'Neil suggested, France should decide to use this opportunity to press the Scots Highlanders into attacking while our soldiers are occupied on foreign soil?"

"I would expect such a suggestion from O'Neil. He will say whatever is necessary to keep our soldiers out of his country."

"Aye." Elizabeth's eyes flashed. "I have no illusions about the rogue's loyalty. But he makes a strong point, Dunstan. Will I be remembered as the monarch who left her realm helpless in its time of need?"

"Are you willing to allow these Ulster chieftains to continue their quest for arms?"

"They are pitifully few in number, Lord Dunstan. Without the aid of Spain, they cannot hope to mount a war against England.''

''Aye, Majesty. But what if Spain agrees to join them?''

Elizabeth began to pace. At length she turned to him. ''My head aches with so many conflicts demanding my attention. Leave me to my rest, Dunstan.''

''Aye, Majesty.''

From his position, Conor watched as Elizabeth offered her hand, then withdrew to her sleeping chambers, while Dunstan took his leave.

As soon as the room grew quiet, he caught Emma by the arm and dragged her along the hallway to her chambers. Once inside, he glanced around and, seeing that they were alone, barred the door.

Emma could read the temper in his eyes and found herself backing away. With each step she took, he stormed ahead.

''Now you will tell me what you were doing.''

She bumped into the wall and froze, then straightened her spine. ''The same, it would appear, that you were doing.''

''Spying?'' His eyes narrowed.

For the space of a moment the word hung between them. Now that it had been spoken aloud, Emma realized the enormity of what she had done. She had been spying on the Queen of England. The penalty for such a crime would surely be hanging. Or the Tower. Then a second thought assaulted her. Her mouth rounded in surprise.

''And you were doing the same, Conor O'Neil. Spying on the queen.''

In the silence that followed, those penetrating eyes seemed to be studying her with calculated interest. And then he said, through clenched teeth, ''Who sent you here, Emma? Who sent you to spy?''

Her chin came up in that infuriating manner. "I didn't admit to being a spy, any more than you."

"You don't need to." Of course. It made perfect sense now. "I suddenly realize why you seemed so unsuitable in this role you've been assigned." He caught her roughly by both shoulders and nearly shook her in frustration. "Tell me who sent you."

Her heart was pounding so violently, she was certain he could hear it. But to her credit she held her silence and forced herself to meet his stormy look without flinching.

"Ah, lass." The hands at her shoulders abruptly softened their grasp. His tone softened as well. "I should have known. That fierce loyalty to Ireland. The way your voice sounds whenever you speak of it. And those connections. Your uncle a bishop. Your great-uncle closely aligned with my father. Our mission, it would seem, is the same."

"The...same?"

He smiled and touched a finger to her lips. "Aye. To spy for Ireland."

Seeing the look in his eyes, Emma averted her gaze. She could tell him the truth this very moment. Or she could go on with this charade and allow him to believe that they were allies. The moment stretched to two, and she knew in her heart that it was already too late. She couldn't bear to see that look of love turn to one of hate. No matter what the cost, she would keep her secret to herself.

"Emma. Emma." He framed her face with his hands, and brushed his mouth over hers. The merest whisper of lips to lips. But it had her breath backing up in her throat. "Now I know why you've managed to touch me as no other woman ever has." He gathered her close and covered her mouth with a searing kiss. Inside her mouth he whispered, "We're kindred souls, Emma."

The pain around her heart was so great, she feared it might shatter like glass.

Suddenly, from the hallway came the sound of the queen's imperious tone. "Emma Vaughn. Awake and open this door at once."

Emma's eyes went wide with fear. "Do you think she knows?"

Conor shook his head. "If she knew, she wouldn't knock. She'd have a guard break down the door."

He thought a moment, then began to tear her gown from her shoulders. Startled, she slapped at his hand. "What are you doing?"

"You heard Elizabeth. She thinks you're sleeping. Quickly now. Get out of these clothes and into a nightshift. And let your hair down."

They raced to the sleeping chambers, emerging moments later with Conor pulling the combs from Emma's hair, while she smoothed down the skirts of her nightshift.

"What about you, Conor? Where will you hide?"

"Don't worry about me. I'm an old hand at spying. Remember?" He dragged her close and covered her lips with his.

Then he released her and strode to the balcony. He stood for a moment, staring down into the darkness, before disappearing over the railing.

Moments later Emma hurried to open the door and admit the queen.

"It's about time." Elizabeth strode into the sitting chamber, followed by her maid and several of the ladies-in-waiting. She turned to study the young woman. "Your skin seems flushed, Emma. Are you coming down with a fever?"

Emma pressed her hands to her cheeks. "I...believe so, Majesty."

"Your eyes seem a bit bright as well. I'll send my physician later with a potion."

"Aye, Majesty. As you wish."

The queen settled herself on a chaise and waited while the others sat or knelt around her. "I have come with some exciting news, Emma Vaughn. I have decided that your service to your queen is sufficient that you will join my other ladies-in-waiting."

Emma kissed the hand that was extended to her. "I am most humbly grateful, Majesty. How can I ever thank you?"

"I shall find a way, I am sure." Elizabeth smiled. "There will be many services you can perform in the days and weeks to come when we leave here."

"Leave here?" Emma looked up in surprise. "I don't understand."

"In a matter of days we will leave Greenwich Palace." The queen looked as delighted as a child with a gift. "And now I must take my leave of you. There is much to be done."

As if in a fog Emma watched the door close behind the queen and the others. Then she walked to the balcony, half expecting Conor to reappear. But all she saw was the darkness below. And above her, a midnight sky laced with stars.

She pressed her hands to her heated cheeks. Her poor head was spinning with all that was happening. In a daze she made her way to her bed, wondering how in the world she would be able to sleep. In the space of an hour, so much had changed. She had gained the queen's confidence. And Conor's. Though it pained her to mislead him, the fact that he believed she was a spy for Ireland would certainly make it easier for her to do Celestine's bidding.

But by far the most distressing piece of news was that, for some unknown reason, they would leave Greenwich Palace. If that should happen, any hope she had nurtured of saving her father and little Sarah would be lost forever.

Chapter Thirteen

"It is called a progress, my lady." Nola explained the queen's plans as she helped Emma with her morning toilette. By now, everyone in the palace knew that they would soon be leaving Greenwich and going into the countryside. "It is necessary for Her Majesty to move from one palace to another."

"But why?" Emma couldn't imagine wanting to leave a palace as elegant as this.

"It serves several purposes, my lady. The most important reason is for the queen to see her subjects, and to be seen by them." Nola led her to the dressing table, and Emma sat while the servant arranged her hair. "But there is another reason. With all the people and animals under one roof, even a home as grand as Greenwich takes on..." The servant wrinkled her nose. "...the odor of a barnyard."

"How far will we travel?" Emma's despair was growing by the minute.

"The rumor is that we will head to the midlands." Nola added a pretty comb to Emma's hair, and handed her a looking glass.

"So far away." Emma looked at her reflection without even seeing. All she could see was a future without her father and little sister, who would be completely lost without her help.

"Not so far, my lady." Nola appeared happier than Emma had seen her since her arrival. "I have family in the midlands. Perhaps I'll have a chance to slip away for a visit." She glanced down. "What is wrong, my lady? You seem unhappy this morrow."

"Nothing." Emma shrugged. "I just wish I weren't going so far from my family."

"We'll be back again within the year, my lady."

A year. Emma put a hand to her mouth to stifle the little cry that sprang to her lips.

"Hurry, my lady. The queen dislikes being kept waiting."

As she made her way to the great hall, Emma felt as if she were carrying the weight of the world on her shoulders. How could she remain here, dancing to the queen's tune, while her family was in grave peril? And yet, how could she leave and risk causing them even greater peril?

Elizabeth looked up as she entered. "Ah, here you are, Emma. Come. Sit at my table. It looks as though your sleep was as restless as mine. There is nothing like a grand adventure to stir the soul."

"Aye, Majesty." Emma's shoulder brushed Conor's as she took her seat, and she felt the first hint of comfort since she'd awakened. His smile added another layer of warmth to her soul. But still her heart was heavy.

Across the table, Dunstan seemed in fine humor. "Your servants do an admirable job of keeping your many guests in food and clothing, Majesty. But I had begun to note that the scullery, the refectory, even the gardens were taking on a rather distinct odor."

"Aye. I'm grateful for your suggestion, Lord Dunstan. A progress to more friendly environs will greatly lift my spirits. My messengers have already reported back that the gentry are eager to welcome their sovereign at every county and village through which we shall pass. We will partake of feasting and celebrations all along the way.''

Dunstan turned to the Earl of Blystone. ''I'm told you have a lovely home in Warwick.''

''It's a pretty enough place, though I rarely go there since the death of my wife.''

''Perhaps you should open your doors to your queen and her company.''

Blystone's smile of pleasure was quick and sincere. He turned to the queen. ''I bid you to allow me to entertain Your Majesty at my home. If you agree, I will send riders ahead this very day to prepare.''

Elizabeth seized upon the invitation, since so many in the realm shrank from the prospect of such an undertaking. ''I would be delighted, my friend. You realize you are inviting a great deal of work upon your staff.''

The earl waved a hand, ignoring the sheer numbers of people, baggage, clothing, animals that would have to be accommodated. ''My housekeeper and servants will consider it an honor, Majesty. As will I.''

''Then it shall be done.'' Elizabeth's smile was positively radiant. Just the thought of moving lifted her out of the boredom which had begun to set in. ''Oh, the parties. The balls. The grand entertainment.''

Out of the corner of his eye Conor could see Emma's consternation, and understood. The thought of leaving her family at the mercy of Celestine was weighing heavily upon her heart. While the others laughed and chatted, he lowered his voice, for her ears alone.

''Don't despair, Emma. We'll find a way.''

''But there is so little time now.''

He yearned to draw her close and offer her the comfort of his arms. But all he could do was whisper, ''We need but a single word from Edward, and we will move with all speed. Take heart, Emma. And keep a good thought.''

She looked up, about to say more, when she saw the queen glancing her way. Thinking quickly she said aloud, ''Aye, my lord. This is all new to me. But, as our queen said, it will be quite an adventure.''

''It pleases me, Emma,'' The queen's voice had the others turning to look at her, ''to see how quickly you have learned our ways.''

''Thank you, Majesty.'' A liar. A spy. A villain with no heart. That was what she had become. And all because of Celestine. The thought of it shamed her. ''I am most eager to please you.''

''You do please me, my dear child.'' Elizabeth got to her feet and the others followed suit. ''Now I must meet with the household staff, to see to the arrangements for our progress.''

Emma breathed a sigh of relief, hoping to find some time to herself. But those hopes were dashed when the queen said, ''I will expect all of my ladies-in-waiting to attend me. There is much we must discuss.''

Emma had no choice but to follow the queen to her chambers.

When they were gone, Conor excused himself from the company of gentlemen and made his way to the stables. He had need of a long, silent ride. Possibly all the way to Clermont House.

''Emma.''

At the sound of a deep, masculine voice whispering her name, Emma sighed in her sleep and burrowed deeper into the bed linens. She had spent the entire day and evening in the company of the queen and her ladies, and had even been forced to take her meals with them, while they had been fitted for suitable wardrobes for their journey.

When Emma had finally been allowed to retire to her own chambers, she had been disappointed to learn that the gentlemen had been dispatched by carriages to a nearby village, for a night of cards, and ale, and presumably wenching. But even though the rogue, Conor O'Neil, had taken himself off for his own pleasures, he was now intruding upon her dreams.

"Emma. You must awaken. There's no time to waste."

She muttered something in her sleep and attempted to shrug off the hand at her shoulder.

Hand? She sat bolt upright, peering through the darkness at the shadow beside her bed.

"Conor? Is that you?"

"Aye. Hurry. You must dress for riding."

"It's the middle of the night."

"That's true. But Edward informed me that his mistress, Lady Vaughn, would be out of Clermont House for the rest of the night."

"All night? Conor, where would she possibly go for an entire night?"

He shrugged and handed her a pair of dark breeches and tunic. "I know not. But put these on and let's be off."

"What are these?" She stared at them with a doubtful expression.

"Proper men's riding clothes. It wouldn't do for one of the queen's ladies-in-waiting to be out at such an hour. And the queen would have both our heads if she discovered me out riding with anyone but a proper gentleman."

Emma studied the clothes. "I'll wear them. But first," she commanded, "turn around."

At her imperious tone, he grinned and did as she bade. Keeping an eye on his broad shoulders she hurriedly stripped away her nightshift and dressed in the strange clothes.

"Where did you get these?" She cast a quick look at herself, then bent to retrieve her boots.

"I persuaded Meade to loan me his, since mine were far too big for you."

"How very generous you are with the stable lad's clothes."

"I paid him a gold sovereign for the use of them. And on the morrow he'll get them back." He grinned at the sight of her. "Now, perhaps you'd best hide those glorious tresses beneath this hat." He removed his own hat and placed it on her head.

When she started toward the door he whispered furiously, "Not that way, Emma. I've barred the door so your maid can't enter your chambers and discover your empty bed."

"Then how...?"

He caught her hand and led her toward the balcony, where a rope dangled from the railing to the ground far below.

"This is how you got up here?"

"Aye, my lady. And how we must both get down."

When she hesitated he added, "Unless you'd prefer to let this opportunity slip by."

She squared her shoulders. "I'm not afraid."

"Good." With the agility of a panther Conor pulled himself over the railing, holding firmly to the rope. When he was safely on the ground, he lifted his arms.

"Come on."

Following his lead, she pulled herself over the railing and slid down the rope. Her heart was thundering, but to her credit she made it down safely until she felt Conor's arms wrap around her. When he released her, she managed to dash toward the waiting horses. Within minutes they were galloping across the hills, on the road leading to Clermont House.

She turned to him as the dark mists swirled around them. "It strikes me that you are quite adept at treachery, Conor O'Neil."

He merely smiled. "It has held me in good stead from time to time." He turned, admiring her silhouette against the night sky. Despite the rough clothing, there was no mistaking the distinctly feminine curves. "For a gently bred colleen from Dublin, I might say the same for you. Why is it that you have no fear of what we're about to do?"

"Make no mistake, Conor. I'm desperately afraid. But my fear for my father and sister are far greater than my fear for my own safety." She looked up and caught her first glimpse of Clermont House in the distance. Her heartbeat quickened. "What is our plan? Surely I cannot pretend to visit, dressed like this."

Conor shook his head. "Nay. It was a good plan, but now, with the queen's untimely meddling, everything must be changed. We'll secure the horses some distance from the house, and then climb the arbor together."

He reined in his mount and Emma did the same. "I'll keep watch in the hallway while you determine the condition of your father and sister."

"The condition?" She felt her breath hitch in her throat.

"Aye, my lady." He slid from the saddle and tied the reins to a tree. "The fact that you haven't been permitted to see them makes me think Celestine's potions are keeping them drugged. If that is so, they may be too weak to leave their beds."

"Oh, Conor." She put a hand to her mouth to stifle her cry.

He reached up and helped her from her horse. "Don't tell me you haven't feared the worst."

"Aye. But to hear it spoken aloud breaks my heart."

"Shhh." He touched a finger to her mouth. Feeling the jolt he lowered his head and kissed her. Just one hard, quick kiss. Then he held her a little away. "Are you able to do this?"

She swallowed, squared her shoulders, then nodded. "I'll do whatever it takes, Conor."

He gave her a smile. "Good. Now follow my lead."

It occurred to Emma that he showed absolutely no hesitation as he raced across the lawns and paused beside the arbor. After one quick test of its strength, he began to climb. When he reached the upper story he beckoned her to follow.

When she was halfway up the arbor he heard her little hiss of pain as she closed her hand over a spike of rose thorns. Reaching down, he grasped her wrists. She was surprised by the strength in his arms. Then she quickly reminded herself that Conor O'Neil was not what he pretended to be. He played the part of a man who seemed to do nothing more strenuous than lift a goblet with the queen. And he played the part well. But he was, in truth, a spy, with all the strength of a seasoned warrior.

He lifted her the final few inches until she was standing beside him on the upper balcony. "Are you all right, Emma?"

She nodded, absently wiping blood down the leg of her borrowed breeches. "As a lass I was always climbing trees and racing across the meadows after the horses. But I'm amazed at how much simpler it is to do these things in men's clothing."

"Aye." He winked, causing her heart to do a series of quick tumbles. "That was the easy part. The hard part is now." He framed her face and whispered fiercely, "No matter what you see, Emma, you musn't cry out. Do you understand?"

She wasn't certain what he meant, but she nodded.

"This nighttime visit is for one reason only. To determine the condition of your father and sister. Once we know what we're dealing with, we'll be better able to make our plans.''

"Are you telling me we can't take them with us tonight? Even if they're able to travel?''

He shook his head vigorously. "Tonight you will see them, speak with them if they're able to hear you, and assure them that help in on its way. And then, though it breaks your heart, you will have to leave them as you found them. Are you prepared to do that?''

He saw the quick flash of pain before she composed herself. "Aye. I'll do what I must. But—''

He cut her off. "Do you trust me, Emma?''

She stared into his eyes, and though she didn't know why, she knew that she did indeed trust him. "I do.''

"That's my lass.'' He squeezed her hand, then turned and led the way through a half-opened window.

The room was a sitting chamber, with several chaises arranged around a fireplace. From the coolness of the ashes, it appeared the fire hadn't been tended in hours.

"These used to be my little sister's rooms.'' Emma looked around in consternation. "But she must have been moved. It's far too cold for a child.''

"Check the sleeping chamber.'' Conor moved to the door. "I'll keep watch in the hallway.''

He waited until Emma made her way to the other room, then, just as he was about to slip out the door, he heard her little cry. Quickly closing the door he hurried to her side.

She was standing beside the bed, holding a candle aloft while she stared down at the still figure of a child. A child with matted hair and glazed, unseeing eyes.

"Oh, Conor.'' Emma couldn't stop the tears that spilled from her eyes and flowed down her cheeks. "What has Celestine done to my sweet, beautiful little sister?''

Conor had to struggle to bank the wave of fury that engulfed him. But this wasn't the time to give in to such feelings. For Emma's sake, for all their sakes, he would put aside emotion and do what was necessary.

He turned away and began to rifle through the things on the table beside the bed. Finding a small vial, he sniffed, tasted, then replaced it as he'd found it.

He caught Emma's hand. ''Remember what you promised. No matter what you see, you won't cry out again.''

''But she's so small and helpless. Look at her, Conor. They aren't even tending to her basic needs. She looks as if she hasn't been fed or washed. And she's cold.'' She closed a hand over Sarah's. ''So cold.''

Conor rummaged through a wardrobe and found a small sheepskin. ''Here. Wrap this around her, then place her bed linens over it. Judging by the signs of neglect, I'd wager that no one will even notice.''

Emma did as she was told, grateful for anything that would ease her little sister's suffering.

''Now.'' Conor caught her by the wrist and forced her to turn away. ''We must find your father.''

Emma followed him from the room, then pointed toward the suite at the end of the hall. ''Those are my father's chambers.''

''They were.'' Conor's eyes narrowed as he considered. ''I doubt Celestine would permit him the largest suite. We'll try these others first.''

On the second try they found Daniel Vaughn in nearly the same condition as his little daughter. The room was cold, the fire burned to ash. In the bed, the aged, withered hulk that had once been Emma's father was now a bearded old man with sunken cheeks and vacant eyes.

This time, though Emma kept from crying out, she sank to her knees beside the bed and began to weep in silence.

Conor searched the contents of the table beside the old man's bed until he found a vial similar to the one in Sarah's room. A quick sniff and taste satisfied him that it contained the same potion. He replaced the stopper, then turned his attention to Emma. Her body shook with sobs as she clung to her father's cold hand.

"Come, Emma. We must leave before a servant comes upon us."

Instead of a reply she brought her father's hand to her lips and began to weep harder.

Conor heard the sound of a door open and close somewhere nearby, and the sound of footsteps echoing along the hall.

"Emma. There is no more time. We have to leave now."

"I cannot, Conor. Don't you see? I can't leave them alone. Celestine wants them dead. Without me they're helpless."

"Aye. But if she should find you here, you'll become like them. There's no time for argument now, Emma. We must go."

As she started to shake her head he lifted her up like a sack and tossed her over his shoulder. At the door he paused, then hearing the footsteps recede, he opened the door and peered around. Seeing no one around, he made his way to Sarah's sitting chamber and crossed to the open window. Once on the balcony, he deposited Emma on her feet and pulled the window closed.

"You can't do this." Emma's tears were no longer tears of sorrow, but of rage. "You can't make me leave them."

"I can and I will."

As she opened her mouth to protest he again picked her up and, as easily as if he were leading a partner through the dance, descended the arbor and ran to where their horses were tied.

Without a word he pulled himself into the saddle and, still holding her prisoner in his arms, caught the reins of her horse and nudged his own into a run.

Chapter Fourteen

"Let me go. You don't understand." In vain, Emma pounded her fists against Conor's chest, as they sped across the darkened countryside. "I can't leave them, Conor. I can't. I'm their only hope of surviving."

"Aye, my lady." His tone was low with suppressed fury over what he had seen at Clermont House. "Which is why I can't allow you to stay."

"Oh, I should never have trusted you." Tears of pain and rage blinded her.

When they were a safe distance from her father's home, Conor reined in his mount and slid from the saddle.

As he reached up to help her dismount, she caught at a riding whip and lifted it to strike him. "I'll not go back to the palace with you. I'm going back to find a way to rescue my father and sister."

"Nay, little vixen. You'll do as I say." He caught her wrist and yanked her none too gently from the saddle, then tossed the whip aside.

Her tears started again. Tears of impotent rage. "How can you be so cruel?"

He brought his arms around her, pinning her to the length of him to keep her from striking out again. Against her hair he muttered, "I tried to warn you, but I see you weren't really listening. Did you think to find your father and sister sleeping peacefully, with nothing but a guard outside their rooms? Did you think that Celestine would leave anything to chance?"

"She's a monster." Emma's words were muted against his chest.

"Aye. A monster who will stop at nothing to have what she wants. Now, Emma, stop and think a moment. Do you really believe your presence at Clermont House could have any effect on a woman like that?"

"At least she'd know that I was aware of her villainy."

"She cares not what you or others think. She cares only for her own pleasures."

Emma brushed at her tears with the back of her hand, then took several long shuddering breaths. "Then what am I to do?"

His tone gentled. "You can begin by trusting me."

She sniffed, nodded. "I do."

"You say that. But your actions say otherwise."

She took a step back, feeling more in control now. "All right, Conor. I give you my word. I will truly trust you. Do you have a plan?"

He led her toward her horse. "Aye. Come. On our return to the palace, I'll tell you what I think we must do."

Dispite the lateness of the hour, candles gleamed in many of the palace windows. When they were still some distance away, Conor and Emma dismounted and led their horses to the stable. A sleepy figure stepped from a stall and, pausing to rub his eyes, took the reins.

"Thank you, Meade." Conor handed him a gold coin. "I'll return your clothes on the morrow."

The stableboy glanced at the shadowy figure beside

Conor. "If the lad wishes to keep them, my lord, I don't mind."

Conor thanked him, handed him a second gold coin and led Emma away before she could speak.

"It's better if he doesn't know who accompanied me on my midnight ride," he whispered. "And since he thinks you're a lad, all the better."

In the darkness she stumbled, and he caught her before she could fall. As he gathered her against him he noted the weariness etched on her face. When they reached the palace courtyard, Conor took hold of the rope which still dangled from the upper balcony.

"Come, my lady. You need your bed."

"Aye." Now that the tears had run their course, she didn't know how she would find the strength to climb. All the energy seemed to have drained from her.

"Here." He lifted her arms around his neck and muttered, "Hold fast to me."

Before she knew what he was planning, he began to climb hand over hand. Again she was aware of his incredible strength. It didn't seem possible that he could be pulling the weight of both of them as easily as if he were climbing the stairs. When they reached the balcony outside her room he paused for a moment, leaving them both dangling in space. She lifted her head and their lips brushed.

"Beware, my lady." His eyes, the color of the midnight sky, held hers. "Whenever our lips meet, I lose all my senses." He smiled, and her heart tumbled wildly in her chest.

Was it this feeling of weightlessness that had her mind spinning, her breath hitching? Or was it the nearness of this dangerous, mysterious man?

The breeze caught them, causing them to sway back and forth. It occurred to Emma that this was the most amazing sensation. Their bodies were pressed tightly together. Her arms were locked around his neck. And all that kept them from being dashed on the paved courtyard below was Conor's strength holding them fast.

Still grasping the rope, he claimed her lips. She felt a rush of heat that left her dazed. And then, with a sigh, she forgot everything and gave herself up to the pleasure.

"I think…" He kissed her, long and slow and deep, lingering over her lips while his blood heated and his heartbeat began to race. "…I'd better get you inside quickly, before I completely lose my senses."

With strong measured movements he clambered over the railing. Instead of setting her on her feet he carried her into her room and deposited her on the edge of her bed. Then, before she could move, he knelt and began to remove her riding boots.

"What are you doing, Conor?"

"I'm putting you to bed, Emma."

"I can do this myself." She touched a hand to his, to stop his movements. "I'm not a child."

"I'm aware of that." He looked up and she felt the jolt clear to her toes. "Too well aware of it."

He slid off one boot, then the other. The touch of his hands, moving along her feet, caused the strangest sensations. As oddly intimate as the kiss they had just shared.

She stared down at his head, the hair gleaming blue-black in the firelight. Without thinking she caught his face between her hands and lifted it to hers.

"Who are you, Conor O'Neil?"

"You know me, Emma."

She shook her head. "I realize I don't know you at all." Her eyes searched his, seeking answers. "Oh, I know Her Majesty's Irish rogue. The fine teller of tales, who can outdrink, outlaugh and outlie most of the peacocks who surround the queen at court. Only now I realize you aren't that man."

"I am that man, Emma."

She shook her head. "You only pretend to be. Who are you really?"

Instead of an answer, he kissed her hard and quick. And then he got to his feet and crossed to the balcony.

"Unlock your door now, Emma, before you retire and then toss me the rope. If I can keep my wits about me, the only one who will enter is your servant, to tend to your needs on the morrow."

He caught hold of the rope and stepped over the railing. And with a soft sound that could have been a chuckle or an oath, he dropped to the ground and neatly caught the rope when she'd managed to untie it.

As silence settled around her, Emma unlocked her door and went to her bed. She sat very still, thinking about all that had transpired this night. She had discovered the truth about Celestine's cruel treatment of her father and sister. And the truth was far more painful than what she had imagined. If Conor hadn't stopped her, she would have ruined everything by confronting her stepmother too soon, before she had a plan of action.

She had discovered something else, as well. The man she knew as Conor O'Neil, was not at all what he seemed.

She leaned back and closed her eyes. As she drifted into sleep, her lips curved into a smile. She was in love, not with the queen's rogue, but with a man of mystery. A man who, whatever else he might be, had proven himself a bold, clever, fearless warrior.

"Oh, my lady. Have you ever seen such excitement?" Nola came dashing into Emma's chambers, her arms laden with clean linens. "The palace is alive with activity. Already the first carts and wagons are being loaded for the journey."

Emma looked up from the basin where she was washing.

"I have heard the rumble of wheels all morning in the courtyard. But I thought it far too soon to begin the progress."

"Her Majesty has decreed that we must be ready to leave Greenwich by the end of the week."

"But that isn't possible." Emma's voice caught in her throat. "Why must we take our leave so soon?"

"I know not. But Her Majesty's maid was overheard telling the earl's maid that the queen expected to be supping in his manor house by week's end."

Emma felt the familiar twinge of fear. So little time. Still, Conor had said he would find a way. She would trust him, as she had promised.

She squared her shoulders and began to dress for the day.

As she entered the great hall to break her fast with the queen, she caught sight of Conor, relaxed and content, looking for all the world like a man who had spent a lazy night in bed, rather than a night of hard riding and dangerous escapades.

"Good morrow, my lady."

He bowed over her hand, and she felt the jolt clear up her arm.

"Good morrow, my lord." She curtsied. "Majesty."

As she took her seat at table the queen said, "I hope you slept well, Emma."

"Aye, Majesty. And you?"

"Nay. I am far too excited to sleep. Blystone tells me his gardens are in full bloom. I am eager to see them."

"And you shall, Majesty." The earl drained his cup. "My messenger tells me that my household is most eagerly awaiting the honor of your presence."

Elizabeth beamed. The thought of the progress had infused her life with new meaning. "I must have a new travel wardrobe. New ballgowns. A warm cloak for cool mornings. And a lighter cloak for warmer evenings." Her mind raced with plans.

Dunstan interrupted. "I am told there is excellent hunting at your estate, Blystone."

"Aye. Our woods are well stocked with deer, with pheasant and partridge."

"The queen loves to hunt." Dunstan turned to her with a smile, and she was quick to embrace the idea.

"Aye. Then I must have new hunting outfits as well. I trust you will arrange a hunting party."

"As you wish, Majesty."

"And a grand ball."

Blystone nodded, becoming as caught up in the excitement as Elizabeth. "The gentry will be eager to greet their monarch."

She gave him a sharp look. "You'll see that they mind the length of their speeches."

He smiled. "I'll caution them to keep their words of greeting brief."

"Splendid." She sipped hot mulled wine, then glanced around the table. "This time next week we will be dining in Warwick."

Emma wanted to groan with dismay. But when she glanced across the table at Conor, he merely winked. Despite her misgivings, she felt a glimmer of hope. She would trust him to set his plans into motion in time.

When the queen pushed from the table and prepared to take her leave, Emma felt a wave of relief. She needed only a moment or two of Conor's time.

Instead, her plans were thwarted when the queen commanded sternly, "Come, my ladies. Our work with the seamstresses has just begun."

Emma trailed the other women, her hopes plummeting. There were only days left before their departure. The safety, the very lives of her father and sister depended on her. And she was being forced to waste her time on such frivolous things as ball gowns and riding cloaks.

Emma sat beside the Earl of Blystone, watching and listening in silence while Conor told an amusing story. All night he had charmed the crowd with his wit and humor. Throughout the endless dinner, and afterward, during the interminable dancing, he had been the life of the party.

Now he sipped his ale and leaned back while the queen added her own bit of narrative to the tale.

All around her, while the titled guests nodded and laughed, Emma felt her composure beginning to slip. In three days Conor hadn't found even a moment to speak with her in private. Three long days. She was beginning to think he'd been avoiding her. What other explanation could there be? Perhaps he had lost his taste for adventure. Perhaps the queen had cautioned him about spending too much time away from her. Whatever the reason, Emma was beginning to lose faith. Just watching him, listening to that smooth voice always saying just the right thing, made her question the wisdom of placing so much trust in the man. Hadn't he admitted to being a spy? Wasn't he a man who seemed to consider nothing sacred? Why should he take on her problems, when they could only lead to trouble?

"...my lady?"

She stared at the outstretched hand for a full minute before comprehension dawned. The earl had just asked her to dance.

"Of course." She accepted his hand and moved into his arms. And all the while, she watched as Conor led the queen through the same dance steps across the room.

Blystone leaned close to whisper, "Are you as excited as I at the prospect of the progress, my lady?"

She struggled to put some gaiety into her tone. "Aye. It should prove to be quite an adventure."

He sighed. "I do so look forward to showing you my home at Warwick."

Emma forced a smile. "I've heard that it's a lovely place."

"It was. And it could become lovely and gay again. It saddens me to see how somber and empty it has become since my wife's death. I have much preferred the liveliness of court."

"Then I'm glad that the queen will now bring laughter and life back to your home."

He tipped up her chin. "It is not only the queen's visit that gladdens my heart, my lady. Part of my excitement is due to you."

"My lord…" Emma found herself speechless.

"My given name is James. Though Elizabeth has always called me Blystone, my friends call me Jamie." His voice lowered. "I hope you will do the same."

She was grateful for the interruption when the queen and Conor paused beside them.

Elizabeth gave Blystone a bright smile. "Dance with me, my friend, and we will talk about the plans you have made."

"Aye, Majesty. With pleasure." Blystone released his hold on Emma and began circling the floor with the queen.

"My lady." Conor held out his hand, and Emma moved into his arms.

"You have been extremely busy, I see." Emma hated the petulant tone of her voice, but there was no stopping it. She couldn't hide her displeasure.

"Aye, my lady." Conor watched until Dunstan and his partner, Amena, moved beyond hearing. Then he bent low and whispered, "Be ready tonight. When the others have retired."

Emma's head came up sharply. Her mouth opened, but

no words came out. Finally she managed to blurt, "How could you calmly sit there...?"

He gave her his most charming smile. "I believe that is another new gown, Emma."

She swallowed. Blinked furiously to keep tears from brimming. "Aye, my lord."

"It is most becoming." He turned her in an elaborate circle, and she felt her head spin.

None of this seemed real. Tonight, while the others slept, she and Conor would ride to the rescue of her father and sister. They would be free of Celestine. All of them. Free.

Including herself. She would no longer have Celestine's threats forcing her to do things she despised. She shook her head to clear it. "All through the evening, I have been entertaining doubts about you, Conor. Allowing myself to think the worst. And all along, you've had your plans in place."

"Forgive me, Emma. There was no way to prepare you. This was why I haven't come near you. I knew it best that we were not seen together for a while."

He had filled his days and nights with dangerous schemes. And she had foolishly resented him.

"My lady, I will bid you good night now." As the music ended, he handed her over to the Earl of Blystone and walked away beside the queen.

Minutes later Conor and Elizabeth took their leave, while the others bowed and curtsied.

Emma struggled to join in the laughter and gaiety of the other ladies-in-waiting and the gentlemen, as they sipped their ale and repeated the latest gossip. But her mind was already on the danger that lay before her this night.

She glanced around at the others and realized that not one of them had an inkling that this was a momentous occasion. If all went well, she and her family would be free of Celestine's tyranny forever. And she would be free of this deceit that had her lying to the man she loved.

The man she loved.

The thought was so stunning, she could do nothing more than stare into the flames of the fire, while a dreamy smile played on her lips.

"Perhaps you will join me in a game of chess, my lady?"

She looked up in surprise. How long had the earl been staring at her?

She pressed a hand to her mouth, pretending to stifle a yawn. "Forgive me, my lord. I must go to my bed."

"Then I will accompany you to your room." He offered his arm and she accepted.

At the door of her chambers she turned and offered her hand.

He closed it between both of his and brought it to his lips. "Perhaps, my dear Emma, you would permit me a brief visit in your chambers?"

"Another time, my...Jamie. For tonight, I find myself far too weary to entertain a guest." To soften the blow she added, "Even one as charming as you."

She was relieved when he didn't press the issue. Instead, he smiled, bowed grandly and turned away.

Once inside, Emma allowed her servant to help her out of her clothes and into her nightshift.

As she sank down on the edge of the bed she feigned another yawn. "Good night, Nola. I will need no further assistance this night. If you don't mind, I do not wish to be disturbed until morning."

"Aye, my lady."

Emma waited until the servant was gone. Then she bounded to her feet and stripped off her nightclothes, replacing them with the breeches and tunic belonging to the stable lad.

That done, she paced her room, pausing occasionally at the balcony to peer into the darkness. And wondering how her nerves would be able to withstand whatever was to come this night.

As soon as Elizabeth entered her chambers, she called to a servant, "Bring us some wine." Then she motioned to a chaise drawn up before the fire. "Sit with me awhile, my handsome rogue."

Conor was puzzled. This was the first time that he could recall the queen veering from her course. Why now, on this most important night of all, had she decided to change the rules of the game?

The servant entered and offered the queen a goblet of ale, then bowed in front of Conor. He accepted the drink, and the servant walked silently away.

Elizabeth turned to him, and lifted her goblet in a salute. "I thought you might care to work a little more of your potent charm before we bid good-night."

"My charm, Majesty?"

"Your wit, your patience, are most persuasive, my rogue."

"Majesty?" His heart lurched. Was she hinting that she wanted him in her bed? There had been a time when he had thought himself capable of any sacrifice for the sake of his countrymen. Even this. But that had been before Emma. Now the thought was so repugnant to him, he found himself cringing. How strange life was. There were dozens, nay hundreds, of men who would give anything for this opportunity. And all he could think about was a sweet Dublin lass who had stolen his heart.

He forced his attention back to the woman beside him.

"Lord Dunstan has given me a very persuasive argument for engaging the Ulster leaders in war." She smiled up into

Conor's eyes. "Is there anything you would like to add before I make my decision?"

He almost sighed with relief. It wasn't affairs of the heart that held her interest this night, it was affairs of state.

"Have you made up your mind, Majesty?"

"I believe so. But I will wait to make my decision known to my advisors. As Dunstan has reminded me, it is a chance to send a message to Philip of Spain. He fears I have bided my time long enough."

"If you agree with Dunstan, I will be greatly sorrowed at your news, Majesty, though I know you will not do this thing merely to harm my poor countrymen. Nor to cause pain to me. But such a decision will do both."

She lay her palm against his cheek. "That is the difference between you and Dunstan. You are too clever to be fooled into thinking that such matters can be undertaken lightly, or for purely personal reasons. Still, Dunstan does have great charm. And there is our long-standing friendship. But when it comes to England, I must think only of my people, and what is best for them."

"I will continue to press for a peaceful solution, Majesty. I fear that if you choose war, you will live to regret your decision."

"We shall see, Conor O'Neil. We will drink, for now, to old friends and new. And may the most persuasive charmer win my heart." She lifted her goblet and drained it, and Conor did the same.

She stood and he followed suit. "Now I must bid you good-night. I need my rest, to prepare for the coming progress."

"Aye, Majesty." He kissed the hand she offered. "May your sleep be peaceful and dreamless."

And his, he realized as he hurried along the hall to his own chambers, would be brief, if at all this night.

Chapter Fifteen

"I see you're ready."

"Oh." At the sound of the deep voice Emma stopped her frantic pacing to turn toward the balcony. "Conor. At last. I thought you were never going to come."

"Forgive me, my lady." He pulled himself over the railing. Up close he could see the worry etched on her brow. He touched a hand to her shoulder. "Did you begin to lose faith in me again, Emma?"

She shrugged in embarrassment. "I tried not to. But I must admit that my thoughts have been in turmoil these past hours. How do we know that Celestine won't return and catch us? And what of my father and sister? I know we can carry Sarah from her bed. But whatever will we do with my father? Conor, he's too heavy to carry from the upper window. And we dare not use the stairs, or the servants will see..."

"Come, Emma. I'll try to put all your fears at rest while we ride. But we must hasten. Already, the nighttime hours are slipping away."

Without another word Conor descended the rope, and Emma followed, dropping lightly into his arms in the darkened courtyard.

She shivered as his arms came around her. There was such strength in them. Such strength of will in this man. And yet she constantly doubted him. Still, the mere touch of him seemed to bring a sense of calm to her troubled heart.

For a moment he crushed her against him, pressing his lips to her temple. "Trust me, Emma. I'll see your father and sister safely free of their prison this night. Or die trying. Now come, lass. We've no time to waste."

They raced toward waiting horses and sped off across the meadows.

Conor's voice beside her was unexpectedly calm. "Edward assures me that Celestine will be gone for the night."

"How can he be certain?"

"He has been a servant in your father's home a long time, has he not?"

She nodded as she guided her horse up a gentle slope.

"Then trust that he knows far more about Celestine's business than you or I."

"But what would take her from her warm bed at this late hour?"

His voice was warm with unspoken laughter. "Perhaps your stepmother has a lover."

He heard her little gasp of surprise and his smile grew. This sweet creature hadn't even begun to fathom the depth of her stepmother's deceit. "That would account for her nights spent far from her own bed."

Though the words stung, Emma had to admit that they made sense. "I've always known that Celestine never loved my father. She merely used him to secure his wealth and title." She paused, considered. "What about Edward? Can you trust him to keep his silence?"

"Though the butler values his position too much to incur your stepmother's wrath, I sense that his loyalty lies with your father. The offer of a few gold coins is little enough to assure that loyalty. And I've promised him more before I leave."

"And there is my next question. Conor, how will we manage to leave with such a heavy burden? There is the matter of the guard posted at the foot of the stairs. How will we ever manage to slip my father and sister past him? And even if we get them out of the house, how do we manage to spirit them away to safety?"

"Have no fear, Emma. Can you trust me a little longer?"

She turned to study his profile in the darkness. How strong he seemed. How determined. Now that he was here beside her, she had no doubt that he would do what he promised.

"Aye, Conor. I do trust you. And whatever you ask of me, I'll do it without question."

Her words warmed his heart as nothing else could have.

At the top of the meadow he reined in his mount and pointed. Up ahead was the darkened outline of Clermont House. Except for an occasional flicker of candlelight, the house and all in it seemed at rest.

Emma shivered as they pulled into a stand of trees and dismounted.

The whinny of a nearby horse startled her. She turned. And found herself staring at a wagon. Standing beside it were two giants.

"You got my message." Conor embraced first one giant, then the other.

"Aye. With little enough time to get here." The voice was thick with brogue. "Couldn't you have given us a bit more notice? It isn't the same as going to market."

"I figured as much. But I live to make your lives miserable."

The three chuckled softly and clapped each other on the back. Then Conor turned to Emma. "This is my father, Gavin O'Neil. And my brother Rory."

The two men inclined their heads slightly as Conor added, "And this is Emma Vaughn."

"A woman, you say?" In the darkness the two studied the shadowy figure in breeches and tunic.

"Aye. Her father is Daniel Vaughn."

"Daniel Vaughn from Dublin?"

"Aye. He and his young daughter, Sarah, have been drugged by Emma's stepmother, Celestine."

"An English woman, no doubt." This from Gavin.

"True enough. She is cousin to the queen."

"Then I'm not surprised at her treatment of a man from Dublin."

Conor ignored his father's remark and added, "They are being held prisoner in that house. We're going to free them."

"And why would we do that?"

"Because he is a countryman. Because it will vex his new wife, who is cousin to the queen you love to hate. And because I ask it."

Rory gave a throaty laugh. "Fine reasons all. Come on then. Let's get to it."

As the three started forward Emma joined them.

Conor paused and placed a hand on her shoulder. "Nay, Emma. You'll stay here with the wagon."

She shook off his hand. "I'll not stay behind. They're my father and sister. My responsibility. I'll see to them."

"It's too risky, Emma. Besides, there are three of us. More than enough to see to this."

"But my father and sister don't know you. I'll not have them frightened by three strangers." When she saw that he wasn't being moved by her argument she added, "I can reassure them that we're here to help them. Without me, Conor, they might cry out in fear and ruin everything."

"She's right," Gavin said. "Better to bring the lass along and not need her, than to wish we'd done so."

Conor gave a sigh of defeat. "All right, Emma. Come along then. But promise me you'll do everything I say."

"I promise." She had to run to keep up with their impatient strides. And blamed that on the thundering of her heartbeat. But there was no denying the nerves that hummed through her as they neared the house.

When they reached the rose arbor, Conor pointed to the second story, then proceeded to climb. When he reached the balcony, he motioned for Emma to follow. By the time she was standing beside Conor, his father and brother had pulled themselves over the rail.

Without a word Conor pried open the window and led the way into the cold, neglected chambers of little Sarah.

In the sleeping chambers they found the child as before, huddled in her bed, her eyes vacant and staring, her hair matted and tangled. When she caught sight of the strangers she became agitated, rolling from side to side as though anticipating pain.

To soothe her, Emma sat on the edge of the bed and gathered her little sister into her arms, crooning softly, but the child wouldn't be still.

Conor turned to his father. "You see the problem. Her crying may attract the attention of the servants. You'll have to carry her down the arbor and across the lawns without being seen. Can you manage?"

The older man's eyes crinkled into a smile. "Do you remember the time, while hunting, when you fell into the swollen river and were being swept downstream?"

Conor smiled, remembering. "Aye. You jumped in and pulled me to shore, while I wailed like a banshee, not out of fear, but because I thought I'd just lost the biggest stag I'd ever killed. And when we got to shore, I realized you had not only dragged me to safety, but the carcass of the stag as well."

Emma listened in amazement to this tale. What manner

of men were these O'Neils? Any man would leap into a raging water to save his son. But to drag the weight of a dead stag as well?

Aye, she decided, they were giants. Very foolish or very fearless giants. But giants who were devoted to one another.

Despite his size, Gavin O'Neil gathered the small bundle into his arms with great tenderness and cradled her against his chest.

"What is her name?"

"Sarah," Emma whispered as she touched a hand to her sister's cheek.

"Have no fear, lass. Sarah is safe in my arms."

Emma felt a tightening in her throat as Gavin strode across the room. How many times, before her father's marriage to Celestine, had she seen him in like manner, cradling his daughter to his chest? And now he lay as helpless as a babe himself.

"Now to the challenge," Conor whispered to his brother.

Following Emma's lead, they made their way along the hallway toward Daniel Vaughn's chambers. Inside they found him in his bed, shivering beneath a thin coverlet.

Emma caught her father's hand. "He's so cold, Conor."

At once Conor leaned over the bed, touching a finger to the old man's throat. "He has grown weaker. Celestine's potions are working their evil magic."

Seeing the stranger in his line of vision, Daniel became agitated and tried to pull away from Conor's touch. In his excitement he cried out and gave a series of low moans.

"He thinks you've come to harm him," Emma whispered. To her father she murmured, "Don't be afraid, Father. It's me. Emma. I've come to help you."

Conor turned to his brother. "Hurry, Rory. Help me lift him from his bed. His cries may have roused one of the servants."

The two brothers wrapped Daniel's blanket around him,

then lifted him as easily as if he were a child. But before they were halfway across the room they heard footsteps approaching.

Thinking quickly, they returned him to his bed, smoothing the blankets, then turned toward a wardrobe. Conor threw open the door of the wardrobe and jumped inside, drawing Emma with him. Though there was little room, Rory leapt in beside them and drew the door closed just as the door to the sleeping chamber was opened.

Emma's heart was thundering so loudly she feared the intruder would surely hear. Held firmly against Conor's chest, his arms wrapped tightly around her, she clung to his strength as the footsteps sounded across the floor.

"Here now. What's the problem?" A servant's voice seemed overloud in the silence. "Having another one of yer fits, are ye? Lady Vaughn left orders that ye were to take this potion whenever ye started yer wailing."

Emma heard the sound of the glass stopper being removed from the vial. Heard the sound of her father's faint struggle. When she instinctively started to push away, Conor tightened his grasp on her and covered her mouth with his hand, to keep her from crying out.

"None of that now. It'll do ye' no good, m'lord. Ye'r wife knows what's good for ye. Drink this now and let me get some sleep."

Conor felt the wetness of Emma's tears spilling over his hand as she wept silently in his arms. To hear such indignities against her own father and to be helpless against them was breaking her heart. It only served to harden his own heart against the woman who had inflicted such pain on the woman he loved.

"That's better. Sleep now, m'lord."

The servant's footsteps sounded as she made her way across the room. The door was opened, then closed.

As soon as the footsteps receded, Rory threw open the door of the wardrobe and led the way to the bedside.

Daniel Vaughn lay silent, his breathing slow and deep.

Emma knelt beside the bed and lifted his hand to her lips. "I promise you, Father, this will be the last time you will suffer at that woman's hands. I give you my word on it."

Conor and Rory waited until she got to her feet. Then they wrapped the blanket around the still figure and lifted him once more from his bed.

"Check the hallway, Emma," Conor whispered.

She opened the door and stole a look before beckoning them to follow. This time they managed to make it to Sarah's room and out the window to the balcony without any further delay.

By the time Emma had managed to close the window, Conor and Rory were halfway down the arbor, balancing the limp figure of her father between them. She watched in amazement, marvelling at their strength.

"Hurry, lass," Rory whispered fiercely.

She scrambled over the edge and followed them safely to the ground.

As she was racing across the lawns toward the waiting wagon, Emma glanced over her shoulder, fearful that at any moment she would see a candle flickering in the window of her sister's chambers. If that should happen, a cry would go up and the entire household would be scrambling to search the house and surrounding grounds.

To her relief, there were no lights. No cries for help. The household lay slumbering.

Her breath was burning her lungs by the time she reached the others.

"Hurry, lass." Rory tucked blankets around the two figures in the back of the wagon, then scrambled to take a seat on the hard bench beside his father. "We have no time to lose. We must go now."

Conor nodded. "You know what to do. We'll follow behind."

"Wait." Emma held up a hand and the men halted their movements.

"Why do you do this? Why do you help me, no matter how dangerous?"

It was Gavin who answered for all of them. "We've always known, lass, that it takes but one man's actions to make a difference in this world. Regardless of the danger, each person must do what he can to right the wrongs. Come now. We have no time to waste."

With a crack of the whip the horses leaned into the harness and the wagon took off with a lurch. Moments later they were swallowed up in the darkness.

Conor helped Emma onto the saddle before mounting his own horse.

As they sped across the darkened landscape, he whispered furiously, "Hurry, Emma. We musn't lose sight of them. The boat can't be kept waiting if anyone is delayed."

"What boat?"

"We've a boat waiting to take you all to Ireland."

Ireland. The very sound of that made her want to weep for joy. Home. Safety. Freedom from Celestine. Freedom from her threats. Freedom from the terrible burden of having to lie and cheat, for the sake of her loved ones.

Emma breathed deeply, imagining that she was already breathing the air of freedom.

Suddenly, over the sound of their horses' hooves, came another sound. A horse and carriage coming toward them from the opposite direction. Beside her Conor motioned for her to follow as he led the way behind a hedge.

They had barely taken cover when a carriage bearing two figures passed by.

"…need something that will convince her that Conor O'Neil is not to be trusted. Else I sense she will be swayed by him and give up the idea of war against the Ulster leaders."

Emma and Conor stiffened. Though the two people were shrouded in darkness, there was no mistaking the voice of the driver. It was Lord Dunstan.

"I know you'll find a way, my love."

Emma turned to Conor with a look of shock. The voice of the woman beside Dunstan was seared into her mind and soul. It was the hated voice of her stepmother, Celestine.

"In fact, I will help you. Stay the night with me, and together we will come up with a way to ruin Conor O'Neil's standing with Elizabeth."

"Oh, you are a clever one, my lady. If anyone can think of a way to drain a man's power…" He leaned over to nuzzle her neck. "…it is you."

The sound of their laughter drifted on the breeze as the carriage rolled past.

In the silence that followed Conor turned to Emma. There was so much he wanted to say to her. So much he held in his heart. But those things would have to wait. As always, there was no time. No time for love words. No time for anything except this thing he must do for Ireland.

"You must ride now, Emma, until you catch up with my father's wagon. For the boat must leave while it is still dark. Once the dawn light streaks the sky it will be too late."

"But what about you, Conor?"

He gave her his most charming smile. "I have something I must see to here."

When she hesitated he leaned over and drew her close for a hard, quick kiss. He felt the flare of heat and the sudden quickening of his heartbeat. For a moment he merely stared at her as if memorizing all her features. Then he slapped her horse's flank and said, ''Go now. Ride like the wind, love.''

There was no time to think. No time to protest. Her horse was already racing along the path.

She turned for another glimpse of Conor. But all she could see was darkness, where moments earlier he had been. Like a creature of the night, he had already blended into the shadows.

Chapter Sixteen

Emma's steed was swift and sure, dancing along the ribbon of moonlight that formed a path toward the looming docks.

She knew why Conor had remained behind. He needed to learn what her stepmother and Dunstan were plotting. Were she in his position, she would do the same. But it pained her to know that he wouldn't be coming with them to Ireland. There was so much she wanted to tell him. So many secrets she'd kept locked in her heart. She wished she could explain why she'd allowed him to believe a lie. And she yearned to reveal the love she felt for him. Love unlike anything she'd ever known before.

When she heard the unmistakable thunder of approaching horses, she pulled her mount from the trail and took refuge in a stand of trees. As the riders drew closer, she could see that they were English soldiers, from the queen's own guard. Their voices carried in the stillness of the night.

"Why has Lord Dunstan ordered us from our beds?"

"He does not wish to find himself facing the sword of a highwayman."

"If that be true, why did he leave the safety of the palace?"

"Because his latest conquest lives outside London. Often they tryst at a tavern not far from the palace. We usually meet him there, allowing him enough time for his... pleasure, and then we accompany him safely back to the palace."

"Then why are we traveling in this direction?"

"Because the woman insists that her husband is now so old and weak it no longer matters if she takes her lover to her own bed."

"I pray I am never that old. Or that weak."

At the coarse words and rumble of laughter, Emma's eyes narrowed with fury. Celestine and Dunstan had made a mockery of all that her father had once held dear.

Hadn't she always known that the marriage was a sham? Celestine had no room in her heart for anyone but herself. She had married only for wealth and titles. Still, it was one thing to surmise such a thing; another to see the proof of her father's betrayal. It was so shocking, so painful, that for a moment all Emma could do was sit and stare as the figures receded into the darkness.

And then another thought intruded. Sweet heaven. These soldiers were heading to Clermont House. Unless she warned Conor in time, he would be caught unaware. And at the mercy of dozens of swords.

She thought of the boat that must set sail before dawn. A boat that would see her safely home with her beloved father and sister. How she yearned for safety. For freedom from this oppressive burden placed on her by Celestine. If she hurried, she would be in Ireland by dawn. But at what cost to the man who had saved her family?

Her orders to catch up to Conor's father and brother were forgotten. As was the freedom that lay tantalizingly just out of reach. Right now, the only thing that mattered was Conor. His safety. Perhaps his life.

* * *

Conor once more secured his horse in the stand of trees, then ran across the sloping lawns toward the house. From his place of concealment he watched as a servant, who had obviously been roused from sleep, crossed the courtyard toward the waiting horses and carriage. With a muttered oath the servant unhitched the horses and led them toward the stables. A short time later, with the horses secure in their stalls, the servant scurried back to the comfort of his bed.

When all was quiet Conor climbed the arbor and made his way along the balcony, until he heard the murmur of voices. Ducking down, he inched his way toward the open window. Then he settled down to listen.

"Don't you want to check on your husband?" Dunstan sprawled on a chaise and watched as Celestine filled two goblets with wine.

"Why should I? The old fool will be snoring."

"Or possibly dead, with the amount of potion you've been giving him."

"Not yet. But soon. I've been careful not to give him too much at one time."

"Very wise." Dunstan gave a snort of laughter as Celestine handed him the wine. "It might have looked suspicious if he'd followed his wife to the grave too soon."

"Aye. This way, all the servants will attest that the old man never left his bed. His death will be deemed a blessing."

"What of the child?"

Celestine chuckled. "A fall from a horse can leave lingering injuries that eventually end in death. No one will dwell on it."

"That leaves only your stepdaughter, Emma." Dunstan watched as Celestine began to undress. She was a woman accustomed to pleasing men. As she slid the gown from her shoulders, a sly smile played on her lips.

"You needn't worry about Emma."

"I won't, my dear. I won't." He thought about Emma's pale, firm flesh. Of the fear in her eyes when he'd ripped the bodice of her gown. When he thought about all that he wanted to do to her, he grew hard. "In fact, when she's served her purpose, I'll dispose of her myself."

"She's done little enough to earn her keep." Celestine stepped out of her petticoats and untied the ribbons of her chemise, baring her breasts.

Seeing the hungry look in his eyes she threw back her head and laughed. "We're good for each other, my love. We each know exactly what the other is thinking. Now…" She sipped her wine, then crossed to him and settled herself on his lap. "…If I help you think of a way to dispose of Conor O'Neil, what will I get in exchange?"

"What you always get, Celestine. My faithful, undying love."

"You're about as faithful as a rutting goat." She wound her arms around his neck and pressed her lips to his. "What I want is an invitation to the Earl of Blystone's home in Warwick."

"Why?" He nibbled her throat.

"So I may begin a search among the nobles for my next husband."

"You mean victim, don't you, my love?" They both laughed. But when he started to lever himself above her she pushed away. "Nay. I want your word. I know you are responsible for Blystone's invitation to the queen and her company."

"Aye. It took little time at all to have him fall into my trap. All I did was appeal to his vanity, and he couldn't wait to invite Elizabeth and her entire court to his home.

Once there it should be an easy matter to put the rest of my plan into motion.''

"I want to be there."

"Why?"

Her voice was smug. "Maybe because I have the Vaughn jewels now, and I want to flaunt them before my cousin." Her tone lowered with venom. "Elizabeth thinks herself above mere mortals. But she'll soon learn that she's just like the rest of us."

"All right. You'll get your invitation. Now, come here." He pulled her close, and this time she relented.

As his mouth began a slow exploration of her body, she smiled. "I believe I've just thought of a way to thank you, Dunstan."

He lifted his head.

"I've just thought of the perfect way to besmirch the good name of your enemy, Conor O'Neil."

Conor went very still. At last. It hadn't taken nearly as long as he'd feared. The thought of sitting through hours of this was repugnant to him. But if they should reveal their secrets quickly, he'd be on his way, leaving them to each other. These two vile creatures deserved each other.

Suddenly Conor heard the thundering of horses' hooves. From his position on the balcony he watched as a contingent of soldiers clattered into the courtyard and milled about.

From inside the room he heard Celestine's voice purring. "I hear your guards."

"They'll wait." There was a muffled laugh. "They'll have to. I can't possibly leave just yet. Not in this... condition."

Conor pressed himself into the shadows, prepared to wait as long as necessary.

From somewhere in the house came a cry. Then a shout.

Doors were slammed. Hurried footsteps sounded along the hallway, then another cry.

A pounding on her door had Celestine muttering oaths usually reserved for sailors and stable hands.

"How dare you disturb me?" she demanded.

"My lady. This is of the utmost urgency." The voice of the servant was muffled behind the closed door.

Conor pressed close to the window to overhear.

"What is it?" Celestine's voice was louder now, as she scurried to pull on a wrap before yanking open the door.

"It's the lord." The servant was clearly out of breath.

Celestine chuckled. "Is he dead?"

"Nay, my lady. He's gone."

"Gone? What do you mean gone, you stupid wench? He can't be gone. The man can't even sit up, let alone walk."

"His bed is empty, my lady. As is little Sarah's."

Celestine's screams brought the entire household to its feet. Doors were slammed. Candles were lit. Conor peered through the window in time to see Dunstan struggling into his clothes, while Celestine raged against the one who had done this thing. The name that brought the most curses was Emma's.

Conor barely had time to pull himself back into the shadows before Dunstan had poked his head out the open window and began shouting orders to the guards in the courtyard to search every inch of the grounds.

Conor cursed his luck. Just when he'd thought to best his opponent, his fortunes had turned. He couldn't stay here any longer. The soldiers would search the balcony as well as all the rooms.

With an oath he watched as dark shadows began circling the house. One soldier had already begun climbing the arbor.

He scrambled across the roof, grateful for the darkness.

Taking refuge behind a turret on the far side of the house, he whirled at a sound behind him.

Two soldiers stood facing him, swords drawn.

"Look what we've found," the first said with a sneer.

"I see. Is this not the queen's own Irishman?" The soldier advanced, the tip of his sword pointed at Conor's heart. "What are you doing so far from the palace, O'Neil?"

"I might ask you the same." Conor measured the distance between soldiers, wondering which one to take first.

"We're here at the invitation of Lord Dunstan. And a lucky thing, I surmise. But you haven't told us what you're doing here, O'Neil."

"Visiting an old friend. Tell me, why is the queen's own guard protecting Lord Dunstan?"

"We do not compromise our duty to the queen. But while she sleeps, Lord Dunstan pays us well to guard his person. And since he is a close friend to the queen, we are simply doing her bidding as well as his."

"I see." He could see something else, as well. The first soldier's footing was none too steady. The fog and mist of night had made the roof slippery. Conor took a step closer.

"Perhaps you'd like to come with us and explain yourself to Lord Dunstan and Lady Vaughn," the soldier called.

"I'd be happy to." Beneath his tunic Conor's fingers closed around the handle of his knife.

As the soldier turned to allow him to move past, Conor reached out a hand. It happened so quickly the man never had a chance to do more than cry out before the knife was imbedded in his heart. As he toppled forward, Conor snatched the sword from his hand and turned to the second soldier, catching him completely off guard.

"You're mad, O'Neil." The soldier raised his sword, prepared to run him through. But Conor was faster, driving the blade of his sword through the soldier's throat.

The man's eyes widened as he struggled in vain to pry

the blade free. His lifeblood draining, he toppled from the roof with the sword still imbedded in his flesh.

Hearing more soldiers scrambling over the roof, Conor looked around for a means of escape. There was a tree, tall enough, and, hopefully, sturdy enough to hold his weight. But not a single branch was close enough to grasp.

As their voices drew nearer, he knew he had no choice. Leaping through space, he reached out and managed to wrap his arms around a branch. For a moment the limb swayed, and he feared it would snap. But as the movements stilled, he continued to cling, and the branch continued to hold his weight.

Hand over hand he scrambled from branch to branch until he caught hold of the trunk of the tree, then climbed down until he was at last on the ground. Keeping close to the hedges, he managed to circle the yard until he reached the spot where he'd left his horse tethered.

Before he could pull himself into the saddle, he felt something heavy crash into his skull. He crumpled to the ground. And though his eyes were closed, he continued to see stars as a voice said, "So. Are you a highwayman? Or just a common scoundrel?"

A soldier stood over him, his sword drawn. A branch as thick as a man's thigh lay by his feet.

Conor shook his head, hoping to clear the fog that seemed to be clouding his vision. He could hear the thundering of his horse's hoofbeats as the frightened animal ran off into the darkness. In some small part of his mind he realized his only means of escape had just been snatched from his grasp. Still, he had to fight for his very survival.

Instinctively he reached for the small, deadly dirk he always kept at his waist. But it was gone. And then he remembered. He'd left it in the heart of the soldier he'd first encountered on the roof.

Setting his teeth against the pain he got to his knees and

shook his head. Lights danced behind his eyes, and he struggled to clear his mind. From the sound of voices nearby he knew the soldiers had fanned out and were combing every inch of grounds. He had to find a way to overpower this lone soldier before the others overheard and came to their comrade's assistance. Once the area was overrun with soldiers, there would be no hope of escape.

"Haven't you heard?" His fingers closed around the tree branch, and he knew he would have but one opportunity to swing it before the soldier's sword found his heart. "I'm Heaven's Avenger."

"Aye." The soldier threw back his head and laughed. "And I'm the King of Spain."

Conor sprang to his feet with surprising agility, and with one blow from the club sent the soldier sprawling in the dirt.

"Sleep long and deep, Your Majesty," he muttered, as he bent and retrieved the fallen man's sword.

"Aye." At the sound of a raspy voice, Conor felt the tip of a sword against his back. "And you're about to do the same. Now lower your sword at once."

Conor felt a rush of anger at his miscalculation. He hadn't heard the approach of another soldier.

He looked around for escape, but there was none now. "And if I should choose not to lower it?"

The man's laugh scraped like a rusty hinge. "Then I'll have to run you through. It matters not to me whether I present you to Lord Dunstan alive or dead."

Keeping his back to the soldier Conor calculated the odds of escape. Of even staying alive. They were becoming slimmer by the moment. When he didn't immediately release his hold on the sword, he felt a sharp, searing pain as the soldier's blade sliced across his hand, knocking the weapon from his grasp. It landed in the grass with a dull thud.

With blood streaming from his wound he turned to face his opponent.

"Prepare to die, villain." The soldier raised his sword for the final blow.

Conor tensed, waiting for the death blow.

Suddenly the man stiffened. The sword dropped from his lifeless fingers. As if in slow motion he staggered, then slumped to the ground.

Bewildered, Conor took a step forward to examine the still figure. Protruding from the soldier's back was the hilt of a knife.

Conor looked up as a shadowy figure stepped from a place of concealment among the trees. A figure in dark breeches and tunic stepped forward, leading a horse.

"Emma." He shook his head, unable to believe what he was seeing. "What are you doing here? I told you to be on the boat to Ireland."

"Aye. And I fully intended to do as you'd asked." She pulled the knife from the soldier's back and idly wiped the blood on her pants before tucking it beneath her waistband. "Come now. I think we'd best ride, before more soldiers come this way, and I have to save your hide again."

"Aye, my lady." With a laugh he boosted her into the saddle, then pulled himself up behind her.

With his arms around her he grasped the reins and urged the horse into a gallop.

Later, he knew, when he'd had time to think all this through, he would have a million questions for this strange little female who had just appeared as if by magic.

For now he would accept the fact that, thanks to shy sweet Emma Vaughn, who seemed not at all shy and sweet at the moment, he had survived to fight another day.

Chapter Seventeen

"Do you think the soldiers follow?" Emma's words were hushed in the darkness.

"Nay." Conor's voice, so close to her ear, made her shiver. "They're still combing the grounds of Clermont House, looking for the intruders who freed your father and sister."

"Then, if it's safe, we should stop here," Emma called over her shoulder. "I'll bind your wound."

"Aye." Weary beyond belief, he reined in their horse and slid to the ground, then reached up to help her dismount.

She shivered at the close contact. Thinking she was cold, he kept his arm around her as they walked a short distance until they came to a shallow stream. They knelt and drank beside their horses. While Conor tethered their horse in a nearby stand of trees, Emma remained by the stream. In the darkness she removed the chemise she wore beneath her tunic. A few minutes later she approached him and ordered him to sit.

"The wound is of little consequence, Emma."

"Still, we can stem the bleeding. Let me look at it."

He held out his hand, and she used a strip of wet cloth

to bathe the cut. Then she carefully bound it with a clean cloth.

"Where did you get these dressings?"

"I used my chemise."

"So." He grinned. "You wear nothing beneath that tunic?"

She gave him a long, steady look. "Nothing, my lord."

The look she gave him quickened his heartbeat. Surely he was imagining things. He would have to remember that Emma was an innocent. The cloak of night's darkness had a way of making a man forget such things.

He studied her while she bent to her task, loving the way her long hair spilled around her angel face like a halo of light. "I can't believe that you turned your back on your one chance at freedom, Emma. You realize there's no escape now. The boat to Ireland is gone."

"Aye. But at least my father and sister are safe."

He smiled. "Not that I'm complaining, mind you. If you hadn't returned, I'd be dead now. Or a prisoner of Dunstan. I owe you my life, my lady."

She gave him a smile that would have melted glaciers. "Then we're even, Conor. For you surely saved the lives of my father and sister. Without you, Celestine would have succeeded in killing them both. It relieves me greatly to know that once they reach our home in Dublin, the servants will see to their needs."

He shook his head. "They won't go there. At least not immediately."

"Why?"

"I instructed my father and brother to take them to our home in Ballinarin, where my mother will watch over them until they're returned to good health."

He saw her blink back tears. "You would do all this for them?"

He touched a hand to her cheek. "And more, if you but asked, Emma."

"Oh, Conor." Though his wound was dressed, she continued holding his hand between both of hers. "You see? It is just another reason why I love you so."

Conor went very still. When at last he found his voice, the words were rough with feeling. "You confuse love with gratitude, my lady."

His words, spoken so fiercely, had her shaking her head. "I know the difference, my lord. What I feel for you could never be confused with gratitude." She lay a hand on his chest, and could feel the thundering of his heartbeat. It matched her own. "I love you, Conor O'Neil."

He couldn't swallow. Could hardly breathe. And couldn't seem to form a single coherent thought.

When he remained silent she whispered, "I had hoped, my lord, that you might feel the same."

He heard her words, but couldn't respond. Couldn't speak a word. Sweet heaven. She loved him. This innocent maiden was offering him the sweetest of gifts. It was almost more than he could absorb. Suddenly this whole night seemed like a special gift. A miracle.

Still, he had to make her see the folly of this situation. "Emma, this is impossible. We can have no future."

"Then we'll have this night, Conor." She brought her other hand to his chest. "And we'll make it enough."

He cleared his throat, struggling to find the right words. For a man who prided himself on his ability as an orator, his gift had suddenly failed him. "You realize that when we leave here, we'll have to return to the palace, Emma. A palace filled with whispers and rumors. And danger at every turn."

"I'll risk it." She brought her lips to his and thrilled to the swift rush of heat. "As long as you're there with me."

On a moan he returned the kiss and thought about crushing her in his arms. But, though the temptation was great, he knew he had to try once more to convince her of the folly of this.

"I can't be with you every minute, Emma." He caught her hand when she pressed it to his cheek. Struggled to remember what he'd been about to say. "There will be long separations. And many dangers."

She saw the way his eyes darkened with a flare of heat. So, he was not immune to her touch. She brought her other hand to cup his face. Then she lowered her mouth to his. Against his lips she murmured, "Is the brave Conor O'Neil afraid of the dark?"

"Of the dark?" He backed away and caught the hands that were causing such a rush of feelings along his spine. "Nay, my lady. It isn't the dark that frightens me. It's the woman who plays the temptress one minute, then hides like a child the next."

Her tone deepened with anger. "I'm not a child, Conor."

"Aren't you?" He stood up and drew her fractionally closer.

"Nay." She lifted her chin in defiance. "I'm a woman, or haven't you noticed?"

"Oh, I've noticed. I've noticed that you change as the mood suits you. Right now you're playing the part of a temptress. But it doesn't suit you at all, Emma. You see?" He tightened his grip. "Here's the proof. Your hand is trembling."

With a boldness she didn't feel, she placed her other hand on his chest. "And your heart is pounding like a runaway carriage. Does that mean I frighten you, too?"

For a moment he didn't say a word, but merely stared into her eyes. Then he dragged her against him and pressed his lips to her temple. "You absolutely terrify me, Emma. God in heaven, how much is a man supposed to take? If I stay here with you, I'll have to kiss you. And if I kiss you,

I'll have to do more. I'll have to have you. All of you. Do you understand?''

She let out the breath she'd been unconsciously holding. "Aye, Conor. I understand perfectly. It's the same for me."

He held her a little away and stared at her as though he'd been struck by lightning.

"The words..." She took a deep breath, then said in a rush, "The words aren't as easy for me as they are for you, Conor. But I love you. Oh, I do love you. Desperately. And have, for a very long time."

For several long moments he framed her face with his hands and merely studied her. Then he drew her into the circle of his arms and covered her mouth with his in a savage kiss.

The heat was so swift, so sudden, neither of them had time to react. The kiss was long and deep and so filled with hunger, that each of them fed from it, frantic to fill the aching void.

Once again Emma was aware of the carefully controlled strength in the arms that held her. And of the carefully controlled passion in him as well. Each time he'd touched her, kissed her, she'd felt it. But this time it was barely contained, threatening to break free at any moment. Her body felt boneless, fluid, as he dragged her against him and savaged her mouth.

She leaned into him, wrapping her arms around his neck, fueling the need. It seemed so right. Though his kiss held no gentleness, though the hands that held her were almost bruising in their intensity, she felt no fear. Though he was still a man of too many mysteries, she knew this much. She loved him. And though he hadn't said the words yet, he loved her. Only her. For now, that was all that mattered.

The need for him grew. The need so long denied. To be held. To be loved. To be cherished.

Holding her firmly against him, Conor could feel her

heartbeat inside his own chest. It matched his. Thundering. Erratic. And her breathing, like his, shallow and strained. He heard a hoarse voice whispering her name and recognized it as his own.

He tore his lips from hers to rush in desperation over her face, her neck, her throat. The need for her continued to grow until it bordered on panic. He had to have her. All of her. Body. Soul. Mind. Or he would go mad.

"Say it again, Emma." He spoke the words against her mouth.

"I love you, Conor. Desperate—"

He cut off her words with a long slow kiss, drawing it out until she sighed and her lips parted for him. His tongue tangled with hers, drawing out all the pleasure until they were both lost in it.

He brushed his lips over her eyelids, her cheeks, the tip of her nose.

"Do you know how precious you are to me, Emma?" Before she could speak he nibbled the corner of her mouth, then brought his lips lower to the hollow of her throat.

This time, instead of words, he was determined to show her all that he was feeling. Despite the hard, driving needs, he forced himself to go slowly, to keep his touches, his kisses, as gentle as possible. But he knew that soon, very soon, she would discover the darker side of his passion. A passion that could very well devour them both.

With his tongue he traced the curve of her ear, nibbling, whispering words that had her shivering with pleasure. When his tongue darted inside she gave a gasp of pleasure and clutched at his tunic. He pulled her closer, burning a trail of fire along her throat. She moaned with pleasure and clung to him, afraid that at any moment her trembling legs would fail her.

As if reading her mind he caught her hand and together they dropped to their knees in the cool, fragrant grass of the meadow. But it offered no soothing balm to the frantic needs that were driving them.

"If you need time, Emma, to think, to change your mind, I'll understand." Even as he said it, Conor cursed himself for a liar. He would have to die if she walked away from him now. He would beg, plead, even crawl to have her.

"I need no time to think. I want you, Conor. I want this." She twined her arms around his neck, offering her lips.

He hesitated, needing this one moment of honesty. "I can make you no promises, my lady. I am committed to this life I live at court. To this queen, who holds the fate of our country in her hands."

She felt the stab of pain. Quick. Jagged. A blow from a sword would have been kinder. She caught her breath on the pain, then forced it aside. "I'll ask nothing more of you than this."

A lie, she knew. She wanted so much more. She wanted it all. Home. Marriage. Children. A lifetime of love with this man. But she would settle for whatever he was willing, or able, to offer.

He took her mouth with a hunger that shocked them both. His kisses were by turn harsh, then gentle, as he struggled with the needs that begged for release. He wanted her. Wanted to take her, here and now. But what she was offering was so precious, so priceless, he owed it to her, to them both, not to waste a moment of it. It wasn't enough to merely take what she offered; he wanted to give in return. As much care as he could manage. As much patience as she deserved. As much pleasure as he could provide.

Around them the night creatures scurried. A bird cried and its mate answered. The leaves of a nearby tree rustled as an owl returned to its nest with food for its young. The horse stomped and tossed its head, sending its mane flying. But the man and woman locked in each other's embrace took no notice. For now the world beyond them no longer existed. They were no longer strangers on foreign soil. The queen and her court were forgotten. As were the life and death schemes that were being played out around them. For now there was only each other and these few stolen moments.

Though he was a man on fire with needs, Conor banked them, determined to go slowly for Emma's sake. He would allow her to set the pace, to savor each moment.

His kisses gentled, as did his touch and his whispered endearments. With teeth and tongue and fingertips he explored her face, her neck, her throat. And with each touch he felt her body grow more tense, her breathing more shallow. As did his own.

Time was forgotten. The rush to return to the palace no longer mattered. The night closed around them, its darkness lending a soothing magic to the moment. They felt alone in the universe. Except for the moon and stars, nothing else existed.

"Do you know how long I've wanted you, Emma? Wanted this?"

She relaxed in his arms, steeped in pleasure. All her fears slipped away. Her family was safe now, far from Celestine's threats. Because of this man. Her duties at the palace no longer mattered. All that mattered was this man. Conor would love her. And that love would keep her safe from all harm.

As his kisses grew more passionate, her breath came more quickly. Her body heated, her blood flowed hotly through her veins.

Conor felt the gradual change in her and thrilled to it. It wasn't surrender she gave. Nor was it surrender he craved. It was trust. Even though there were still so many things about himself he couldn't share with her, she was willing to trust him. It humbled him. And filled him with a strange sense of wonder and pride. Though she knew not where he was leading, she trusted him enough to follow.

He reached for the rough tunic and breeches that hid her beauty. With infinite patience he undressed her. As he did so, he allowed his lips to brush her naked flesh. She trembled and sighed in his arms, which only excited him more.

He held her a little away and studied her in the thin ribbon of moonlight. "Emma." His voice was barely more than a whisper on the breeze. "You're so beautiful, so perfect, you take my breath away."

No one had ever seen her as he had. Nor had anyone ever spoken such words. She kept her eyes steady on his as she reached for his tunic. As she slid it from his shoulders she brushed her lips across his hair-roughened chest. She felt a flutter of excitement when he moaned and trembled. It was her touch that thrilled him. Her kiss that filled him.

Drunk with such power she reached for the fasteners at his waist. When her fingers fumbled, he helped her until his clothes were discarded carelessly with hers, forming a cushion beneath them.

They knelt facing each other. Without a word he combed his fingers through her hair, pulling her head back, staring deeply into her eyes. He covered her mouth with his in a kiss that spoke of hunger, of needs so long denied. Of a need to touch and be touched. A need to give and take. A desperate need to share.

She wrapped her arms around his waist and pressed her mouth to his throat. At that simple contact she felt his muscles contract. And then his hands were moving over her, arousing, enticing, until she felt her body straining with need.

Now his touch was no longer gentle, but rough, almost bruising. His kisses grew fierce, demanding. Now she experienced the darker side of this man. The darker side of his passion. The face he showed to the world was of a charming, smiling rogue. But the stranger who emerged was now an insistent lover who began to take, to feast, to devour. He excited her, even while he frightened her. And the knowledge that it was her touch, her taste, that aroused him made her bold.

She pressed kisses to his neck, his chest. At his moan of pleasure she grew bolder still, running moist kisses across his stomach, exploring him as he was exploring her. With each sigh, each moan of pleasure, she grew bolder still.

Together they feasted, they devoured. Each gave and took until, half-mad, they felt themselves slip over the edge of reason.

Conor was beyond thought. His body was alive with needs. Needs that only she could fill. He had intended to go slowly, but he could no longer rein in his smoldering desire. With her passion unleashed, he was at last free to take her to places she had never gone before.

Straining with need he lay with her in the grass and brought his lips to her breast. Her nipple hardened at his touch and he feasted until she writhed and moaned. He moved to the other breast to nibble and suckle until she cried out for release.

Her breath was coming harder, faster now, as she clutched at him and sobbed his name.

The night air around them was cool, but still the heat rose up between them, clogging their lungs, leaving their skin damp with sheen.

She trembled as he moved over her, his flesh damp and abrasive, adding to the exquisite pleasure. He felt her stiffen and gasp his name as, with lips and fingertips, he brought her to the first peak.

Her body was still shuddering. He gave her no time to think, to breathe, as he continued to move over her. His voice was low now, rough and urgent, as he touched her in ways she'd never even dreamed of. Each touch brought more pleasure. Intense pleasure that bordered on pain.

"Conor. Please. Now. I want you. Now." She kept her eyes steady on his, though they were glazed now with passion. She hadn't thought it possible to want more. But she did.

He let the madness take him over the edge. When he entered her she wrapped herself around him, wanting to hold on to him like this forever.

And then she was moving with him, matching his strength.

He watched her, wanting to see her, to fill himself with her, with the touch of her hands warm upon him, and the taste of her, like the sweetest of wildflowers filling his lungs.

He knew that, in years to come, while he was far from home and fighting to keep his country free, when he was missing Ballinarin and all that he held dear, he would think of her, and this night, and be warmed by the memory.

And then there was no time to think as they began to move together toward a distant star. He whispered her name like a litany, over and over, as their bodies shuddered and seemed to splinter. And then they were soaring, floating, drifting. Still holding tightly to each other, afraid if they let go, for even a moment, they would shatter like fragile glass.

Chapter Eighteen

For the longest time they lay, unable, unwilling to move, their breathing shallow, their bodies slick with sheen.

With great effort Conor managed to lift his head. "Am I too heavy for you?"

Emma was afraid to speak. Afraid if she did, her voice would tremble and he would realize how overcome with emotion she was. Instead she merely shook her head.

"If you're cold, love, I could toss my cloak over us."

Love. His easy use of that endearment brought the tears ever closer. She merely waved a hand, then let it fall back limply.

Alarmed, he levered himself above her and stared down at her. Seeing the glimmer of moisture on her lashes he felt as if he'd taken a knife to the heart. "Ah, no, Emma. I've hurt you. I've been a brute. I don't know my own strength sometimes. I'm so sorry."

"Conor." She lifted a hand to his cheek. "You didn't hurt me. I'm not really crying. Well, I am. But ever since I've met you I seem to do that. It's just…" She sighed. "It was so incredible. I hadn't known it would be like that."

"Truly? That's the only reason for the tears?"

She nodded.

He felt his heart begin to beat again. Touching his forehead to hers he whispered, "Then you're not sorry?"

"Sorry? Oh, Conor, how could I be sorry about what we've just shared?"

He rolled to one side, cradling her against him. "You know Emma, I knew you were a maiden. I really didn't mean to...I hadn't planned this..."

She placed a hand over his mouth. "Shh. I know. I was the one who planned it."

He gave her a long measuring look. Then a smile touched the corners of his lips. "Aye. You did, didn't you? Why, if I didn't know better, I'd say you seduced me, Emma Vaughn."

"I?" She sat up, unmindful of her nakedness. Her hair spilled forward around her face. "Are you saying a sweet innocent maiden from Dublin seduced the very handsome, very charming, very worldly Conor O'Neil?"

He couldn't help looking just a bit smug. "Is that what you think of me? Handsome, charming and worldly?"

"Did I say that? That wasn't what I meant. That's how you appear to others. As for me, I find you merely a...rather plain, rather simple bumpkin."

He was grinning now, his heart so filled with love he felt as if he couldn't contain it all. "A bumpkin, am I? Well this bumpkin was the innocent party in all this. Why, you had me so dazzled with your charm and beauty, I couldn't even think."

She actually glowed at the unexpected compliment. He thought her charming and beautiful.

"According to the ladies at court, men don't think with their brains anyway. It seems another part of their anatomy rules their head."

"Is that so?" He burst into gales of laughter. "What else have those ladies at court been telling you?"

"Well." She looked away, while her fingers continued

to play through the mat of hair on his chest. "I did hear that some men…some extraordinary men," she added with a dimpled smile, "are capable of loving many times through the night."

He wondered if she had any idea what she was doing to him. He caught hold of her hand to stop its erotic movements.

When she looked up, she caught sight of the smoldering look in his eyes.

"And you want to know if I'm one of those…extraordinary men?"

She looked at him from beneath her lashes. "Are you?"

He pulled her down on top of him and gave her a lingering, heart-stopping kiss. She realized at once that he was fully aroused. That only caused her to move over him in a most provocative manner until he moaned softly.

When at last the kiss ended he muttered against her mouth, "I suppose you have your answer now, don't you, imp?"

"Aye." She swallowed.

Then, feeling even more playful, she continued wriggling over him while her hair swirled around, tickling his face, veiling her eyes in a most seductive way.

"I believe you're trying to seduce me again, Emma."

"And if I am?"

With a groan of pleasure he muttered against her lips, "Woman, I can see there's only one cure for this." He rolled her over and kissed her until they were both breathless.

And then, with long sighs and whispered love-words, they tumbled once more into that wonder-filled world reserved for lovers.

The first pale ribbons of dawn streaked the sky. A chorus of birds entertained in the nearby trees.

Conor studied the woman who slept in his arms, tucking the edge of his cloak around her for warmth. All night they had loved, then snatched a few hours of sleep before loving again. It had been the sweetest hours of his life, learning all the secret delights of this extraordinary woman. He had thought himself a worldly man, knowledgeable about the ways of love. But, though Emma had been at first shy and sweet, she had soon discarded her inhibitions and had become a source of amazement. He could no longer recall who had led and who had followed.

She was so loving. So generous. So honest.

Honest. He felt a twinge of guilt. There was so much about himself that he couldn't share. But he owed it to this woman to at least bare a few of his secrets.

"So serious, my lord." Emma studied him from beneath her lashes, then touched a finger to the little frown between his brows. "Is it because of me? Are you having regrets?"

"Nay, Emma." He caught her hand, pressed it to his lips. "How could I regret what we've shared? These have been the sweetest hours of my life."

"And mine, Conor." She stretched, yawned, then wrapped her arms around his neck and pressed a kiss to his lips. "I have never known such a night."

"Nor I." He paused, considered the implications of what he was about to reveal, then decided to plunge ahead. "But there is something I must tell you. Something I fear may change how you feel about me."

She placed her hand over his mouth. "First, I have a confession of my own. It weighs heavily on my heart." It had been the last thought before she had slept and her first thought upon awakening.

He nodded reluctantly. "All right. I'll be a gentleman and allow you to go first."

She took a deep breath, avoiding his eyes. "Not far from

my home in Dublin there is a small village called Glencree. Do you know it?''

Unsure where this was leading he tensed. Nodded.

''A lass there was attacked by a band of English soldiers. Before they could harm her, a man wearing the garb of a friar burst upon them and slit all their throats, saving her virtue.''

''Heaven's Avenger.'' Conor carefully kept his tone devoid of inflection.

''Aye.'' Twisting her hands nervously, Emma glanced at him, then away. ''He was tall as a giant, his arms and shoulders corded with muscles. Eyes bluer than the heavens. And though most of his face was hidden by hood and cowl, he was the handsomest man ever seen in all Ireland.''

''And how do you happen to know all this?''

''I...I was that lass.''

''You, Emma?''

She nodded. ''I didn't mean for it to happen, but right then and there I lost my heart to Heaven's Avenger. And I vowed that no other man would ever share my dreams. He was the reason I began to carry a knife, and the reason why I mastered the art of tossing it.'' She turned to him then, with a look so troubled, he couldn't help but be moved by it. ''Forgive me, Conor. I am tempted to argue that I was younger then and easily swayed by romantic notions. But the truth is, though I truly love you, a part of my heart is still owned by Heaven's Avenger. His cause is so noble, his deeds so pure, and his courage so selfless, it fairly takes my breath away. It doesn't mean,'' she was quick to add, ''that I will love you less. Only that I will think of him sometimes in my dreams. And wish him godspeed on his mission of mercy.''

When he remained silent she turned away, relieved and yet shamed by her admission. In a very small voice she whispered, ''I can see that my story troubles you. I'm sorry if I've caused you pain.''

He sat up and pulled her against him, pressing his mouth to the back of her neck. Though she couldn't see his face, his words were warm with unspoken laughter. ''Oh, Emma. This is the terrible secret you had to share?''

''Aye.''

''Then I must share one of my own.'' He closed his arms around her, his hands resting just below the fullness of her breasts. Against her ear he muttered, ''If I must compete with another, at least I'm grateful it isn't with a mere mortal. As long as you give your heart and soul and body to me, I cannot be jealous if this legendary warrior owns your dreams.''

''Truly?''

''Aye.''

With a sigh of relief she leaned against him, feeling the familiar rising passion as his lips nuzzled her neck, and his hands began their lazy exploration of her body.

''Oh, Conor. See why I love you so? No other man could ever be so understanding.'' She turned, offering her lips.

As he drew her down to the cloak and kissed her, she managed to ask, ''Now. What did you want to tell me?''

His own confession was quickly discarded. It would now ring hollow and empty. He pressed soft moist kisses to her forehead, her cheeks, the corner of her lips. ''Only this, my love.'' He nuzzled her lips until they opened for him. Inside her mouth he breathed, ''You are the most amazing woman I've ever known. I will never have enough of your love.'' He felt his blood heat and allowed himself to be swept along on the tide of passion. ''If I live to be a hundred, I'll not have enough of your love.''

''Come, love.'' Conor nibbled the corner of Emma's lips. ''The sun will soon be up and our empty beds at the palace will be discovered by servants unless we make haste."

"Wait." She pulled him back to her and whispered, "Say that again."

"The sun…"

"Nay. What you called me."

He smiled. Against her lips he whispered, "Love. You are my love, Emma. My own true love."

"Oh, Conor." She kissed him, long and slow and deep, on a sigh of pure pleasure. "Just hearing that word on your lips will make the day so much sweeter."

He returned her kiss with a passion that left them both gasping. Then, gathering his wits, he forced himself to his feet and helped her to stand. "Unless we leave now, our secret will become the latest rumor to sweep through the palace."

"Aye." She hurried to the stream to wash before pulling on her breeches and tunic. When she turned, Conor was already leading the horse. He lifted her into the saddle, then pulled himself up behind her. With a last look at the flower-strewn meadow where they had spent such pleasant hours, they turned their mount toward Greenwich Palace. And whatever dangers lay before them.

"Stay here," Conor warned as they neared the stables. "It wouldn't do for the lads to catch sight of you dressed like this."

He slipped to the ground and helped Emma dismount. While she remained crouched in the tall grass, he pulled himself into the saddle and turned his horse toward the waiting stall.

"Good morrow, my lord." With a smile Meade reached for the reins. "You must have been up before dawn."

"Aye. I saw no need to disturb your rest." Conor glanced over, catching sight of Nola's skirts just inside one of the stalls. "Especially since your time was being put to better use."

The lad blushed and turned away. Conor blessed his good fortune. Not only had the little maid offered him an excuse, but she would be far too busy pulling herself together to catch Emma sneaking into her own chambers.

As soon as he was out of sight he caught Emma's hand, leading her toward the empty courtyard. "Come, love. We must hurry."

"How will we get to our rooms without being seen?"

"The same way we left them last night."

"But that was under cover of darkness." She paused as he caught the rope, tested its strength. As he gathered her close she whispered, "Conor, if anyone should glance out their balcony windows, they'll see us."

"It's our only hope. The hallways of the palace will be filled with servants. They might not take notice of me, but seeing one of the queen's own ladies-in-waiting wearing a man's breeches and tunic would certainly start tongues wagging."

She knew he was right. Still, as she wrapped her arms around his neck, and he began climbing the rope to her balcony, she felt as if the whole of England was watching.

When at last they reached her balcony, he lifted her over the rail and carried her easily inside. Once more she was reminded of his incredible strength, and she had a quick mental image of the way he had looked, running across the lawns of Clermont House, as if he were out on a simple jaunt. Perhaps it was one more reason why she loved him. In her youthful romantic fantasies, this was exactly the way Heaven's Avenger would have behaved. Then she admonished herself for giving in to such a fantasy. She fervently hoped it didn't demean her love for this flesh and blood man.

"Here we are, love. Safe and sound after our adventure. And no one is the wiser."

No sooner were the words spoken than they heard a knock on the door and Nola's voice, soft and muted calling, "My lady. I would enter your chamber and help you with your morning toilette."

"Aye, Nola." She watched as Conor headed toward the balcony. "Give me a moment."

When she reached his side he pulled her to him with a wicked grin. "Not a moment too soon. I'll bid you goodbye for now, love." He covered her mouth with his, lingering over her lips.

"Hurry, Conor. Before someone comes and notices the rope dangling in the courtyard."

"Aye, my love." But instead of leaving, he kissed her again. "I'll pray the day goes swiftly, so that I can lie with you again this night, and show you once more how much I love you."

And then he was gone. Over the railing. Down the rope. As soon as he jumped clear, Emma untied the knot and tossed the rope down to his waiting arms.

He blew her a kiss and was gone.

"My lady," came Nola's insistent voice from the hall.

Emma stripped off her tunic and breeches, and buried them in the back of her wardrobe. Then she slipped on her nightshift and glanced around, to see if there might be anything out of place. Satisfied that all was in order, she released the latch on the door and pressed a hand to her mouth as though stifling a yawn.

"Forgive me, Nola. I fear I was deep in a wonderful dream when you first called to me."

"I can see that, my lady."

"You can see my dream?"

"Aye." The little maid studied Emma until she flushed and turned away. Nola stepped inside and made her way across the room to pour water into a basin. ''For your eyes have a warm gleam to them. Why, even your skin seems to glow this morrow, my lady.''

Touching a finger to her lips Emma walked to the balcony and studied the empty courtyard below. Though Conor O'Neil was nowhere in sight, she could still taste him. A taste that was dark and mysterious. And she could still see in her mind that wicked smile that had a way of tugging at her heart and making her whole world tilt at a precarious angle.

''Perhaps, Nola,'' she said on a sigh, ''if I'm lucky, I'll enjoy that same dream again this night.''

Chapter Nineteen

"Well, my Irish rogue, once again you are late." Elizabeth looked up from the table to watch as Conor crossed the great hall and made his way to her side.

Across the table, Emma watched as well. As always, Conor cut a splendid, dashing figure that never failed to make her heart beat a little faster. Just the sight of him had her spirits soaring. And thinking about the night of loving they had shared had her blushing furiously.

"Good morrow, Majesty." He paused and pressed Elizabeth's outstretched hand to his lips, before greeting the others around the table.

When he caught sight of Emma seated between Dunstan and the earl of Blystone, he forced himself not to stare, though he longed to linger a moment and just drink in her beauty. She had been the sweetest surprise. The night they had shared was still uppermost in his mind. And judging by the flush on her cheeks, she was sharing the same sweet thoughts.

"How does your planned progress go, Majesty?"

"Smoothly, Conor." Elizabeth touched a proprietary hand to his arm when he took the seat beside her. "I was just telling the others to be prepared to leave on the morrow.''

''So soon?''

''Aye. Lord Dunstan wagered one thousand gold sovereigns that I could not possibly be ready to leave that soon. It was all the reason I needed to move ahead with all speed. You know how I detest losing.''

''As does Lord Dunstan.'' Conor tensed when he looked across the table at Dunstan, remembering what he'd overheard on Celestine's balcony. It was Dunstan's suggestion that Blystone invite the queen and her party to his estate. Now he was pressing to get her there with all speed. But why? What was Dunstan's plan?

The words Conor had overheard last night began to play through his mind. At the time he'd been determined to learn what Dunstan had in store for him. When he'd learned that Dunstan intended to harm Emma, all else had vanished from his mind. But now he struggled to recall what else had been said. How could Dunstan benefit from the queen's visit to his rival's estate? It made no sense. If anything, Dunstan should have wanted to show off his own wealth and power by inviting the queen and her company to one of his many estates.

Conor cursed himself for his carelessness. He should have paid more attention, despite the distractions. Now he would have to go back in his mind to recall every word, every phrase.

He was too deep in thought to realize that Dunstan was studying him carefully.

Dunstan's words brought Conor out of his reverie. ''You look a bit weary this morrow, O'Neil. Was it ale, cards or women?''

Emma gasped while the others laughed.

Conor merely gave him a lazy smile. ''I could boast that it was all three. But in truth, I slept like a babe.''

"As did I." The queen's voice was a purr of contentment as she touched a hand to Conor's in a most suggestive manner.

While the others winked and nodded at the queen's words, Dunstan steepled his fingers and narrowed his gaze on the man beside her. It was going to give him such satisfaction to watch this Irishman squirm when he found himself no longer under the protection of England's monarch. Oh, it would be sweet vengeance indeed.

"Come. We have tarried long enough." Elizabeth stood and her ladies formed a circle around her as she walked away. "We have much to see to before we take our leave of Greenwich on the morrow."

Seeing the smug smile on Dunstan's lips, Conor became even more determined than ever to watch, to listen, to go over every word he had overheard last night. If there was the slightest hint of what Dunstan and Celestine were planning, he had to move quickly. Not only did Emma's safety depend on it, but possibly the safety of the queen as well. That could mean an end to all he had worked for. The safety, the very survival of Ireland, might depend upon what happened in these next days.

"I have never seen such an uproar," Nola muttered as she gathered up yet another batch of gowns and cloaks.

"Aye," grumbled another servant. "Now that the queen has moved up the date of our departure, there's not a moment left to catch my breath."

Servants scurried from room to room, collecting armloads of clothing and bed linen. The cooks had been working night and day, baking breads, roasting meats, to feed the army of men and women who would accompany the nobles on their journey. The stable lads were busy preparing dozens of horses for the trek into the countryside. Many wagons and carts, laden with household goods, had already been hauled away. Every so often the rumble of wheels would announce the departure of another.

Through it all Emma worked alongside the other women, preparing the queen for her public appearances. Though her thoughts often strayed to Conor, Emma managed to feign interest in the mundane problems of the queen's wardrobe. When the others admired Elizabeth's satin cloak lined with ermine, Emma agreed it was the loveliest she had ever seen. And when the queen asked her opinion on which riding outfit to choose, Emma boldly suggested the russet gown and cloak, to compliment Elizabeth's hair.

There were slippers and jewels to be matched to each gown. Coats and bonnets and ribbons and combs.

At long last, day inched toward darkness, and the queen announced that she would sup in the privacy of her chambers to preserve her energy for the morning's journey.

Emma was delighted to retreat to her chambers, where Nola was already preparing a simple supper on a small table set before the fire.

The servant looked up when Emma entered. "Shall I stay and serve you, my lady?"

Emma shook her head firmly. "You need your rest, Nola. Her Majesty has declared that we must be prepared to move out at first light."

"Aye, my lady." Nola fairly flew across the floor.

As she drew open the door, Emma called to her retreating back, "Bid Meade a fond farewell from me, as well, Nola."

The little maid paused, her cheeks flushed with color. "How did you guess where I was headed, my lady?"

"It is obvious to anyone who sees you, Nola. Go now. And try to get at least a little sleep tonight."

"Aye, my lady." With a giggle, she was gone, the door closing firmly behind her.

Emma was still smiling when she felt arms close around

her and a deep voice whisper in her ear, "I thought she'd never leave."

Conor's voice sent shivers along her spine.

She leaned back against him and gave a sigh of pure pleasure. "How long have you been here?"

"Not long. I climbed to your balcony just before your servant arrived with your meal. I thought it best to remain concealed until she was gone."

"A very wise decision, my lord. Else her shouts would have brought down the entire palace." She turned and touched a hand to his cheek. "How long can you stay?"

His smile held a hint of danger. "That depends, my lady. How long can you stand to have me here?"

"Oh, Conor." She threw her arms around his neck and kissed him with a fervor that made both their heads spin.

He hadn't expected such a rush of passion. It heated his blood, clouded his vision. With his mouth on hers he backed her up until she was pressed firmly against the wall.

His words, which only moments earlier had been spoken lightly, were now rough with urgency. "I've thought of no one but you all day." His mouth savaged hers. His lips, his hands took her on a wild, dizzying ride. "All I could think of was you. Of this. Only this."

She had thought, after the night they had spent together, that there was nothing new he could show her. But this was no slow, sweet journey of love. This was passion. Raw. Wild. Unleashed.

With every touch of those strong fingers, with every taste of those clever lips, he drove her higher, giving her no chance to recover her senses. With each sigh and moan of pleasure, she soared higher, then higher still, until, desperate for release, with his name torn from her lips, she felt herself slipping over the edge of a cliff. And falling. Falling.

She was wonderful to watch. All her feelings were mirrored in her expressive eyes. Her excitement fueled his own, driving him beyond all limits. When she reached the crest, he covered her mouth with his and took her with a fierceness that bordered on madness. And left them both shattered.

Drained beyond belief, they dropped to their knees. Conor gathered her into his arms and felt her breathing slowly return to normal.

"I can't quite believe this," she managed over a throat still clogged with passion.

"Nor I." He kissed her eyelids, her cheeks. And then, with laughter rumbling in his chest he muttered, "Do you realize that we have never yet enjoyed the comfort of a bed?"

She joined his laughter. "Perhaps, after we sup, we could try it?"

He surprised her by lifting her in his arms and carrying her across the room. He settled her gently in the bed, then lay beside her.

Against her mouth he muttered, "It seems a shame to waste time with food. Don't you agree?"

"Aye. I do indeed."

It was the last word she managed before his mouth claimed hers again.

With soft sighs and heated touches, they came together once more, shutting out the world around them. But this time it was a slow, patient journey of two lovers who had all the time in the world.

"Tell me what to expect on the first day of the queen's progress." Emma lifted the goblet of wine to her lips and drank, then offered it to Conor. Though the hour was so late that all in the palace were asleep, they found themselves wide awake after hours of loving. The remains of their supper rested on a tray between them.

"It will not be difficult." He held a biscuit dipped in honey to her mouth and watched as she took a bite. Then he bent to taste the sweetness that lingered on her lips. "Warwick is but a day's journey from here."

"Then why must we leave at dawn?"

He polished off the rest of the biscuit, then sipped more wine before handing the goblet back to her. "The village elders will wish to greet their queen with long, boring speeches and many gifts of gold and precious jewels. And then there will be the formal supper with all the nobles from nearby villages and shires. Elizabeth enjoys these spectacles. But she also knows that it will be very late before she can retire to her bed. The sooner we start, the sooner the celebration will end. And then she can enjoy several days at Blystone's estate, doing as she pleases."

"Such as?" Emma removed the tray and filled their goblet from a crystal decanter.

"There will be a hunt, of course, for Elizabeth dearly loves to hunt." As she climbed back into bed Conor paused and lifted his arm, drawing her close against his chest. When she held the goblet to his lips he sipped. "And a grand ball. As you've noticed, our queen loves to dance."

"Aye. She especially loves to dance with her charming rogue."

He winced as she offered him a sip of her wine. "Do you know how much I detest that name?"

"I don't know why." Emma fought to keep the laughter from her tone. "After all, you are charming. And, as everyone knows, you are quite a rogue."

"And you are a most annoying wench." He took the goblet from her hand and set it on the table beside the bed. Then he turned and dragged her into his arms, kissing her until she had to struggle for breath.

"I hope that will remind you to find a new name for me. I'll no longer answer to the queen's title."

"Aye. Enough, Conor." Laughing, she pushed free of his arms. As soon as he released her she added teasingly, "My charming..."

Before she could scamper from the bed he caught her by the ankle and began to tickle her foot.

"Come here, wench," he growled in mock anger. "It's time you were taught some manners."

Amid squeals of laughter she managed to ask, "By the queen's charming...?"

"That does it." He knelt up and, holding her foot firmly in both hands, began raining kisses along the sole of her foot until she was writhing and giggling.

"Stop. Oh, Conor, stop. I can't bear it." She giggled again. But, as his lips began a slow, torturous journey up her calf to the back of her knee, her laughter suddenly faded.

By the time his lips were moving along her inner thigh, she was sighing. And then, as he brought his mouth higher still, she gave a gasp of surprise that soon turned into a little moan of unbearable delight.

She hadn't thought it possible to experience anything this intense. Pleasure bordering on pain. A feeling so exquisite, she felt lost in rapture.

"Conor. Conor." As if in a haze she whispered his name as he brought his mouth up her body, further exciting her, until he claimed her lips. With a savageness that stunned them both, he took her.

She moved with him, driven by incredible strength. Conor watched her, loving the way she lost herself in him. In the pleasure. In the passion. And then he found himself drowning in her. In her voice calling his name. In this tide that was so compelling, he felt himself tossed and buffeted and finally, shattered.

Spent, they lay in each other's arms and drifted slowly back.

Still locked in an embrace, they slept.

* * *

Dunstan stood very still, listening outside Emma's door. So, it was as he'd suspected. Emma Vaughn and Conor O'Neil were lovers. But, had the girl merely followed orders and seduced the Irishman for the sake of her loved ones? If so, that would have to mean she didn't yet know that her father and sister had escaped Celestine's clutches.

Or had she lost her heart to O'Neil?

No matter. The fact was, she wasn't as sweet and innocent as she'd pretended. Whether it was duty or love that sent her to O'Neil's bed, one fact remained. The queen's lady-in-waiting had betrayed her monarch with the hated Irishman.

Dunstan walked away, a sly smile touching the corners of his lips. What sweet revenge he would enjoy. For Emma Vaughn and Conor O'Neil had just given him a powerful weapon to use against them.

Chapter Twenty

"Where are you going?" Emma awoke to find Conor already dressed.

"It's almost dawn, love. Your maid will be here soon. You wouldn't want Nola to find me in your chambers." He crossed to the bed and gave her a soft, lingering kiss. "This may have to hold us for days, until we find a moment alone."

"Oh, Conor." She knelt up in the bed and wrapped her arms around his neck, returning his kiss with a passion that was nearly his undoing. "I wish you didn't have to go. I miss you already."

He moaned and took the kiss deeper, resenting the time and circumstances that conspired to keep them apart. "It will only be a day or two. I'll come to you, love, even if I have to slay a few dragons to do it."

She shivered at the deep timbre of his voice. "Don't say that. Even in jest."

He couldn't help teasing her. "I'll wager you wouldn't be so concerned for Heaven's Avenger."

"Nay. But he's a fighter, and you're a lover. My lover." He gave her a heart-stopping grin and kissed her one last time, then forced himself to step back. Unless he left right this minute, he'd never make it out of here.

He crossed to the balcony, grasped the rope, then disappeared over the railing. By the time Emma raced across the room and looked for him, her man of mystery had been swallowed up by the swirling mist.

"There, Majesty." Conor, astride his horse, pointed to the turrets in the distance. "There is the earl's estate at Warwick."

"At last." The queen, weary after hours in her carriage, brightened.

The procession had been slowed considerably by the throngs of people who lined the roads. Young boys waved from the high branches of trees. Women stood on tiptoe, for a glimpse of their monarch. Fathers held shrieking children on their shoulders to salute their queen.

Elizabeth fanned herself. "I have been greatly cheered by the warmth and adulation of the crowd. But now I want nothing more than a refreshing basin of water to bathe away the dust of the journey, and a glass of ale for my parched throat."

"Then you shall have them, Majesty." Conor gave the order to a servant, who took off toward the manor house in a flurry of hoofbeats.

Within minutes their procession had entered the grounds and began winding its way along a curving ribbon of road toward the turreted house beyond.

When they arrived the servants were lined up in the courtyard behind their master, as he waited to receive his regal guest. The Earl of Blystone's voice was warm with affection as he presented his household staff to their queen. He watched with pride as the men doffed their hats and bowed and the women curtsied.

Then, while the other guests were being helped from

their carriages, the queen gratefully entered the privacy of the earl's home. She was taken at once to her sumptuous quarters, where she could refresh herself after the long journey.

Emma, who had been forced to ride with the queen, stood to one side in the sunshine, watching as trunks were unlashed and dropped to waiting servants, who carried them inside. Amid all the bustle, she saw Conor walking toward her. At once her weariness vanished as he greeted her with a smile.

"How did you fare, my lady?"

"It was not a difficult journey. And the queen's servants saw to our every comfort."

"I'm happy to hear that." He leaned close. "I wish I could touch you. Just for a moment."

"Then you shall." She placed her hand on his arm and began to walk beside him.

As they stepped through the arched doorway, Conor managed to pull her close. His lips brushed hers. A mere whisper of mouth to mouth, but they both felt the heat and were warmed by it.

"If only we could slip away to a distant meadow, my lady, so I could show you just how much you were missed."

Emma heard the frustration in his tone. It mirrored her own. "Perhaps later we can find a moment. But I fear the welcoming festivities will last far into the night."

With matching sighs they stepped apart and continued on to their separate chambers, to oversee the unpacking and to prepare for a lavish banquet and ball for the royal visitor.

Conor, dashing in black satin tunic and breeches, stood in the great hall. All around him, the crush of invited guests milled about, accepting goblets of ale and wine from the liveried servants who moved among them. Though he continued chatting with the lord mayor of a nearby village, he was aware of the exact moment when Emma entered the room. He felt his heartbeat quicken.

She wore a gown of palest pink, the shade of a blushing rose. The low, rounded neckline revealed the swell of high, firm breasts. Her tiny waist was encircled with a girdle of pearls. The full skirt, dotted here and there with more pearls, fell to the tips of fine kid slippers. The full sleeves, inset with pearls, billowed to the elbow, then were tapered to the wrist and banded with a rope of pearls. Her hair was a mass of thick ringlets, pulled to one side with mother-of-pearl combs, the burnished curls spilling over her breast. She wore no jewelry at her throat or ears or on her fingers, which only seemed to add to her unassuming beauty.

Conor saw the admiring glances of the men, and heard the whispers of the women as Emma passed. How he longed to take her hand and acknowledge his love for her. Instead, he had to be content to merely offer a simple greeting.

"Good even, my lady."

She paused, smiled. "My lord."

"Ale, my lady?"

She accepted the goblet from his hand, enjoying the brush of his fingers on hers before acknowledging the introduction to the lord mayor.

Conor saw Lord Dunstan walking toward them and whispered, "Brace yourself, Emma. Dunstan's looking far too smug."

"Ah. Emma, my dear. And O'Neil. How fortunate that I should find you two together. You're just the ones I'm looking for. You're in for a most pleasant surprise this night."

Conor gave him a steady look. "Surprise?"

Before Dunstan could reply, the earl entered the hall and announced the arrival of the queen. All conversation ceased. The men bowed, and the ladies curtsied, as Elizabeth made her way through the crowd.

Elizabeth accepted a goblet of ale and took her place in an ornate chair positioned on a raised platform where she could be seen by everyone in the great hall. From the elders of the neighboring shires to the titled noblemen and their ladies, all eyes were fixed on the queen.

She summoned Emma and the other ladies-in-waiting to join her, then beckoned to Conor.

"Is this not a lovely place in which to refresh ourselves?"

Conor nodded. "Indeed, Majesty. The outpouring of love from your people has been amazing."

"I quite agree." Elizabeth turned to her host and in regal tones announced, "My dear Blystone. Your queen's heart is so filled with joy at this magnificent setting, that I shall grant a number of favors to the assembled. Let those who wish to petition their queen step forward."

There was a moment's pause as the people glanced around, trying to summon the courage to approach their monarch. Though it was a common practice for the queen to grant such favors, many were too timid to take advantage of the blessing.

While they murmured among themselves, they noticed a slight commotion near the back of the great hall. As a woman made her way forward, the crowd began to part. When she drew near, Emma and Conor were stunned to recognize Celestine, looking every bit as smug as Dunstan.

Celestine wore a gown of rich cloth-of-gold, and over it, a cape lined with ermine. At her throat were dazzling diamonds, with more diamonds at her ears and about her wrist. She looked far more regal than the queen herself.

Hearing Emma's little gasp of surprise, Conor turned. In her eyes was a look of pain.

"What is it, my lady?"

"Those were my mother's diamonds," she managed to whisper. "My father gave them to my mother on her wedding day. Before she died, she gave them to me."

It was, Conor knew, one more reason to despise Celestine.

Elizabeth seemed surprised to see her cousin so far from London. But she quickly composed herself and offered a warm greeting. "I see you have journeyed to Warwick to make me welcome, cousin. How gracious of you."

Celestine curtsied and kept her eyes downcast. "I do indeed bid you welcome, Majesty. But I have made the journey for another reason as well. I would ask a favor."

"Then ask it. For I am feeling most generous."

Celestine lifted her head and stared past the queen to where Emma stood. Her lips curved into the merest hint of a smile. "I ask that, since my husband has abandoned me, I be given all his titles, estates and goods here in England."

"What do you mean, you have been abandoned?" The queen shot a questioning glance at Emma, who kept her gaze lowered.

"My husband committed a most cruel and heartless act. He fled in the night, taking with him my beloved little stepdaughter, and all the wealth he could carry, leaving me alone and penniless, except for these clothes and jewels which were on my person. Without the protection of my husband's wealth and title, I will be at the mercy of those to whom he owes tremendous debts. I could even end up in debtors' prison."

Emma seethed with impotent rage. There was no way she could expose Celestine's lies without implicating herself.

"What about Daniel Vaughn's other daughter, Emma?" the queen demanded.

Celestine stared directly at Emma. "Has she pleased Your Majesty with her service?"

"Indeed she has. I find her both sweet and selfless."

"I am gratified to hear that." Celestine's voice quivered with emotion. "My stepdaughter, Emma, will always have a place in my heart and in my home. Why, she is like my own dear child."

Elizabeth nodded, pleased at Celestine's response. "Very well, cousin. Have my lord secretary draw up a list of Daniel Vaughn's titles and holdings in England. They shall be yours."

Celestine gave a deep, dramatic bow, which nearly hid the satisfied smile that curved her lips. But Conor saw it, and clenched a fist at his side. The woman was a clever actress. And a shrewd thief.

He glanced at Emma's pale face and could see how she struggled with shock and horror. Risking the queen's wrath, he touched a hand to hers. It was cold as ice.

"What a cruel, spiteful woman," she whispered. "She strips my family of everything of value."

"Nay," Conor muttered fiercely. "Don't despair, love. All she takes are worldly possessions. They have no true value. Don't you see? You and your father and sister have the things that matter. Love, family, loyalty. Celestine can never touch those."

Emma swallowed back her tears and nodded. It was true. She had the best of life. She would waste no more regrets on the things that didn't truly matter.

Conor stood in the darkness of the courtyard, studying the balconies above him. It had taken all of his considerable skill to excuse himself from the queen's chambers. Invigorated by the journey, and by her warm reception here at Warwick, she had danced late into the night. Even after she had made her grand exit, so that the guests could take their leave and return to their beds, she had been too excited to give in to sleep. Instead, she had insisted that Conor escort her to her private chambers, where she hoped to continue the festivities.

"What is it, my charming rogue?" she had demanded when Conor had suddenly slumped against the wall.

"I fear I've enjoyed the wine a bit too much, Majesty. Or perhaps it was the fine food. Whatever the reason, I am feeling indisposed. Can you forgive me?"

"There is nothing to forgive. You will rest. And on the morrow, you will join me for the hunt."

"Aye, Majesty." He'd kissed her hand. "It will be my great pleasure."

And now, as the candles were being snuffed throughout the household, he studied one balcony in particular, and tested the rope in his hand.

It pained him that he couldn't take advantage of the night and go to Emma's bed. The need for her was like an ache. But he had to get into Dunstan's chambers. He was quite certain that was where he would find Celestine. And where he might learn what other secrets she and Dunstan had in store.

He tossed one end of the rope and felt it circle the railing before dropping into his hands. Securing the rope, he tested its strength, then began to climb. It was an easy matter to reach the balcony. From there he studied the two shadowy figures in the bed, then, needing to be closer, he slipped through the window and crept across the room.

A quick glance around showed him the perfect hiding place. But as he crawled toward the armoire, he paused at the sound of Dunstan's voice. "Did you see the look on Emma's face when the queen granted your request?"

"Aye." Celestine gave a throaty laugh. "She thought she had bested me, spiriting away her father and sister in the night."

"You can't be certain it was Emma."

"No matter who did the deed, the plan was Emma's. I'm

sure of it. She was always too headstrong for her own good. But no matter. Now the little fool will learn a very painful lesson. No one crosses swords with me. No one.''

"You are a most spiteful creature, my love." At Dunstan's low growl of laughter, the mattress shifted, and his voice was muffled against her skin. "Which is probably why you and I are so evenly matched."

Conor seized the momentary distraction to open the door to the armoire. But as he stepped inside he realized he wasn't alone.

Someone was already concealed inside. Someone wearing black breeches and tunic, in order to blend into the darkness. Someone whose breath came out on a hiss of surprise. And whose hair and skin smelled of lavender.

Emma felt a big hand close over her mouth, shutting out the little yelp of surprise that bubbled in her throat. Her eyes rounded in shock, before narrowing.

"Not a sound," Conor whispered against her ear.

Slowly he removed his hand, and she took in several gulps of air to steady herself.

She was sweating, she realized. And it had nothing to do with the heat and stuffiness of the armoire. There was nothing she could do now but hunker down beside Conor and wait for this interminable night to end.

"What have you planned for the morrow?" Celestine's voice was a low murmur as if filtered through the door of the armoire.

"The same as before." Dunstan's voice was pleasantly calm, with an air of assurance. "Only this time I won't miss."

"Who will take the blame? Another peasant?"

"Not this time. There will be no need. I intend to lay the blame directly at Blystone's feet."

"He's certain to protest his innocence."

Dunstan chuckled. "Dead men don't protest. As soon as

I've finished with our queen, I intend to put an arrow through his heart as well. And then, when Huntington is king, I expect his first act to be to declare war against that upstart little island across the sea. Conor O'Neil will be the first victim of our war with Ireland. I'll ask that our new king have him beheaded.''

"What about Emma?'' Celestine's voice was filled with venom. ''I want her dead as well.''

"Never fear, my love. She will join her lover in death.''

"Her lover?''

"Aye. She and O'Neil have been carrying on their affair in Greenwich Palace, right under the nose of the queen.''

While the two shared a laugh, Emma shivered, and Conor drew her close against him in the darkness of the armoire.

Dunstan's voice was low with pride. ''And while our soldiers are crushing the Irish peasants, your brother, the new king, will see that Blystone's titles and estates are confiscated and apportioned to the hero who brought down Elizabeth's assassin.''

Hearing those words, Emma gasped. Beside her, Conor pressed a finger against her lips.

Dunstan laughed again. ''I've always wanted to be an earl. And I've always coveted Blystone's estate here at Warwick.''

Celestine clapped her hands in delight. ''Oh, my love. We are a pair, aren't we?''

The bed creaked as the two came together in a storm of passion.

While the two were distracted, Conor caught Emma's hand and dragged her from their place of concealment. Minutes later they descended the rope and stood in the darkened courtyard.

Conor's voice was low with anger. ''Do you know what

a foolish, dangerous thing you just did? What were you doing in their chambers?"

Emma stood her ground. "The same thing you were doing. Listening to their plans, in the hope of finding a way to restore my father's estates."

"I told you to trust me to find a way. If you'd have been caught in there, you would have tasted Dunstan's sword."

"As would you, Conor."

"If only he would try," he whispered fiercely. "It would make for an enjoyable interlude. Nothing would make me happier than to finish what we once started."

She fingered the glint of silver at her waist. "As for me, I have my knife. Now I'm going back up there and cut out Celestine's thieving black heart."

He caught her roughly by the arm, halting her before she could step away. "There are more important things to worry about than revenge upon your stepmother. Do you understand what they plot?"

"Aye. To kill the queen and blame her death on Blystone."

"It's up to us to stop them." Though he spoke the words softly, she could hear the steel in his words.

"Then it will give me great pleasure to cut out both their hearts. But I will do it for myself, not for the Queen of England."

He gave a long, deep sigh, wishing there were time to tell her everything. But all he could say was, "We must keep Elizabeth safe from harm."

"The English queen? How can you, who spy for Ireland, say such a thing?"

"If Elizabeth dies, Huntington and Dunstan will wage a bloody war in Ireland. There's no time to waste. Something Dunstan said reminded me of what I'd forgotten. Now," he said impatiently, "I must ride."

"Ride? I don't understand. Aren't you going to go to Elizabeth and tell her what you've heard?"

"If I go to Elizabeth with this wild tale, she will confront Dunstan with my accusations, and he will simply deny. I need proof. I now realize where I must go to seek it."

"Where will you go, Conor?" Too much was happening too soon. She couldn't seem to keep up with his sudden shift in plans.

"To Fleet Prison. Pray I find what I'm looking for. And pray I make it there and back before the queen leaves on her hunt. Or all I've labored for over the past years will have been in vain." As she turned away he caught her by the arm and kissed her long and hard. Against her mouth he muttered, "I love you, Emma. No matter what happens, never forget that."

"And I love you, Conor. With all my heart."

He stared into her eyes. "If I don't return in time, you must warn the queen about the attempt on her life. She is not to go on the planned hunt. And you must caution her not to confront Dunstan with your accusations until I have returned. Do I have your word?"

She gave a reluctant nod of her head. "You know I can refuse you nothing. Since you ask it, I'll warn her. But hurry back, Conor. For I know not what we're about."

"That makes two of us," he muttered under his breath as he turned away and hurried toward the stables.

Chapter Twenty-one

As the rooftops of London came into view, Conor leaned low over his horse's neck and urged him into a gallop. His heartbeat kept time to the pounding of hoofbeats. And in his mind, the same phrase was repeated like a litany. No time. No time. Not nearly enough time.

He thought about the years he had spent preparing for this mission. In a matter of hours all could be lost. He found it ironic that he, who had pledged his life to the freedom of Ireland, would feel compelled to save the life of the English queen. But unless he was successful in his attempt, everything he had worked for would be in shambles.

The successor Dunstan had chosen, Huntington, had already made it clear that he was sympathetic to the cause of those who desired war in Ireland. A war that would further Dunstan's ascent to wealth and power.

Dunstan was a man driven purely by greed. He had spent a lifetime using his friendship with royalty to enhance his own fortune. What a fortune he would amass if he could assume the estates of the vanquished Ulster leaders.

Conor knew that many lives were depending on the outcome of this ride. Especially the lives of his father and brother. Their safety and that of his countrymen, was always uppermost in his mind.

He swore viciously and urged his mount even faster.

"My lady, I was worried about you." Nola, embarrassed at having been caught napping on the chaise, got to her feet when Emma entered her chambers. "I couldn't imagine where you could be at this hour…" Her words died in her throat as she stared in surprise at her mistress's strange garb.

"I…" Emma saw the way the little servant was studying her. "…went for a moonlight ride."

"I see." Rather than ask questions, the maid bustled about, laying out Emma's nightshift and pouring water into a basin. "Let me help you prepare for bed."

The two worked in awkward silence.

When she had finished her ablutions, Emma crossed to the bed and climbed between the covers. "Thank you, Nola."

"You're welcome, my lady. Will I lay out your hunting outfit?"

"Aye. Thank you, Nola. Good night."

"Good night, my lady." The servant set out her mistress's clothes for the morning, then crossed the room and let herself out.

Emma lay in the darkness. But her mind was too restless to permit sleep. She had known from the day her father wed Celestine that the woman was heartless. And her first encounter with Dunstan had left her no doubt that he was a blackhearted villain. Still, he proclaimed himself friend to the queen, while plotting her death. Had Emma not heard his admission with her own ears, she would find it ludicrous. That would be the reaction of the queen, as well. She would demand a confrontation with the one accused of such a horror. And unless Conor could find the proof of such a thing, Elizabeth would dismiss their claims as the ravings of lunatics. Emma prayed Conor would make it back to Warwick in time.

There were so many things about him that were a mystery. Why he stayed in England, when his heart lay in Ireland. Why he agreed to this life as a spy. Perhaps the biggest mystery of all was Conor himself. Though she had no doubt that he loved her, she had no idea who he really was. Beneath that charming, cultured person was someone much tougher. He was more than a spy. Much more. There seemed to be something dark about him. Something totally ruthless.

Who was this man who had won her heart? One thing was certain. He was not merely the man he showed to the peacocks at Court. A man who spent his life doing nothing more compelling than telling humorous stories. A man who chose to live far from the home and family he claimed to love, in order to win a few smiles from a shallow, selfish queen.

A man of many secrets.

Still, that wasn't as terrible as it sounded, she reminded herself. After all, she, too, had become adept at lying, thanks to Celestine. And lately, she had learned to swallow her fear and do things she would once have never dreamed of. Things like sneaking away from the palace to save her family. And hiding in a wardrobe in order to overhear the whispered secrets of two villainous lovers.

If truth be told, she was learning to enjoy the keen edge of danger. Though her heart often threatened to explode with fear, she was discovering new strengths within herself. Strengths she hadn't even known existed.

As she hovered on the verge of sleep, she played over in her mind all the amazing things that had happened to her in the past months. Of all of them, the most amazing was the love of Conor O'Neil.

* * *

As dawn light threaded its way through the darkened sky, Conor pulled himself into the saddle and turned his mount toward Warwick. Even as he pushed the horse to its limits, he knew he was fighting a losing battle. There was no way he could make it in time to stop Dunstan. But his one consolation was Emma. He offered a prayer of thanks that he had one member of the queen's court in whom he could place his trust. Were it not for his beloved, he would be fighting this battle all alone. And losing.

He leaned low over the horse's head and raced across fields and meadows. He hoped Emma would be clever enough to stay close to the queen once she had told her the tale. There was no telling what Dunstan would do when he learned that his plan had been foiled. Desperate men often took desperate measures. And a man as evil as Dunstan, once the truth was known, would be dangerous indeed.

The sun was high in the sky by the time Conor arrived at Blystone's estate in Warwick. When he reached the stables, he noted that most of the stalls were empty.

With a feeling of dread he slid from the saddle and made his way to the queen's chambers. Inside he found her maid folding linens.

"Where is Her Majesty?" he demanded.

The servant glanced up. "Why, she is hunting, my lord. Her Majesty was quite annoyed that you absented yourself without her leave…".

Conor spun on his heels, without even acknowledging the rest of her words. He stormed down the hallway until he came to Emma's chambers. When he threw open the door, Nola looked up in surprise.

"Oh, my lord. You startled me."

"Where is Emma?"

"Why, she's hunting, my lord. With the queen's party."

"And she left no message for me?"

"Nay, my lord."

Conor spun away, hurt, puzzled. Why would Emma have broken her promise to him?

Nola, watching him leave, called after him, "My lady wasn't going to go on the hunt at first."

Conor paused, turned. "At first?"

"Aye, my lord. She had me take a message to the queen that she wished to speak with her about some urgent business. But when I went to relay her message, Lord Dunstan met me in the queen's outer chambers and demanded to know the manner of my business with the queen. When I told him, he said he would personally relay my lady's message to Her Majesty."

Conor's heart nearly stopped. "And then what, Nola?"

"When I returned to my lady's chambers, Lord Dunstan and Lady Vaughn were already here. They said that the queen had asked that they personally escort my lady to the stables."

"Did she go with them willingly? Did she say or do anything that would indicate that she was in any danger?" Conor's throat was so constricted he couldn't seem to catch his breath.

Nola thought a moment. "She spoke not a word. But she seemed…a bit confused. She stumbled near the door, and both Lord Dunstan and Lady Vaughn had to assist her as they took their leave."

Conor caught sight of the tray on the bedside table. It held three goblets, but only one was empty. "Did you bring this?"

"Nay, my lord. It was here when I arrived."

He lifted the empty goblet and smelled it and knew instantly that it contained the same potion Celestine had used on Emma's father and sister.

Nola remarked absently, "They left in such a hurry, they left my lady's hunting bonnet here on the bed."

Conor stared at the bonnet, with its adornment of feathers and lace, remembering the last time Emma had worn it. And then, in his mind's eye, he saw the way she had looked when she'd taken that hideous tumble from the back of her horse.

That was nothing compared to what Dunstan would do to her now, knowing she was privy to his plans.

He whirled and fled along the hallway and out the door to the stables. On his face was a look of fierce determination.

"You must have ridden your mount at great speed, my lord." The stable lad looked up from the stall, where he was busy toweling Conor's lathered steed.

"Aye." At some other time, Conor might have bristled at the note of censure in the lad's tone. But right now he was nearly crazed with thoughts of Emma and the queen. Spotting another horse nearby, Conor grasped the reins and pulled himself into the saddle. "Where does the queen and her party hunt?"

"In the north field, my…"

Conor nudged the horse into a run, heading straight for a hedge. The animal easily cleared it, then raced on, splashing through a pond, scattering ducks and geese as he went. Horse and rider sped up a hill, then tore across a meadow. And all the while, Conor scanned the distance, hoping to catch a glimpse of the queen and her party.

Far ahead he could see a flutter of cloth. A skirt perhaps. Or a bonnet belonging to one of the ladies-in-waiting. He urged the horse even faster, his heart pounding as loudly as the horse's hooves upon the hard-packed earth.

When he drew near he recognized the young woman, who was riding slowly beside a handsome duke.

"Amena." His tone reflected his relief at seeing a familiar face. "Where is the queen?"

Surprised, she merely stared at him for a moment before saying, "Her Majesty is greatly annoyed at you, my lord."

"Aye. So I've been told. Where is she?"

The young woman pointed. "Far ahead, my lord. She leads the hunt."

"And Emma?" He held his impatience in check.

She shrugged. "I have not seen her, my—"

He didn't wait to hear more. With a flick of the reins, his horse broke into a run. When Conor spotted more horses up ahead, he urged his mount even faster.

The party of hunters looked up at the solitary rider approaching. Conor scanned their faces, feeling a wave of bitter disappointment. Neither the queen nor Emma was among them.

"Where is the queen?" he called to her ladies-in-waiting.

"Her Majesty has gone ahead with the Earl of Blystone and several of her soldiers. The hunt master spotted a magnificent stag in the forest. The queen demands the right to fire the first arrow."

"And Emma?"

"Emma Vaughn did not ride with us, my lord," one of the women called.

"Have you seen her?

One by one the women glanced at each other, then shook their heads.

One of them said, "I saw her early this morrow, riding with her stepmother, the queen's cousin and Lord Dunstan."

"And you haven't seen her since?"

The woman shook her head.

The dread within him was growing, like a boulder lodged in his chest. He headed his mount toward the looming forest. His heart was being torn in two. He could search for the queen, and, hopefully save her from assassination. Or he could search for Emma, in the hope of sparing her life. Common sense told him he couldn't possibly do both. Besides, he had no way of knowing if Emma was still alive.

I would know, he thought fiercely, as he urged his horse faster. *If Emma were dead, how could my own heart continue beating?*

In the end, it wasn't common sense or even love that decided his choice. It was, as always, determined by duty.

"Stop your struggling. It will do you no good." Lord Dunstan hauled Emma roughly from the saddle and dumped her unceremoniously in the wet grass. He checked the bindings at her wrists and ankles, noting the bruises where she'd fought furiously to free herself. All to no avail. Now he drew the bindings so taut, her hands and feet began to turn blue. Blood oozed from a dozen different scratches and cuts, inflicted by thorns and brambles.

Satisfied that she couldn't work herself free, he got to his feet. "Your stepmother should have given you a stronger dose of the potion. I warned her you were a headstrong little fool."

"Celestine is no longer my stepmother." Though her words were slurred, and her movements halting, Emma continued to rail against her bonds. Much of the morning was a blur to her. She remembered struggling with Celestine and Dunstan, and being forced to swallow a foul-smelling liquid. But now, gradually, her senses were returning. "Celestine is nothing to me now."

"And you are less than nothing to her. She will not grieve when you are…disposed of. Nor will anyone else, for that matter." His eyes glinted with an evil light. "A pity I don't have more time. I'd finish what we started that night in the palace." He saw the telltale flush on her cheeks and felt a stab of pleasure that, even now, he could hurt her. "After I kill the queen, I'll be forced to put an arrow through your heart and the heart of Blystone as well. And when I return to Warwick with Elizabeth's body, all of England will hail me a hero, for having killed the traitor, James Blystone, who robbed them of their beloved queen. As for you, Emma, when the forest predators are through with your carcass, no one will even recognize you. Nor will anyone ever hear of you again."

At his words Emma shivered. They had traveled deeply into the forest. If it weren't for a shaft of sunlight filtering through the trees, she wouldn't know if it was daylight or dusk. She heard the rustling in the brush as creatures of the wild watched from all around them.

Nearby a bird shrieked, sounding for all the world like a woman screaming. The sound would drown out any attempt she might make to call for help. She knew it would also compete with any sounds that might alert the queen to danger.

The queen, Emma thought with a wave of guilt. She had been so reluctant to agree to come to the queen's aid. She had only agreed for Conor's sake. She closed her eyes and struggled against the tears that threatened. For Emma, this was the most painful thing of all. Knowing that Conor would forever hold her responsible for the queen's death, and the collapse of all his carefully laid plans for the freedom of Ireland. He had warned of a bloodbath if Huntington were to assume the throne of England. And now, because of her weakness in the face of danger, all was lost.

She watched as Dunstan picked up a bow and tested its strength. Satisfied, he bent and retrieved a quiver of arrows. Then he walked a short distance away and positioned himself behind a tree, to watch and wait for Celestine's signal.

Emma began frantically rocking to and fro, struggling to

loosen the bindings just enough to reach the small knife concealed at her waist, though she feared it was an impossible task.

The forest was so dense, Conor had been forced to dismount and lead his horse. At first, all he could hear was the silence around him. But gradually, as his senses sharpened, he became aware of so many things. The whir and hum of insects. The cry of a bird, and the answering call of its mate. The rustle of leaves and underbrush as small animals scurried out of his path.

And then something else. Not so much a sound as a blur of movement.

He tensed, then let out his breath when he caught sight of Celestine up ahead. She wasn't alone. A man in the garb of a huntsman was with her.

Leaving his horse, Conor dropped to the ground and began crawling forward. Concealing himself behind a log he watched and listened.

"You say the queen is coming this way now?" Celestine's voice was a conspiratorial whisper.

"Aye, my lady. The beaters are driving the stag toward yonder wall of rocks. There it will be trapped, and thus easy prey for the queen's arrow."

"And her soldiers?"

"They will remain some distance behind, to give Her Majesty the chance at first arrow."

"You will never know how grateful I am." Celestine took a heavy pouch and opened it, spilling gold coins into the man's hand.

The gold disappeared instantly inside his tunic. "You realize I could lose my position with the earl if he should learn that I permitted you here, my lady?"

"Aye." She gave him her most radiant smile. "But the queen will be so pleased to see her cousin, and to hear the joyous news of my betrothal, she may even give you more gold herself.''

''Then I am delighted to serve you, my lady.'' He paused, then nodded toward the line of trees. ''I hear the beaters. They draw near.''

''You have done well. You may go,'' she said.

Within moments the huntsman had disappeared into the forest.

A smile played on Celestine's lips. She wondered where in England the huntsman could manage to hide, once it was discovered that the queen had been assassinated in his forest. And all because of his greedy desire for gold.

From his place of concealment Conor stared around, wondering which direction would lead him to Dunstan. From the conversation between Celestine and the huntsman, he realized that she was here for only one reason— to give a signal when the queen approached.

Conor couldn't wait a minute longer. If the queen should appear, it would be over in a matter of seconds. Elizabeth would be dead. And Emma. His beloved Emma's fate was tied to the queen's.

As he studied the surrounding forest, he caught a sparkle of sunlight through the foliage. It could be the reflection off a smooth surface, such as a rock or pond. Or a knife, he thought with sudden clarity. Emma's knife. Sweet heaven, could it be?

He felt the familiar rush of excitement that always occurred in moments of crisis. And then the sudden, icy calm that he had experienced since he was no more than a lad. The certain knowledge that he would win at all costs. Or die trying.

He began crawling in the direction of the glint of sunlight.

* * *

Emma could no longer feel her fingers or toes. At first she was grateful, for it meant that she was no longer bothered by the pain of her torn, bloody flesh. But as she continued to struggle, she felt a slight loosening of her bonds. Not enough to be free, but enough to allow her to slip her hand low enough to reach under the damp sash at her waist.

As her fingers closed around the hilt of the knife, she felt a moment of wild relief. If she could cut but one binding, she would be able to work herself free. But as she began to saw through the rope, the knife slipped from her nerveless fingers and fell to the ground. She nearly wept in despair. Then, choking back a sob, she rolled onto her back and began fumbling through the wet grass, in a vain search.

Just then she saw Dunstan hurriedly fit an arrow to his bow, then painstakingly pull the bowstring back and take careful aim.

Tears of pain and rage and frustration welled up and spilled over. She had failed Conor. She had lost. England had lost its monarch. And Ireland had lost its best hope for freedom.

Chapter Twenty-two

Moving with the swiftness of a deer, Conor slipped deeper into the forest, heading toward the spot where he had seen the flash of sunlight.

As he stepped between twin mounds of boulders, he stopped short at the sight that greeted him. Emma, bound hand and foot, was lying in the grass. For the space of a heartbeat he froze, afraid that he was too late. When her head came up, he felt his heart begin to beat once more. Praise heaven, she was alive. That was all that mattered to him.

She turned her head in a silent signal. Following her lead he turned and spotted Dunstan several yards away, his gaze fixed on a spot in the distance. Everything about the man, the rigid stance, the bow in his hand, the bowstring pulled tautly, told Conor that there was no time to take even a moment to aim. In one smooth motion he withdrew the small, sharp knife from his waist and tossed it. At that moment Dunstan caught a blur of movement and turned. Instead of piercing his heart, the blade caught Dunstan's uplifted hand, causing him to drop the bow. Upon impact, he let out a shriek of pain. The sound seemed to reverberate through the forest. When Dunstan glanced back to the spot where the queen had been, he could see that she was now surrounded by armed soldiers, who had formed a protective ring around their monarch.

"O'Neil." On a torrent of oaths he plucked the knife from his flesh, unleashing a river of blood. He spat the word from between clenched teeth, then unsheathed his sword. "You've thwarted my plans for the last time. How I will enjoy killing you."

Conor unsheathed his own sword and stood waiting. Though he moved not a muscle, there was about him such strength, such power, that Dunstan hesitated. But only for a moment. Then, in a blinding rage, he charged across the distance separating them.

"Beware, O'Neil. This duel will be with swords, not words."

"Aye." Conor's eyes narrowed. "It will give me the greatest pleasure to finish what we once started."

Dunstan drew closer. "Perhaps you should summon the queen's army to assist you." With a swagger he attacked. Shocked, he found himself facing the most skilled swordsman he'd ever encountered.

Conor's blade flashed with frightening speed, tearing a wide swath in Dunstan's tunic, slashing his sleeve until it hung in tatters. It was plain that Conor was toying with him, which only added to Dunstan's anger.

With every thrust, every parry, Conor backed him across the clearing, until, with his back against the trunk of a tree, Dunstan had nowhere left to go.

"Who are you?" Dunstan demanded as he was forced to gasp for breath.

"You know who I am." Conor smiled dangerously. He'd needed this. Needed the release of a good, hard fight. He'd been itching for it all these long, tedious months while he'd played the part of a peacock at Court. Now, finally, he was free to be himself.

"Nay. I don't know you. You're not the queen's rogue. For that man could never handle a sword as you do. And your knife. The way you tossed it…" Dunstan's voice went shrill with the sudden realization. "Who but Heaven's Avenger uses a knife in that manner?"

Instead of a reply, Conor merely moved in for the kill.

Across the clearing Emma's eyes widened. The moment Dunstan spoke the words, she knew them to be true. This skilled swordsman was so much more than the queen's rogue. In fact, he bore little resemblance to the man he showed the others at Court. This sleek, frightening creature was, without a doubt, the legend who had fueled her dreams.

Dunstan's fear had suddenly become a palpable thing. He was sweating profusely, looking for a means of escape.

Seeing Emma, he made a desperate move. He reached out, catching her roughly by the arms and dragging her in front of him as a shield. Then, holding the sword against her throat, he shouted, "Unless you drop your weapon at once, O'Neil, I'll kill her."

Emma shook her head. "Don't do it, Conor. You know he'll kill us both."

At that, Dunstan tightened his grasp and pressed the blade against her flesh until a thin line of blood stained the bodice of her gown.

Conor gauged the distance between himself and Dunstan, cursing himself for his carelessness. He should have seen to Emma's safety first. Now she was the one to pay for his miscalculation.

"Drop your weapon, O'Neil. Quickly, for I grow impatient." To prove his point, Dunstan dug his fingers into Emma's hair and yanked her head back viciously, exposing the wound in her throat. "If you really are Heaven's Avenger, you know better than any man what she will look like with her throat slit."

Conor tossed aside his sword and lifted his hand in a sign of defeat. "Your fight is with me, Dunstan. Let the woman go."

"Gladly. Now that you're unarmed." Dunstan tossed her aside and advanced upon Conor, who stood perfectly still until the last moment. Conor managed to avoid the first thrust. But when he danced aside a second time, Dunstan's blade caught him in the shoulder, opening a wound that spurted a torrent of blood.

Setting his teeth against the pain, Conor dodged a second attempt and brought his fist up, catching Dunstan under the jaw, snapping his head back with a vicious jab.

"So. You think your puny fists can defend against my blade?" Dunstan threw back his head and roared. "I would expect such a thing from an Irish peasant. Cowards. The lot of you." He advanced, his lips curled in a sneer. "It won't be as satisfying to kill you as it would have been to kill our gutless queen. But, so the day isn't wasted, I'll take your life slowly and painfully. A cut here..." He slashed out, laying open Conor's arm. Blood stained Conor's sleeve and dripped from his fingers to soak the ground at his feet. "...another cut there." Again he sliced, catching Conor's thigh with such brutal force it sent him dropping to his knees.

Emma struggled frantically against her bonds as Dunstan advanced, his sword raised. With a roar of cruel laughter he stood over his opponent. Suddenly his smile faded. His eyes narrowed. "I tire of this sport, O'Neil. I think perhaps it is time to end it." Lifting his sword high in the air, he moved in for the kill. "Now, O'Neil, prepare to die."

He was smiling in satisfaction at the thought of what he was about to do.

Suddenly, shattering the stillness of the forest was the queen's voice. "The two of you will explain yourselves at once."

Elizabeth sat regally upon her mount, surrounded by Blystone and her soldiers, surveying the bloody scene in the forest.

One by one, the titled ladies and gentlemen who had been invited to join the hunt began to arrive and could do nothing more than gape in silence.

With a look of hatred at his enemy, Dunstan lowered his sword and bowed to his queen.

Elizabeth could barely contain her temper, hurling her words first at Dunstan. "How dare you spoil my shot with that fearful scream! That was the finest stag I've ever seen. And now I've lost him."

"I was caught by surprise, Majesty, when O'Neil viciously attacked me."

"Attacked?" Her eyes narrowed with fury, and she turned on Conor. "And you! Look at you. Fighting in the dirt like a peasant. First you leave the palace without my permission, ruining my morning. And now you steal my chance at a trophy. This time you have gone too far, Conor O'Neil. Do you think my affection for you is so great that I will forgive anything?"

"Nay, Majesty." Blood oozed from Conor's wounds, staining his torn clothing. But all he could see was Emma, lying on the ground, bleeding from a wound to her throat, her hands and feet still bound. As he started toward her, Dunstan strode forward and cut her bonds, freeing her.

Emma lay in the grass, struggling to restore feeling to her raw, wounded wrists and ankles. Though she struggled to remain alert, she seemed to fade in and out as the voices were raised in anger around her.

Elizabeth was in a regal temper. "You will explain at once what the two of you were fighting about."

Before anyone could speak the queen's soldiers came riding up, forcing Celestine to walk in front of them at swordpoint.

"Majesty," the captain of the guards called, "this woman was found hiding in the forest. She claims to be your cousin."

The moment Celestine stepped into the clearing and caught sight of Dunstan, she threw herself into his arms.

"Oh, my love," she cried. There had been plenty of time for her to prepare her defense. As her beloved brother had taught her, the best way to deflect criticism was to attack. "What has this traitor done to you?"

"Traitor?" Elizabeth eyes were growing stormier by the moment. All around them, the crowd fell silent. "What do you mean by that, cousin?"

"That one." Celestine pointed a finger at Conor. "He calls himself your loyal subject, Majesty. But while Conor O'Neil pretended to be devoted to you, he was, in truth, plotting your death."

"My death?" Elizabeth went deathly pale while the crowd began murmuring among themselves.

Then the queen nodded, remembering. "Indeed, an arrow sang over my head and landed harmlessly in some foliage in the forest. It happened just as Blystone and I heard that horrible cry."

Dunstan, taking his lead from Celestine, nodded. "I blame myself, Majesty. I have long believed that O'Neil still owed his allegiance to the land of his birth. It was only recently that I began to realize that what he really intended was to spy on you."

"Spy?" Elizabeth turned to Conor with a look of shock and dismay. "I had thought this to be nothing more than a feud between two rivals. But now…" Now, as the enormity of the situation began to sink in, she was feeling more than a little dazed.

"You must believe me, Majesty." Celestine even managed a tear, which rolled down her cheek. "When Lord Dunstan and I learned what Conor O'Neil was planning, we hurried out here, risking our own lives, to stop him before he could carry out his murderous scheme.''

The murmur of the crowd grew louder.

Dully, Elizabeth looked around, seeing the things her soldiers had brought forward. The bow and quiver of arrows which the soldiers had found beside the tree. A knife. Two bloody swords. It did indeed look as though there had been a life-and-death battle waged here.

She turned to Conor and demanded imperiously, ''Do you have anything to say to my cousin's charges?''

Conor's voice was deadly soft. ''It would seem that Celestine is a far more accomplished liar than I've given her credit for. And today, she piles lie upon lie, until, if she should succeed, all of England will believe her.''

Elizabeth fixed him with a look of hatred. ''Why should I not believe my own cousin?''

''Think, Majesty. None of what has happened in the past months was an accident. Not the marriage of Celestine to Emma's grieving father. Nor the poisoning of Daniel Vaughn and his little daughter, Sarah.''

''Poisoning?'' Elizabeth's head came up sharply. ''What is this? How can you possibly accuse my cousin of such a thing?''

''I saw Daniel and Sarah, Majesty. The vacant stares, the pasty flesh, the gradual weakening of their limbs until they couldn't even stand without support.''

''How could you have seen them? When was this?''

Though he was aware of the muttering of the crowd, he met her angry look without flinching. ''When I helped Emma spirit them to safety.''

Holding a square of linen to her bloody throat, Emma managed to get to her feet to stand beside Conor. If she couldn't speak, at least she could lend her support in some small way.

Elizabeth pointed one bejewelled finger. ''You spirited

them away? They didn't just abandon Celestine as she'd claimed?''

"Nay, Majesty." Though he was growing weaker, Conor caught Emma's arm, holding her when she staggered. "I sent them where Celestine could never harm them again."

The queen's voice issued a challenge. "And where would that be, Conor O'Neil?"

"To Ireland, Majesty. To my family estate of Ballinarin."

"Why did you do this, Conor O'Neil?"

Before he could reply, Dunstan said, "Because he and Emma Vaughn have become lovers, Majesty."

Nobody spoke. Nobody moved. The silence said more than any words.

At last Elizabeth nodded. "So." The word came out in a long, slow sigh. She looked at Conor as though seeing him for the first time. "Everything that my cousin tells me is true. You are devious. Clever. A traitor and a spy."

"I am…" Conor struggled to hold on, though the pain of his wounds had his head spinning. It was absolutely imperative that he deliver the proof of Dunstan's crimes into the queen's hands. He actually reached a hand to the scroll hidden inside his tunic. But his mind refused to obey. He could feel himself slipping away. He stumbled and caught at the stump of a tree for support. "I am, as always, your devoted…"

Celestine squeezed Dunstan's hand and shot him a sideways smile. Even though their plot had failed, all was not lost. Not as long as she and Dunstan could manage to salvage their reputations and distance themselves from this disaster. She had no care about sacrificing the life of this Irishman, as long as she could live to try another time. All that mattered now was that her brother get his chance to be king. It was all she'd ever wanted. And it could still be within her grasp.

Elizabeth gave a long, deep sigh. "Conor O'Neil, your traitorous behavior has proven what I have always known. A queen has no true friends."

Celestine grew bold. "Then you believe me, Majesty?"

Elizabeth waved a hand. "I know not whom to believe."

"Then believe this, Majesty." Dunstan bent and retrieved Conor's knife, sticky with blood and grass, and held it up like a trophy for all to see. "This Irish spy is also the scourge of English soldiers, both on this shore, and in Ireland. A barbarian who has been slitting the throats of our brave young men."

"What are you saying, Dunstan?" Elizabeth's eyes widened. She brought a hand to her throat in a gesture of horror.

"I am saying that I have personally captured Heaven's Avenger. And I proudly deliver him into your hands for justice."

The crowd reacted with shock and revulsion.

Conor's head came up, and in the instant that he met the queen's eyes, he knew. He had been unmasked. His identity had been laid bare for all to see.

Elizabeth stared at the accused. The look on her face mirrored stunned surprise, then anger, then, worst of all, pain and humiliation that she had allowed one of England's worst enemies into her personal circle of friendship.

Eager to escape to the privacy of her chambers she motioned to her soldiers. "Take this monster to the dungeons. We will return to Greenwich Palace on the morrow, where, I assure you, justice will be swiftly and surely meted out."

Emma was weeping uncontrollably. It was the only sound as Conor's hands were bound.

Seeing it, Celestine smiled and leaned close to whisper, "Now, Emma Vaughn, will you feel the sting of my vengeance."

Celestine put a hand on Conor's arm as he was being

led away. In a voice just loud enough for Emma to hear she said, "One more thing, O'Neil. Know this. Emma never loved you. She seduced you only because I ordered it. Because she is a spy, in my employ."

She had the satisfaction of seeing Conor's eyes narrow in fury before he turned to meet Emma's eyes.

She mouthed the words, "Forgive me, Conor," as he was led away.

Then, while Emma stood to one side, weeping as though her heart would break, Celestine giggled with delight.

She had planted the seed of distrust. It would grow. Until it choked them both. She caught Dunstan's hand and said smugly, "You see? I told you. We make the perfect couple. We both know but one thing. How to win."

Chapter Twenty-three

"Please, my lady." Nola hovered over Emma like a mother hen. "You must eat something. At least a biscuit and some honey."

Emma lifted a hand. "Take it away, Nola." The thought of food sickened her. How could she eat when the man she loved was locked in a cold, damp cell beneath the palace?

She opened the door, peered around, then gave the little servant a gentle shove out the door. "You must leave before anyone finds you here, or your punishment will be severe."

"I'm sorry, my lady." Nola left, weeping silently. Over her shoulder she called, "I will not permit you to endure this alone. I'll see that a priest is sent to give you comfort."

"Thank you, Nola."

Emma closed the door and leaned against it, listening to the sound of the servant's footsteps echoing along the hallway. She had been stripped of her duties as lady-in-waiting, and had been confined to this small attic room until the queen decided her fate. Dunstan had argued that Emma should be delivered into the hands of her stepmother. Emma knew that if that happened, she would suffer the same fate as her father and sister. But this time there would be no one to spirit her to safety.

It mattered not to her now. She cared not whether she lived or died.

She had paid the jailer to take Conor a missive. But it had been returned unopened. Not that she blamed Conor. Celestine's words still echoed in her mind, causing a pain as deep as if they'd been carved with a razor. She didn't know what hurt more—the fact that Conor believed the lies Celestine had spoken, or the fact that he'd kept his true identity secret from her, even after they'd become lovers.

Heaven's Avenger. How could she not have recognized him? She'd seen those piercing blue eyes when she was but a lass. The fire in them, and the compassion, had stayed with her for all these years. It was, in fact, the first thing she'd loved about him. But in truth, she'd looked into Conor's eyes with her heart, not with her eyes. And she'd been swayed by the glib words, the golden tongue of an orator. Heaven's Avenger had never been known to speak a single word. Now she understood why. Conor O'Neil knew that it was one thing to hide his face behind a monk's cowl and hood. But his orator's voice was too well-known to hide. And so, as Heaven's Avenger, he had chosen the part of a mute.

"Oh, Conor." On a little moan she stood and walked to the balcony, where she stared into the distance, hoping for a glimpse of her beloved Ireland. But all she could see was the mist settling over the land as the evening shadows gathered.

She forced herself to turn her head and look at the scaffold that had been erected for the public hanging. The proof of Conor's guilt had been found in his chambers. Hidden in his wardrobe had been the coarse, bloodstained garb of a monk. The citizens, alerted to the fact that Heaven's

Avenger had been captured, were demanding his public execution.

There was an air of gaiety, not only within the walls of the palace, but in all of London as well. Banners hung from windows, proclaiming a hero's welcome for Lord Dunstan and Lady Celestine Vaughn, who had unmasked England's most hated outlaw.

Elizabeth had withdrawn to her private quarters, permitting nobody except her most trusted advisors into her inner chambers. Those who had seen her declared that she looked pale and sick at heart. But despite her humiliation, she had already declared that the hanging would go on as scheduled.

Seeing a blur of motion out of the corner of her eye, Emma turned just as the executioner tested the rope dangling from the highest beam of the scaffold.

Her heart contracted painfully, and she burst into a fit of tears and dropped to her knees, burying her face in her hands. She'd never known such a feeling of hopelessness.

Then she thought about her father and sister, and how desperate their situation had been. Had it not been for Conor and his family, they would now be dead.

What was it Gavin O'Neil had said that night? *Regardless of the danger, each person must do what he can to right the wrongs of this world.*

She got to her feet and brushed aside her tears. This was not the time for weakness. She had to find a way to save Conor's life. Even if it meant sacrificing her own.

Conor leaned a hand against the cold, damp stones of the cell and lifted his head. It was impossible to see the morning sky, but he could catch a small glint of sunlight if he angled his head just so.

He thought of the morning he and Emma had awakened together after their first night of passion. He'd never known such joy. Such love. And now, ever since Celestine's words, he'd been plunged into the depths of despair.

He was still wearing the torn, bloody garb of battle, his wounds untended and festering. It mattered not to him now. Nothing hurt as much as the knowledge that he'd been duped into believing that Emma truly loved him. How could he have been such a fool? Perhaps because he'd wanted so desperately to believe. Even now, when he thought about Emma, he found it impossible to believe that she could have been acting. Her love, her passion, had seemed so genuine. Still, he couldn't deny that it was she who had seduced him. Not that he hadn't been a willing, eager participant. But the truth was, while he'd been trying manfully to calm the raging passion, Emma had done all in her power to fan the flames.

What hurt the most was that, even now, knowing the truth, he loved her. And would take that love to the grave.

He heard the sounds of the hammers and knew that the scaffold was in readiness for what was to come.

He closed his eyes, refusing to think about what would be done to him this day. He would get through it with as much courage and dignity as he could muster. He knew one thing. The crowds that gathered wouldn't be treated to words from the famed orator, Conor O'Neil. Instead, they would witness the silent death of the mute, Heaven's Avenger.

The door to the cell was scraped open, and Conor looked up as the jailer entered, followed by several armed soldiers. In their midst was a robed monk.

"O'Neil," the jailer called. "Your priest will hear your confession and offer you absolution before you go to your death." His mouth curved into a humorless smile. "Then we'll show you as much mercy as you showed our comrades."

The soldiers trooped out, slamming the heavy door to the cell. The key turned in the lock.

In the silence that followed Conor turned his back on the monk. "Save your prayers, Father. I can't ask forgiveness, for I have no remorse for the things I did."

"Not even for the heart you broke?"

At the sound of Emma's voice, Conor whirled.

Emma tossed back the hood of her robe. "An excellent choice of disguise, Conor. I thought, since it had worked so often for you, I'd try it myself."

"You little fool." He grabbed her by the shoulders and shook her. "What do you think you're doing?"

"Trying to save your miserable life." For a moment she closed her eyes and savored the touch of him. When she'd first entered his cell he'd looked so bruised and broken and bloody that she had nearly cried out at the sight of him. But at least he was alive. For now. And it was up to her to see that he remained so.

She shook off his hands, flung aside the cloak and handed him a sword she'd concealed beneath. "Take this. You're going to need it."

"You don't really think I can fight my way through all the queen's soldiers?"

"Nay. Not by yourself. That's why I'm going to be standing beside you." She touched a hand to the knife at her waist.

"Emma. You can't mean this."

"Aye. I do." She opened her palm to reveal a key to the door. "Now. Unless you have a better plan, I suggest you stop arguing and come with me."

She fumbled with the key until the door opened. Hearing it, a soldier who had been standing guard nearby came running.

"Here now. What's this?" As he raised his sword, Conor dispatched him in one quick blow.

The sound brought several more soldiers. When they saw their fallen comrade, they lifted their swords and charged ahead.

Conor was able to take down the first two with his sword. A moment later he felt the tip of a sword against his back. But before the soldier could finish the deed, there was a gasp and he dropped to the floor. Emma nervously bent and pulled her knife from the man's back.

"This is the first time I've ever...killed a man at close range," she muttered between chattering teeth.

Conor understood. It was one thing to toss a knife; quite another to plunge it into muscle and bone and flesh. "I know, love. But hold on. We'll soon be free of this place."

They looked up at the sound of running feet.

"Or perhaps not," Conor muttered.

The jailer was headed directly toward them, his sword at the ready. Conor, whose sword was still imbedded in a fallen soldier's back, shoved Emma aside, prepared to take the blow. Just as the jailer lifted his sword, Emma stepped from a place of concealment and drove her knife through his heart.

As the jailer fell forward, blood gushed from his wound, bathing Emma's tunic and breeches. At the sight of it, Emma stood perfectly still, her eyes beginning to glaze. She was thrust backward in time, reliving another time when she'd been bathed in blood and rescued by Heaven's Avenger.

Recognizing the signs of shock, Conor bent and retrieved their weapons, then caught her hand and pulled her along with him.

She struggled to keep up, her breathing labored. But when they came to a turn in the darkened hallway, she dug in her heels, refusing to go on.

"What is it, Emma? What's wrong? We can't stop now."

"Wait," she whispered, struggling for control.

Their nostrils were assaulted by thick black smoke.

"Fire," someone cried.

"This way," another shouted.

At the sound of running feet, Emma and Conor flattened themselves against a wall and watched as soldiers began racing past.

"Is the palace on fire?" Conor asked.

"Nay." Emma managed a weak smile. "But a good many of the queen's favorite gowns and fur-lined cloaks are. A pity. Her seamstresses will have to work day and night to replace them. But it was the only diversion I could think of."

Conor glanced at her with new respect. "I believe you've become quite a clever scoundrel, Emma Vaughn."

"Aye. I had a good tutor."

As soon as the soldiers disappeared, Emma and Conor raced off in the opposite direction, along a maze of darkened tunnels beneath the palace. Finally Emma paused outside a small door. After Conor gave it several fierce tugs, the door opened to reveal a cellar of sorts, which led to a garden at the rear of the palace.

She pointed to a small stand of trees just beyond the garden. "I've tethered two horses there. Hurry."

They crouched low in the garden, darting among the flowers and herbs as they made their way unerringly toward the trees. By the time they reached their goal, they were struggling for breath.

"At last," Emma cried as she started to pull herself into the saddle. "Hurry, Conor."

"Aye. Hurry, Conor." At the sound of Dunstan's mocking voice, they both looked around in horror. He hauled Emma from her horse and wrapped one arm around her while holding a knife to her throat with the other. "You wouldn't want to be late for your own hanging, would you?''

Dunstan was dressed in his finest attire, as befitted a hero of the realm. Brilliant blue satin breeches and a crimson-and-blue brocade jacket over a shirt of lawn with a high, ruffled neck. The knife in his hand bore a regal crest and jeweled hilt. Sunlight glinted off the finely honed blade as he pressed it to Emma's throat.

"Let her go, Dunstan." Conor's voice was deadly calm. But beneath it was pure steel.

"Oh, I will. In time. First, toss down your weapon, O'Neil."

Without a word Conor did as he was told.

"Now take Emma's knife from her waist and toss it aside as well."

Conor watched Emma's eyes as he pulled the knife from her sash and let it drop. The fear in them had his heart aching.

"Let her go, Dunstan. You've won. I'm about to hang. Isn't that enough?"

"Nay." Dunstan's eyes glinted with madness. "I've decided that I want more than your blood, O'Neil. I want to see you beg and crawl."

"That I will never do."

"Oh, I think you will." Dunstan laughed, a high, shrill sound that scraped over their nerves and sent ice along their spines. "I know just how to make you do my bidding." He tightened his hold on the knife, pressing it against Emma's delicate flesh until a thin, red line of blood began to seep down her neck. Her little cry of pain made Conor's hands knot into helpless fists of rage.

"You see?" Dunstan laughed again. "I think it's only right that the man who slit all those throats to save innocent maidens should have to watch while his own sweet maiden is ravished. And who better to have his way with Emma Vaughn than I? After all, you interrupted me once.'' His tone hardened. ''And I've never forgotten. Nor forgiven.''

''What's to keep me from killing you while you're… otherwise occupied?'' Conor could barely get the words out from between clenched teeth.

''You won't try. Not while I have this knife at her lovely throat.'' Dunstan made a sudden move with the knife, slicing the front of Emma's tunic. As it fell open, he ran the blade of the knife along the edge of the delicate chemise.

''Such lovely, unblemished skin, my dear.'' He flashed a grin at Conor. ''It would be a pity to carve up such pretty flesh, wouldn't it?'' In one quick movement he sliced through the chemise, baring Emma's breasts.

''Ah.'' He circled one breast with the tip of his knife, his eyes boring into Conor's as he did. ''This is even better than I'd hoped. Just seeing the look on your face, O'Neil, makes this infinitely more satisfying than your hanging will be.''

Conor gauged the distance between them, wondering just how much damage Dunstan could inflict before he could disarm him. It would surely cost Emma some pain. But perhaps, if he were quick enough, he could save her life. He had to risk it. Not for himself. He was already a dead man. But for Emma's. For he knew, with all certainty, that Dunstan would never permit Emma to live when this was over.

He had to distract Dunstan. ''It was Celestine who forced Emma to spy, wasn't it?''

Dunstan laughed. ''An easy matter, really. Though sweet Emma protested, she was far too tenderhearted to put up much resistance.'' He moved the knife across the flat planes of her stomach and laughed when she flinched. ''Celestine was quite surprised when I told her the two of you had become lovers. She thought our sweet Emma too shy for that.''

Conor kept his eyes on Emma's, fervently wishing he could let her know what he planned. "So, Celestine was lying when she said she'd ordered Emma to seduce me."

Dunstan threw back his head and laughed. "You mean you believed her?"

"Of course he believed me, you fool. What right do you have to say otherwise? Now you've spoiled everything."

At Celestine's voice, Dunstan turned. That was all the distraction Conor needed. He lunged forward, snatching Emma from Dunstan's grasp.

"No. Damn you!" With a savage oath Dunstan advanced, aiming his knife for Conor's heart.

Conor dodged, then brought his head up under Dunstan's chin, hearing bone grind against bone as Dunstan's jaw was broken. The knife slipped from his fingers and fell in the grass.

With a cry of rage Dunstan managed to wrestle Conor to the ground with a knee to his midsection. As the two men rolled around, they fumbled for the knife. When Dunstan managed to snag it, he lifted it in triumph, prepared to plunge it deep into Conor's chest. But just as he raised his hand, he suddenly stiffened, then fell forward. In his back was Emma's knife.

"Oh, my love. No," Celestine screamed as she darted toward him.

Conor disentangled himself from Dunstan's body, then looked up in surprise as Emma swung a heavy tree limb, catching Celestine at the back of the head. She slumped forward, her body resting atop Dunstan's.

In the silence that followed, Emma dropped to the ground, her face pale, her breathing shallow.

Without a word Conor knelt and gathered her into his arms, where he rocked her gently, while his hands moved over her, rubbing heat back into her cold body. Against her temple he whispered, "It would seem that I owe you a tremendous debt, my lady. For once again you've saved my life."

Despite the tremors that thundered through her, she managed a husky laugh. "Would you mind if I wait to collect that debt? I'm a bit too weak right now."

"Aye. Take as long as you wish."

He reached inside his tunic and removed a scrolled parchment, setting it alongside Dunstan and Celestine.

"What is that, Conor?"

"The proof of my claim that it was Dunstan who plotted the death of the queen. The prisoner in Fleet told me all, in the presence of his jailer."

They both looked up at the sound of voices growing near.

Seeing her exhaustion, Conor lifted Emma into his arms and pulled himself up to the saddle. Minutes later, the horse and riders blended into the line of trees and disappeared deep into the forest.

The boat sliced silently through the black waters, leaving the lights of London far behind. Though it was a dark, moonless night, the fisherman needed no stars to guide him. He'd made this journey hundreds of times.

Boats passed him. Fishing boats. English merchant ships. Each time, he saluted smartly, then continued casting his nets before moving on. All night the little boat bobbed in the choppy waters, braving the chill wind off the Irish Sea. Then, just before dawn, the motion of the boat gentled. The fisherman leapt over the side and began to haul his craft to the shore of a rough cove.

Once the boat was on dry land he tossed aside the pile of hides, revealing two bloody figures huddled beneath.

"'Tis safe now, my lord."

"Thank you, Brian."

Conor stood stiffly, then helped Emma over the side of the boat. As soon as they disembarked, the fisherman shoved off, heading back to deep water.

Conor and Emma stood in the shallows, letting the cold water splash against their aching flesh as they watched the little craft ride the waves.

Then they turned and made their way to where an old farmer stood beside his horse and cart.

He doffed his hat, then helped them into the back, where they nestled into a mound of soft hides. As he flicked the reins, the horse started forward. The gentle motion of the horse and cart lulled the two instantly to sleep.

It was the change in the air that had Conor instantly awake. He sat up, brushing the hair from his eyes. Beside him, Emma awoke and lay a minute, struggling to get her bearings.

The little cart was passing through a gap in the mountains. The sides of the hills were clothed with stunted, twisted shrubs and trees, although the more sheltered places in the valley were ablaze with vast clumps of rhododendron. Pink. Purple. White. Red. The colors were so rich they almost hurt the eye.

Waterfalls tossed themselves from the heights, falling into a river far below.

"Croagh Patrick," Conor breathed as he caught the first glint of high peaks shimmering in the late afternoon sunlight.

The horse and cart broke free of the pass and rolled along a curving ribbon of road into a green, green valley, dotted with farms and tidy houses. Flocks of sheep undulated over the hills, and cows moved slowly through the fields toward home, with dogs running alongside.

A housewife gathering vegetables from her garden

placed them in her big apron, then straightened just as the little cart clattered by. She looked up, and seeing Conor, let out a shout.

"Conor O'Neil. Is it you?"

"Aye, Mistress Malloney. It is."

"But we'd heard you were dead."

"A fabrication, as you can see."

At her shriek of joy, more heads poked out of windows and doors, and before long, men, women and children were lining up along the road, calling out greetings, laughing, shouting as the horse and cart rolled past.

Most of them continued running alongside, while others ran ahead to tell the lord of the manor the good news.

By the time the cart rolled up the road leading to the keep, dozens of villagers trailed behind.

Conor pointed, and Emma followed his direction.

"There's Ballinarin." He spoke the word like a prayer, and Emma felt her throat tighten.

Even before the farmer drew his horse and cart to a halt, people began spilling out of the keep. Maids, cooks, stable hands. All stood back as the O'Neil family hurried forward.

"Oh, Conor." Moira O'Neil, tears streaming down her cheeks, gathered her son close and sobbed against his chest. "We'd been told you were hanged."

"You know better than to listen to such nonsense, Mother." He pressed his lips to her temple, marvelling that she hadn't seemed to age a day since he'd left.

He managed to keep his arm around her when his sister, Briana, barrelled into him and wrapped her arms around his waist, blubbering like a baby.

"You've come back," she was sobbing. "And this time, you'll stay. Promise me, Conor."

"Aye, lass. I promise," he muttered.

"Conor." Gavin O'Neil embraced his son in a fierce hug

before holding him at arm's length. "From the looks of you, you've engaged in a bit of brawling."

"Aye." Conor grinned. "A bit."

"Well, boyo." Rory bounded forward to slap his brother on the shoulder. "You escaped the hangman's noose, did you?"

"Aye. Barely." Conor nodded toward Emma, who was standing beside the cart, looking a bit dazed. "Thanks to my fellow scoundrel."

"Emma!"

Hearing her name, Emma turned to see her father and little sister, Sarah, standing in the doorway. With a cry she flew to their arms. Moments later she held them a little away, her heart suddenly filled to overflowing. "Oh, look at you. You look even better than I remembered."

"Aye. We've been well cared for here at Ballinarin," her father assured her. "But we've missed our home. Now that you're back with us, Emma, we'll return at once and be a family once more. And this time, I promise you, we'll never be separated again."

From his position with his family, Conor went suddenly very still. Though all around him everyone was laughing and talking, his eyes took on a sad, haunted look.

He owed Emma his life. And though he wanted, more than anything in this world, to spend the rest of his life with her, how could he now intrude upon her homecoming and ask her to be separated once more from the people she most loved?

He turned away, and vowed to hold his silence. She'd given enough. Sacrificed more than any woman should ever have to. He would ask no more of her.

Epilogue

Emma stepped into the rose garden and breathed deeply, filling her lungs with the fragrance of hundreds of roses. She was desperate for some time to herself. From the moment she and Conor had arrived at Ballinarin, they hadn't had a single minute alone. Last night there had been a celebration feast in the great hall, with half the village present. There had been speeches, and minstrels, and even a chorus of village youth serenading them.

This morning she had been thrust into the chaos of servants and trunks and packing. Today, she and her family would be leaving. That thought cut like a knife. She and Conor would be separated again. This time for good.

Why had he not spoken for her? She had hoped, when her father had retreated to the library with Gavin O'Neil and his sons late last night, that they might discuss marriage plans. But when the men had emerged hours later, they had merely smiled and nodded and bid each other good-night.

She had waited, like a lovestruck fool, for Conor to come to her bed. But she had waited in vain.

She circled the garden until she found a stone bench tucked away behind a fragrant arbor. From somewhere nearby a fountain splashed. She settled herself in a patch of sunlight and hoped the pleasant surrounding would soothe away some of her agitation. But she knew nothing would heal the ache in her heart.

"What's happened to my sweet-tempered brother?" Rory clapped a hand on Conor's shoulder as the two stepped into the garden. "Is it because you are forever banned from England as an enemy of the Crown?"

Conor shook his head. "You know I have no desire to see England again."

"Aye, but I would have thought the news that Dunstan and Celestine have been proclaimed guilty of treason would bring a smile to your face. Surely the fact that Dunstan's properties have been confiscated by the Crown, that Daniel Vaughn's estate has been returned to him, and that Celestine awaits her punishment in the very cell you once occupied, should bring you a measure of satisfaction."

"It does."

"But still you do not smile, Conor. If anything, your return to Ballinarin ought to have your heart leaping for joy."

"It is."

Rory grinned. "Well, if that's how you look when you're joyful, I'd hate to see you when you're in a temper."

"Leave me be, Rory. I'm in no mood for your clever remarks right now."

"I can see that." Rory's smile faded. "What is it, Conor? What's got you looking as though you've just lost your best friend?"

"I have. Or at least, I'm about to."

"Ah." As understanding dawned, Rory nodded. "Sweet Emma Vaughn."

"Aye. Emma." Conor wasn't aware of how his tone softened as he spoke her name. Or of the light that came into his eyes.

But Rory saw. And was moved by it. "If she means that much to you, why don't you ask her to stay and share your life?"

"I want to. More than anything in this world. But it wouldn't be fair to her father and little sister. They've just been reunited after such a long, painful separation. I can see how much they depend upon her. What would they do without her?"

Rory studied his brother, and saw the pain in his eyes. "The question is, what will you do without her?"

Conor shrugged. "I'll live. I've lived through worse."

"Aye." Rory put a hand on his brother's shoulder. Squeezed. "I know how much you've sacrificed for us. And you've never complained. But now you deserve some happiness. Listen to me, Conor. Stop being so damnably heroic and go to Emma's father. After all we've done for him, he'll have to give his blessing."

"That's just it. He'd feel obligated to agree, whether or not he approved." Conor shook his head. "That's why I can't go to him. I won't."

Rory turned away. "Suit yourself, brother. Personally, I don't know whether you're being heroic, or playing the part of a fool. I do know you'd better prepare yourself for a life of emptiness, if you let the woman you love walk away."

"We'll speak no more of this." Conor abruptly turned away.

"Where are you going?" Rory called to his retreating back.

"To my chambers. Where I can brood alone."

Emma sat perfectly still, mulling all she'd overheard. Conor's admission had left her stunned and reeling. Even though he loved her, he was going to let her go. And all because he thought her father and little sister needed her more than he did.

She got to her feet and began to pace.

How could she make him see that her place was here with him? Oh, that blind, pigheaded fool. What was she to do? Oh, what to do?

Suddenly she stopped pacing and began to run from the garden. It wasn't much of a plan. But it was all she could think of. There was so little time left before her father's carriage would be starting off for Dublin.

Conor had tried everything he could to stay busy, so that he wouldn't have time to think. He'd loaded trunks into wagons until his muscles ached. He'd ridden into the fields with Innis to choose a special filly that would accompany Sarah back to her home. The orphaned lad, adopted son of Rory and AnnaClaire, had formed a bond with Emma's little sister, and she with him. They had already made a pact that they would meet often, so their newly blossomed friendship would grow.

Conor stood on the balcony of his chambers watching the activity below. Very soon now, Emma would take her leave of Ballinarin. If it killed him, he'd try to let her go gracefully.

But his heart was so heavy, he could hardly bear the pain.

How had Emma managed to get under his skin like this? He hadn't wanted it. Had fought against it. But there was something so seductive about that strange little woman.

There was a quick knock on the door, then it was flung open. "Ah. Here you are."

At the sound of that sweet voice he turned. And blinked. Emma was wearing breeches that were too big for her, and an oversized tunic that hung to her knees. That glorious tangle of red-brown hair had been tucked beneath a battered cap, pulled down low over her ears. On her feet were dung-spattered boots.

She stepped closer and gave him a bright smile. "What do you think?"

"I think you must have lost your mind. Where did you get those clothes?"

"From young Innis." She kept her voice deliberately cheerful. "What a lovely lad. I think he's sweet on my sister."

"I think so, too." Conor's eyes narrowed. "Why are you dressed like that?"

"I thought this outfit would become my disguise."

"Your disguise?"

"Aye. Heaven's Avenger wore a monk's robes to hide his identity. I thought this would become my special garb."

"Special garb for what?"

"For when I'm spying."

"Spying?" His frown grew.

"Aye. I've decided I like the life of a spy. It's probably that edge of excitement. And you said yourself that I've become very good at it. But I can't dress like a female. No one would take me seriously. So this will be what I'll wear."

"And what is it you hope people will call you?" He looked pointedly at her boots. "Avenging Dung perhaps?" His lips twitched with the beginnings of a smile. "Spy of the Stables?"

She put her hands on her hips. "I can see you don't intend to take me seriously. You'll not be so amused, I think, when you hear of the brave spy who plies her trade throughout France, Spain, Italy."

"You plan to visit all those faraway lands, do you?"

"Aye. Now that I've had a taste of danger, and excitement, and world travel, I must have more."

"And what of your father and sister? You've only just returned to them. Don't you think you owe them some of your time?"

"It's a pity I'll be so far away from them. I'll miss them. But they've already learned to get along without me. I'd only be in the way. So I've decided to live my own life. My own way. For I've decided that life is meant to be lived, not squandered."

"I see." He was beginning to see much more. Her smile was a little too bright. And her voice a little too high. "Emma." He stepped closer, and put a hand over hers. "Your hands are shaking. Not a good thing for a spy."

She pulled away, held them up. "They're not shaking. Well, just a little." She tucked them behind her.

"And you seem out of breath."

She turned away, to avoid his eyes. "Only because I've been running."

"Ah. Running. I see." He dropped a hand on her shoulder and felt her trembling response. "I think, if you hope to become a really good spy, you'll have to learn to control those reflexes."

"Aye. I'll...work on it."

He placed his other hand on her upper arm, and drew her back against the length of him. Her breath came out in a long, shuddering breath as he pressed his lips to her temple.

"And you'll have to do something about that heartbeat." He wrapped his arms around her, his hands resting just beneath the fullness of her breasts. "When it races like that, anyone can see that you're unnerved."

"Aye. I am...just a bit."

He nibbled her ear and her pulse rate accelerated. "So am I. Just a bit. Not a good thing for a spy. But most acceptable for a mere man. Really quite understandable, considering what I'm thinking of doing."

"What..." She could barely get the words out, over the wild beating of her heart. "What are you thinking of doing?"

"This." His lips nuzzled her ear, his teeth nipping lightly at her lobe. "For I have a terrible weakness for women in breeches and tunic." His clever fingers began unbuttoning the tunic. As he slid it from her shoulders he turned her into his arms and brought his mouth to hers. "And I must do this." He kissed her long and slow and deep, until she gave a little moan of desperation and had to clutch at him to keep from sinking to her knees.

"Oh, Conor. Why didn't you come to my bed last night?"

"I couldn't bear to think it would be our last time together. And now, of course, I can see that it was a wise move indeed," he muttered against her lips, "seeing that you've decided to become a spy and go off to all those far-flung countries."

"I suppose I could be persuaded to change my mind." Her fingers curled into the front of his tunic. She could actually feel her toes curling as well. "That is, if there were any good reason for me to stay."

"You need reasons. Hmm." He slipped the cap from her head and watched as a riot of rich auburn tangles fell to her waist. He couldn't resist plunging his hands into them and drawing her head back so he could kiss the smooth column of her throat. "Would it be enough if I asked you to stay?"

"Are you asking?"

"After a lifetime away, I've been thinking that I'd like to spend some time here in Ballinarin." He brought his mouth upward to drop a kiss to her nose. "Perhaps build a home in the high meadow." He brushed his lips over her cheek. "Take a wife." Kissed the corner of her lips. "Have a few children." He lifted his face and gave her a wicked grin. "But I suppose, to a worldly spy like you, that sounds far too mundane."

"Oh, Conor." She sighed and pressed his head down until his mouth was on hers again. "It sounds like heaven."

"You wouldn't regret the loss of excitement?"

"My only regret," she whispered, "will be if you let me go."

He threw back his head and laughed in delight. "I had intended to. I really thought I could. But you've just made me realize something. How could I spend the rest of my life without you, Emma Vaughn? Who would make me laugh? And who would ever love me like you?"

"No one." She blinked. "Do you mean it, Conor? Are you asking me to stay?"

"Nay, Emma, I'm not asking." At her look of surprise he smiled. "I'm begging you."

She let out a long, slow sigh of relief. "And you'll speak to my father?"

"Aye." His smile faded as he lowered his mouth to hers in a kiss so filled with need, it made her heart stutter. "I'll speak to your father. As soon as I take care of a little business."

"Business?"

"Aye." He began unfastening the oversize breeches. "This business of a disguise. It's all wrong for you, Emma. In fact, you'd look best if you'd wear nothing at all."

"I think…" She was already kicking off the boots and stepping out of the breeches. "…I quite agree." She reached for his tunic and nearly tore it in her haste.

"You won't feel you've squandered your life here with me in Ballinarin? There'll be little enough excitement."

"You're all the excitement I ever want or need, Conor O'Neil."

His clothes joined hers at their feet. There were no more words between them. Just soft sighs and whispered promises as they came together in a storm of passion.

As Conor lost himself in her, he realized that what had

once been but a distant dream was now reality. He had truly come home. To Emma. To Ballinarin. And here he would stay. With the only woman who would ever own his heart.

*   *   *   *   *

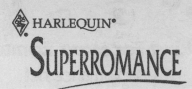

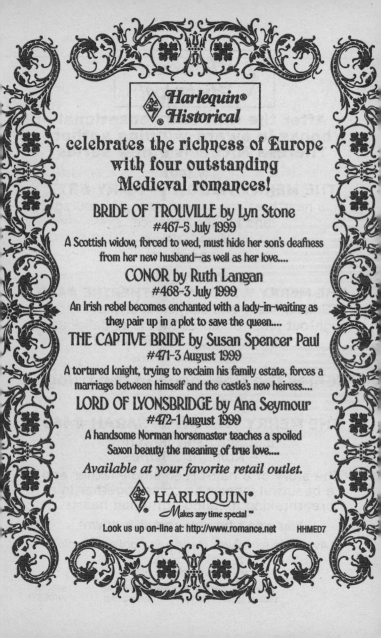

Harlequin® Historical

After the first two sensational books in award-winning author Theresa Michaels's new series

July 1997
THE MERRY WIDOWS—MARY #372

"...a heartbreaking tale of strength, courage,
and tender romance...."
—Rendezvous

and

February 1998
THE MERRY WIDOWS—CATHERINE #400

"Smart, sassy and sexy...one of those rare,
laugh-out-loud romances that is as delicious as
a chocolate confection. 4☆s."
—Romantic Times

Comes the final book in the trilogy

July 1999
THE MERRY WIDOWS—SARAH #469

"Extraordinarily powerful!"
—Romantic Times

The story of a half-breed single father and
a beautiful loner who come together in a
breathtaking melding of human hearts....

You won't be able to put it down!

Available wherever Harlequin books are sold.

HARLEQUIN®
Makes any time special ™

COMING NEXT MONTH FROM

HARLEQUIN HISTORICALS

- **THE CAPTIVE BRIDE**
  by **Susan Spencer Paul**, author of BEGUILED
  In this "captivating" continuation of THE BRIDE TRILOGY,
  an ex-nobleman trying to reclaim his ancestral castle forces a
  marriage between himself and the castle's beloved mistress.
  HH #471 ISBN# 29071-3 $4.99 U.S./$5.99 CAN.

- **LORD OF LYONSBRIDGE**
  by **Ana Seymour**, author of FATHER FOR KEEPS
  A sinfully handsome horse master teaches a spoiled Norman
  beauty important lessons in compassion and love.
  HH #472 ISBN# 29072-1 $4.99 U.S./$5.99 CAN.

- **HEART OF THE LAWMAN**
  by **Linda Castle**, author of TERRITORIAL BRIDE
  In this spin-off of *Fearless Hearts*, a woman falsely accused of
  murder is released from prison and reunited with her daughter,
  who has been raised by the local sheriff.
  HH #473 ISBN# 29073-X $4.99 U.S./$5.99 CAN.

- **PLUM CREEK BRIDE**
  by **Lynna Banning**, author of LOST ACRES BRIDE
  In this heartwarming story set in Oregon, a bitter widower falls
  in love with a persistent nanny who cares for his newborn
  daughter.
  HH #474 ISBN# 29074-8 $4.99 U.S./$5.99 CAN.

DON'T MISS THESE FOUR GREAT TITLES AVAILABLE NOW!

HH #467 BRIDE OF TROUVILLE
Lyn Stone

HH #468 CONOR
Ruth Langan

HH #469 THE MERRY WIDOWS—SARAH
Theresa Michaels

HH #470 THE RANCHER'S WIFE
Lynda Trent